THE STONE OF LAUGHTER

THE STONE
OF LAUGHTER

HODA BARAKAT

Translated by Sophie Bennett

A Novel

INTERLINK BOOKS

An imprint of Interlink Publishing Group, Inc.

NEW YORK

First American edition published in 1995 by

INTERLINK BOOKS
An imprint of Interlink Publishing Group, Inc.
99 Seventh Avenue
Brooklyn, New York 11215

Arabic text © Hoda Barakat 1990, 1995
Translation © Sophie Bennett 1995
Introduction © Fadia Faqir 1995

First published in Arabic as *Hajar al-Dahk*
by Riad El-Rayyes Books, London, 1990
Published simultaneously in the U.K. by Garnet
Publishing Ltd.

All rights reserved. No part of this publication may
be reproduced, stored in a retrieval system, or transmitted
in any form or by any means, electronic, mechanical,
photocopying, recording or otherwise without the prior
permission of the publisher.

Library of Congress Cataloging-in-Publication Data
Barakāt, Hudá.
    [Ḥajar al-ḍaḥk. English]
    The stone of laughter: a novel / Hoda Barakat; translated by
Sophie Bennett. — 1st American ed.
       p. cm. — (Emerging voices. New international fiction)
    ISBN 1–56656–197–3 — ISBN 1–56656–190–6 (pb)
    I. Title. II. Series.
PJ7816.A672H3513 1995
892'.736—dc20   95–14090
                                        CIP

Printed and bound in the United States of America

10 9 8 7 6 5 4 3 2 1

Introduction

At a time when civil war is raging in Europe, and when we are witnessing autogenocide in the former Yugoslavia, it is appropriate that this novel should appear in the Emerging Voices series of new international fiction. It depicts another religious war: namely the recently resolved civil war in Lebanon, which lasted for 14 years and claimed an estimated 100,000 lives.

Hoda Barakat wrote her first novel, *The Stone of Laughter*, to enter into a debate with the dominant culture of war, a debate in which writing was the only source of power available to her. In a basement apartment in Beirut and under fire, she wrote away the war. In the following testimony she explained why she writes: "I write of wars because I have no power; no arms or soldiers. I belong to the dark dampness and to the forgetfulness of those making history in the streets . . . Under the boots stepping over my head, I still write as if I am an empress or a dictator."[1] This novel, which won the Al Naqid Literary Prize for First Novels, one of the most prestigious prizes in the Arab world, was hailed by many critics as one of the best novels set against the background of the Lebanese civil war.

Should Carlos:

a ask his dad to go with him to **prove** that he is very careful?

b scoot off, even though his dad shouts "Stop"?

Barakat created a male character, Khalil, whose personality's feminine side is stronger than the masculine side, who is obsessed with cleanliness and order in a country plagued by disorder and destruction. Because Khalil is feminized, he is excluded and alienated from his own society. Khalil objects to the cyclical violence around him and tries to keep the personal and public spheres in his life separate. While the country is engaged in the most atrocious civil war, he spends his time shopping, cooking, cleaning the house, daydreaming about male loved ones, replacing broken window panes, and reading. These are futile attempts to keep at bay a war that has lost its logic.

Khalil, after a long struggle to keep the war outside his private space, is tragically claimed by it. The temptations are too strong: acquiring basic commodities, personal safety, status, and a more acceptable sexual identity. A change in the social construction of identities and relationships is not possible in this patriarchal tribal system, so the only way out is to repress the feminine in the self, which might be considered the first sexist act any man or woman can commit. The public domain invades the private, which cannot resist indefinitely. Khalil surrenders and assumes the identity of a patriarch, leaving the woman author lamenting the loss of the gentle, androgynous Khalil whose "legs are not long enough" that she had created at the beginning of the novel.

In a society that was bent on self-destruction, the war assumed an unreal quality where incidents seemed to be isolated and without a context. So Barakat wove a net of scenes which might seem disjointed, trivial, and personal, in order to block out the ugliness of war outside. Incidents, fantasies, obsessive thoughts, flashbacks, and digressions appear to be disconnected, but taken together the whole picture of a helpless individual caught in the grip of a country tearing itself apart becomes clear.

One of the main characters of this novel is the beleaguered city of Beirut, where the change from a cosmopolitan capital city to one of deserted buildings and shanty towns is traced. With the bombardment from the outside, a fascination with kitsch and cheap artifice consumes people's passions. When the author describes the plight of the city, her voice becomes entwined with the voice of Beirut. She then draws back to give accounts from the point of view of a non-partisan observer with a black sense of humor.

Throughout the novel, Barakat sees the war as nonsensical and farcical. Khalil, consequently, cannot make sense of the emigration of friends, the death of loved ones, and the use of death as a weapon of political point-scoring by the different factions. The media collude with the war-lords by blocking out the reality of the civil war and enforcing another, artificially happy, picture. In *The Stone of Laughter* all parties of different persuasions are mocked and ridiculed. From the sidelines, Barakat blasts her city with words, trying to "betray" it in order to reconstruct it.

Using Miriam Cooke's classification, Barakat can be considered a Beirut Decentrist,[2] who writes of the dailiness of war where grand ideological struggles and bombastic politics have lost their meaning. She writes to "gnaw" at the foundations of a society built on divisions, power struggle, and a structure of submission and domination. She writes from the margin, compelled to participate in a war that was imposed on her.

Arab women are treated as a minority in most Arab countries. They feel invisible, misrepresented, and reduced. Perceived as second rate natives, they are subjected to a peculiar kind of internal Orientalism. Native males assume a superior position to women, misrepresent them and in most cases fail to see them. This parallels the Orientalist attitudes with which westerners have treated the Arab world for so long. Arab women are therefore hidden behind a double-layered veil.

Arab women writers have created a different language where the patriarch is lampooned and ridiculed, and where women's daily experiences and oral culture are placed at the epicenter of the current discourse. Since the dominant language excludes them, they have pushed standard Arabic closer to the colloquial in order to be able to present their experiences as completely as possible. They gnaw at the foundations of the societies that marginalize them. Arab women writers reject standard perceptions about masculine and feminine language. From a third space within the language they question a culture that is based on exclusion, division, and misrepresentation of their religious, sexual, and political experiences.

Translation is an act of negotiation. "A translators job is like buying a carpet in an Oriental bazaar. The merchant asks 100, you offer 10, and eventually you agree on 50."[3] This delicate balancing act entails being faithful to the spirit of the Arabic text and to its perceived English-speaking audience. The translator becomes something like a double-agent, with a sense of split loyalty; the negotiation is yet more exacting in the context of the "third space" from which Hoda Barakat writes.

Sophie Bennett has managed to strike a good balance with her accurate and idiomatic translation of an extremely complex text. It is difficult to find a good translator from Arabic into English, a problem partly responsible for the absence of Arabic culture from the international arena. This translation, however, to which Sophie Bennett also brings her research specialization in gender and identity in modern Arabic literature, stands out.

Now I invite the reader to open the book of Arab women's stories. This book is part of a secular project, challenging the foundations of a patriarchal tribal system bent on violence and self-destruction. It also sets out to challenge westerners' perceptions of what Arab women think and feel. If you lift the double-layered veil, you will see the variant, colorful, and resilient writings of Arab women, the fresh inner garden. You can hear the clear voices of Arab women singing their survival.

Fadia Faqir
Durham, England, 1995

1   This and other quotations are taken from *In the House of Silence: Conditions of Arab Women's Narratives*, Fadia Faqir, ed., a collection of testimonies by Arab women novelists to be published by Garnet Publishing, Reading, England.

2   Miriam Cooke, *War's Other Voices: Women Writers on the Lebanese Civil War*, Cambridge University Press, Cambridge, 1988.

3   Umberto Eco, "A Rose by Any Other Name" in *Guardian Weekly*, 16 Jan. 1994.

I

1

Khalil's legs were not long enough.

While Naji tossed his head, scattering the raindrops, Khalil panted behind him, on the step before last, stamping his feet to get rid of the mud on his shoes before he caught up and went into the apartment with him . . .

2

Naji was talking in full flow, so Khalil took refuge in silence, trying to make his face blank, neutral; he breathed deeply, letting the muscles of his face go, draining his eyes of any response that might check Naji's flood of words, for Naji was one of those who speak little, who do not believe that man's heart is a vessel that fills and flows over to others . . .

Khalil was afraid for Naji, for it seemed, whenever he looked at him, that there was something strange about him. Strange, for when Naji was bursting with vitality, he made Khalil feel that in some way he was ill . . . not with a disease . . . more the way a mother might feel towards her child when she sees he has no part to play in children's games . . .

Now they are both in Khalil's room, on the ground floor. Khalil is no longer listening to Naji's words, but he lets the warm waters of his voice wash over him until he feels drowsy, while his eyes follow the smooth line of Naji's leg . . . a bit of his leg is showing between his trousers and his long socks. Naji is sprawled out comfortably across the bed, leaning against the wall with his arms folded behind his head, resting one leg on the other, which touches the ground. His skin is so white—Khalil thinks—even in this dim light that the window up there on the wall opposite is letting in . . . his hair is jet black, gleaming, chaotic, like his eyes . . . his thoughts falling between us are like grains of sugar . . .

Naji crosses his legs over the other way without interrupting his staccato speech, and the fine hairs of his leg slowly settle back to their natural place, pointing down towards the foot, while the line of the sock elastic stays where it is. There's something elegant about Naji—Khalil thinks—that would be hard to imitate. He's always dressed simply, in sports clothes that stay like new even when they've gone through and through the wash. He does not have many clothes, perhaps as many as Khalil, who tries, whenever he wants to buy something new, to choose it with Naji's eyes . . . but whatever he buys soon loses its vitality, reverts to an indistinct, gray mess, and is absorbed among Khalil's other clothes. Perhaps the secret is in the symmetry of Naji's body, or perhaps in Madame Isabelle's way of washing and ironing the clothes, and folding them . . .

There are many things about Naji that Khalil could never imitate . . . Naji's passion for the taste of food, for example, his ability to tell apart spices and seasonings or to tell how ripe something is, although he only eats a little, which makes Madame Isabelle worry all the time and usually makes her invite Khalil to eat, so as to whet her son's appetite . . .

Naji knows many small things and Khalil has no idea where he gets the time to find out about them . . . it seems to Khalil these are the sort of things you couldn't find out from books or newspapers, and certainly not from anything in the house . . . once it occurred to Khalil that the source of the "difference" between him and Naji was "Baby Rose" or "le Jardin d'Enfants," the kindergartens in the convent schools with their big, light, colorful rooms . . . children begin to learn there in a way Khalil cannot imagine . . . Naji started reading and writing then, as he himself had begun to now, a man of his age . . .

Naji stops talking. He stops for a long time and Khalil is afraid he has annoyed his visitor, who comes but rarely, and that he will suddenly leave, so he gets up to make some tea. But Naji says he doesn't want any, claiming he only drinks ordinary tea when he is ill or has a cold, and otherwise, China tea with jasmine. Khalil makes no comment but smiles mockingly, puts the small jug on top of the big jug and lights the small gas ring, to spin out the time . . . he switches on the light and goes back to his chair, while Naji gazes at the window where the things in the small room are now reflected . . .

Naji starts grumbling again about his mother putting pressure on him to visit his sister in Saudi Arabia . . . he's thinking about getting up to go home—Khalil thinks—but tells Naji, Madame Isabelle is quite right to worry about you, you can see for yourself how much worse things are getting every day . . . but soon, he regrets trying to give the impartial advice of a friend, for he fears he may convince Naji to go away and he loathes the idea of Naji going, of Naji not coming back to see him . . .

What about the acupuncture, asks Khalil, still trying to tempt Naji to stay a little longer. It's incredible, replies Naji, I can't tell you how much better her leg is . . . Khalil's stratagem works. Naji stays, enumerating the merits of eastern medicine and natural food and the wisdom of the oriental ancients. He works himself up, repeating "we orientals" over and over, and Khalil lets him forget the dark cup of tea which is beginning to grow cold . . . slowly.

Now they are both walking in the cold breeze, Naji always slightly ahead of Khalil, which allows him to secretly enjoy looking at Naji's shoulders and back from behind. Naji stops talking, as if he has come home after being away. He turns up the collar of his jacket, puts his hands in his trouser pockets and begins to gather speed, while his feet make no sound on the soaking tarmac. He walks firmly along the narrow street, unaware that there are fewer and fewer passers-by, as if lost in thought about something important, and he raises his head from time to time as if searching in the lilac sky for something that might make his mind up for him about the idea that is turning over in his head.

Naji's face breaks into a broad smile, and he puts his hand on Khalil's shoulder. Khalil draws level with him and turns to him expectantly, but Naji says nothing . . . what's he thinking? . . . it must either be something against me, or something I'm against, he's smiling to try and get on my good side, and he doesn't even know it . . . well that's something, he can keep it up . . . but it's a shame, he probably thinks I haven't any right to share his thoughts with him . . . like most of his thoughts . . . sometimes he tries to convince me of them, but he gets bored halfway through . . . smiles . . . and tries to get on my good side . . .

—They'll come back. You'll see, Naji says suddenly . . .

Khalil sees Rita. He doesn't see all of her. Just a bit of her. He sees her lips which never stop moving although he has not spoken to her, not once. Or rather, she has never spoken to him, not once. Khalil realizes that he has never seen Rita speak to anyone, ever. All he has ever seen her doing is walking along the street, or going into the building on her way back home . . . once he saw her on the balcony of her apartment on the fourth floor, throwing something wrapped up in a nylon bag to her younger sister, then quickly going back inside. Perhaps because she was still in her nightclothes. Naji said he used to speak to her from time to time, but he never said anything in particular. He just used to turn even paler when Rita passed or when the two of them met in the entrance of the building. Khalil found it strange that Naji made no attempt to flirt with her, for what did he lack? Khalil was certain that Rita was in love with Naji . . . he used to wink at Naji and nod his head in her direction and Naji would smile, pretending not to understand, but Khalil was becoming more and more convinced . . .

When they left the house and she got into the car in front of the furniture van with her mother, Naji's scornful tone was unconvincing: they're mad . . . completely mad . . . what's become of people . . . her father, he's a sick man, a bullish fanatic, he's been devouring the papers lately, staying at home in his pajamas with his hair in a mess dozing over the radio set and he never stops shouting . . . he's been nursing his pet delusions like rare beasts, ecstatically . . .

"They'll come back" . . . not one of those who had left had come back . . . the flowerpots on the balconies were parched and dry . . . when the mistress of the house came back on a fleeting visit she would throw them on the rubbish heap and take fresh bags and packages with her as she bade the neighbors goodbye, hastily leaving the house to their care . . . they were sorry to see her go, but she would barely give them the chance to finish saying their goodbyes or telling her, invoking their usual proverbs, to take it easy, that they were sorry she was leaving and that they hoped she would come back soon . . . she would kiss the children and curse having to be separated from them, curse the circumstances and the times as she hurriedly ran down the stairs . . . while the neighbors would heave a sigh of relief and slowly close their doors, or look at the sky in fear of a sudden rain of bullets on the crossroads that she would have to pass on foot . . . on the way to the eastern quarter . . .

"None of those who left came back" . . . Khalil thought of replying when Naji laughed scornfully and slapped him on the back. But he used to feel deeply sad whenever he saw Rita's lips which never stop moving—which completely vanish in the dome of the sky that has now turned black, at which Naji is gazing again having shaken Khalil by the shoulder asking him to hurry back . . .

A white dog passes and raises one of his broken legs, strutting as if he did not care . . . a bewildered man in front of the black iron door of his building smiles when they pass, as if apologizing for having lost the key . . . a plump woman comes out with a bag of rubbish and throws it far away, where it splits open on the spreading heap. She goes back slowly . . . two young men in military clothes are singing and laughing . . . they stroll aimlessly into Flippers, the shop at the end of the street . . .

3

Khalil soaped his hands once again then raised them to his nose, checking for traces of the smell of the putty. He went back to the window which he had just fastened shut, fetched a chair, and began to scrub the flecked pane with an ancient newspaper soaked in water and methylated spirit, his hands covered in the black ink that ran from the newsprint. When he went back to the sink, the light shone through the single window again, sharp, as usual.

Whenever a battle draws to an end, Khalil feels the need for order and cleanliness and the feeling grows, spreads until it becomes almost an obsession. After every battle, his room is clean and fresh again like new, as if the builders had just left. The tiles shine and the room gives out a smell of soap, of polish, of disinfectant.

The line of the striped blanket on the bed is exactly parallel to the ground. On the table with the gas lamp is a newspaper, still folded, and the whiteness of its pages, like the gleam of the dishes and little cups on the clean polished edges hidden away in the corner, suggests that a woman, a housewife—or a snow-white old maid—has lived for some time, quietly, in this little house. After every battle, Khalil's room is transformed into a little house that lacks nothing, save—were it not for the harsh circumstances—a small vase of pretty, colored flowers in a corner.

The battle ended. Naji came. He stayed for a while. He felt that Khalil was very preoccupied, taken up with setting things straight and that he was not in the mood . . . he made sure he was alright and went home. He told his mother that Khalil was tense and sad . . .

Khalil was not tense at all. It occurred to him to make a cup of tea but he preferred to make the room tidy, taking pleasure in its matchless order a little longer. Naturally, he was not sad either; whenever he cast an eye over the shining room he felt happy and satisfied, even exhilarated.

He sat on his bed and began gazing out of the new glass as he heard the sound of shards of glass being swept up that came from every direction in the calm street . . . a calm that seemed to come from a distant sky, from another world, the calm that descends upon the city after a battle . . . a submissive calm, as if a great vision has entered into the head of the city and emptied it of all it has passed through . . . even the dogs respectfully swallow their barking, drowning in deep astonishment . . . just the sound of shards of glass, from time to time . . . and some distant coughing . . .

It seemed to Khalil that the new kinds of glass were better and more transparent. The amount that was consumed had trained their hands to skills they did not possess before . . . before, they used to throw away the broken panes . . . now they had become expert in recycling and, no doubt, were sorry for everything that had been wasted in vain . . . now, everything takes its turn to enter the large cycle of life . . . they began by buying empty bullets from the boys who, in their turn, began taking up their small places in that large cycle.

When Khalil rubbed the skin of his cold hands he saw blood. Streaks of dark, dried blood and other, fresh streaks, red and sticky, covered a trickling wound on his thumb.

Khalil threw himself onto the bed, trying hard to bring his agitated breathing back to normal. He put his hand far away from him then thrust it under the cover . . . he wished someone would knock on the door, now . . . then he fell into what seemed like a deep sleep.

While Khalil is asleep, stretched out on the narrow bed, he gives himself better to the eye, that is to say, the eye can observe him more clearly, since his solidity and neutrality make it quite unlikely that the senses, which are usually fooled by a movement of the body, by the magnetic pull of the eye, may be deceived.

Khalil has wide eyes, lost somewhere between gold and green, which make one fancy, for example, that he is a little taller than he actually is. The way he moves his body, always cutting short a movement before it comes to an end . . . the deliberate way he moves his body, perhaps because of his intense shyness, gives his face something of a maturity it does not naturally possess.

Khalil, now, seems solid and attainable, even if he is not yet fully old enough to be reckoned a mature man. Looking at that body, one would think it the body of an adolescent that would be considered, once Mother Nature had finished her job, once the trunk has branched and raised its swelling coronets, to have a symmetry evocative of the marble statues the ancients used to carve in celebration and worship of that which the beauty of radiant masculinity may attain when it is ripe.

But, when one looks at his narrow shoulders, no wider than the little pillow where he lays his head, one is led to question the wisdom of Mother Nature when, sometimes, she stops a stage short and fails to send on hidden desires to their appointed ends.

The traces of pallor on his sleeping face, so peaceful, so vacant, hint that Khalil may on some hidden level be aware of the matters that questions such as these suggest, hint at his sad yielding to them, since in its solidity, in its sleep, the body usually speaks of a detailed knowledge of its sufferings, its weaknesses, its pleasures and pains. The sleeper's body tells of his intuitive knowledge of its invisible functions, functions of which he is not consciously aware but which struggle towards the surface of his conscious recognition and which, by this very movement, give him a fleshly knowledge of their existence . . . as the pregnant woman knows the sex of her fetus in her sleep, so the body in decline senses its cancerous cells beginning to explode . . .

In any case, the eye only has to fall upon him in this light sleep of his for the heart to be moved, for you to imagine yourself to be Khalil's father, filled with regret for the excessive violence with which you punished him for some foolish mistake that you took as a pretext to vent your spleen upon him. All you wish to do now is put his little head in your lap and stroke his hair, soft and honey-colored as the hair of children is, while tears of remorse bathe your eyes in the wish that he have sweet dreams, a wish that lifts you out from the pit of guilt and sets him gently back in the blithe garden of childhood where, as he should, he gallops around among his companions.

Khalil's companions could really be divided into two groups. The first group, which looks like him, is made up of youths a lot younger than he, who have broken down the door of conventional masculinity and entered manhood by the wide door of history. Day by day they busy themselves shaping the destiny of an area of patent importance on the world map, concerned with people's public and private lives, even with water, with bread, with dreams, with emigration. The second group, which does not look like him, is made up of men of his own age who have got a grip on the important things in life, and who, holding the tools of understanding, awareness, and close attention to theory have laid down plans to fasten their hold on the upper echelons . . . in politics, in leadership, in the press . . .

But the doors of both kinds of manhood were closed to Khalil and so he remained, alone in his narrow passing place, in a stagnant, feminine state of submission to a purely vegetable life, just within reach of two very attractive versions of masculinity, the force that makes the volcano of life explode.

Yet this ambiguity is now only discernible in that which Khalil's sleeping body, solid, still, unconscious, betrays . . . when he is awake he is aware of none of all this save his strong inclination to peace, to safety, his lack of desire to go out into . . . his inability to stand the sight of blood, of . . . save his sense of loneliness, which peace and quiet never manage to dispel from his confused and troubled soul . . .

II

1

A set of armchairs—six, it appears—French *style* of various thicknesses, next to which are little tables with legs that match the legs of the armchairs and glass covers topped by fat, colored ashtrays made of plaster or glass and, hanging directly above, hideous mock crystal chandeliers.

In the background there is always, behind the big armchair, a wooden or bronze metallic picture frame holding a landscape, a Spanish woman with a guitar, or a paper gazelle with tearful eyes.

The color, on the whole, always tends towards olive or burgundy and gives the impression of large, open flowers or abstract arabesques. As for the curtains, they have little tassels and arches that hide the metal curtain rail. Right opposite, there is—always—the dining table, which eats up the rest of the space, and its enormous chairs covered in the darkest of cloths which mercilessly take the eye back to the armchairs . . .

All this is crammed into miserable spaces. The modern architectural engineer employs all his art and talent even in the design of the corridors, but the housewives who live in the houses he designs invariably thwart his cunning and fill the corridors—with shady potted plants, or cheap and enduring plastic imitation plants—which have become widespread in our city in recent years . . .

Our beautiful, Mediterranean city has grown too much over the last few years. It is a small city that was not, probably, ready to grow in this way and at this pace . . . the small villages that were displaced for various reasons and the villages that are tempted by the captivating charms of the city have made incursions. The city had to manage as best it could so it stretched and spread and grew more crowded, with the help of God. It was on account of this that these buildings sprang up, then these houses—or rather these apartments—and that they came to resemble one another to a nightmarish extent.

It seemed to be due to nothing more than a simple lack of time, rather than a lack of control. As if the rich were in a hurry to spend, perhaps, on the most important, the most famous, the most established things in life. It was the same with the young engineer, of course . . . with the furniture workshops . . . with the people in the apartments . . . it seemed as if the whole city—a little short of breath—wanted to get the things it did on the side out of the way so it could spend, when they were done, on the things it really longed for . . .

Madame Isabelle's home is completely different from these apartments that people seem to pass through rather than live in, these apartments that one can scarcely imagine having kitchens or wardrobes or attics or memories . . .

Madame Isabelle's home contains furniture so heavy and old that it seems to have grown into the building, so that the huge dresser with the curved mirror, for example, has come to stand in place of the lower half of the wall, blocking the hole that gapes out onto the empty street . . .

It is a comfortable home, whose owner took his time building it before he died a death as natural as falling asleep, surrounded on his deathbed by his children and grandchildren who had benefited from his patient wisdom . . . this is what one would suppose, looking at the starched, winged, cream lace and crochet coverings, or the dark silk coverings spread over the little tables, over the surface of the old television, over the arms of the low armchairs, over the corner lamp at each end of the sitting room or over the spacious French wardrobe, which gives Madame Isabelle something of the wisdom of the building's original owner and makes it easier to picture the layers of wisdom, of contemplation, piling up with the stitches, stitch by stitch, evening by evening, at a time when time was worked with fine fingers and fine needles. Time often turns to wisdom and wisdom to time . . .

The little green plants under the butterfly collection seem to be the only things living by their own effort although their clean, shiny leaves show that they are cared for. They live happily alongside faded, colored flowers, skilfully fashioned of silk cloth and hidden wires . . .

The well-preserved furniture is not really grand. True, the apartment is now empty of people, Madame Isabelle and her son Naji, and his two sisters. Before they finally got married and the first went to Saudi and the second settled in the eastern quarter of the capital, the house used to be alive with noise and guests . . .

2

What does a house lose, exactly, when the people who live there leave it empty?

The stale air in the rooms and corridors and the thick layer of dust that had gathered on the furniture since the air was emptied of human breath were enough to banish any idea Khalil may have had in his head that Madame Isabelle would enter with her slow, huddled gait, or lean back on the sofa next to the door. She will not whisper in that quiet, frail voice of hers which had become, as old age drew closer, more clipped and neat like her little body, like her bluish gray plait that was always tied up behind like a cake and which she fixed in place with a little black silk net.

The apartment seemed completely empty, but empty of more than the presence of its owners, even though the things in it remained exactly where they were. It was only the rugs, which had been taken up after the end of spring and put in the corners of the inner rooms, that gave the house the air of being in more of a hurry than anywhere else to let summer loose in its rooms, for the neighbors' rugs were still sunning themselves on the balconies and summer seemed hesitant to enter the city, for it was well-known that the city was high on the list of places in deep trouble.

Khalil kept putting off going to Madame Isabelle's home as if, in some way, he wanted to avoid admitting that the apartment was empty, as if he would rather keep the intimate picture, which made it unique, in his mind. As if he would rather avoid placing Madame Isabelle's apartment alongside all the others, avoid the similarity that this place will assume, in time, with the rest of the houses whose owners have left. He went up to visit the apartment because he knew that the window panes overlooking the street had been completely smashed after the car-bomb that was intended for a famous leader passing through the area. By a miracle he had survived and he realized, as did the residents of the quarter, that from now on the leader would, practically speaking, be estranged from the local people who were of the stipulated majority creed (while the leader was of another persuasion . . .).

The chance passing of the leader's car, Khalil knew, would speed up the effects of external time upon the interior of the house as, now the glass that looked out on the street was broken, the dust would get in more easily and cause more damage at this time of year, so the house would come more and more to indicate the absence of its owners and, consequently, confirm the impossibility of their coming back.

Madame Isabelle and Naji had guarded against openly saying good-bye to Khalil. Madame Isabelle acted as if she were going to visit the neighbors . . . she quickly patted Khalil's shoulder as she handed him the key and asked him to water the plants and she took care to go out of the door before him . . . even her clothes were not really clothes for going on a long journey. She just changed her woolen slippers for a pair of black shoes with a low heel . . .

Naji was more clipped than she was. Whenever she moved or took a few steps in some direction he would keep saying, firmly: leave everything where it is . . . and she would reply in a voice only she could hear . . . of course . . . of course . . .

Khalil did not quite know what to do. He fetched the broom from the kitchen and began gathering up the broken glass, a distant, single player in the subdued street orchestra . . . a crippled musician following, mimicking the tune that his companions, gathered together on

19

some distant platform, were playing . . . he took the glass out onto the little balcony where he piled up the splinters and powder in a corner . . . as he was watering the plants, he felt sorry for having neglected them so long for they seemed on the point of perishing. Then he went to collect the lace covers, the faded silk flowers and the little picture frames and put them hurriedly in the dresser drawer in the dining room. Madame Isabelle's room was completely tidy. Everything was in its place, carefully hidden away . . . the room, stripped of anything personal, seemed as though relatives had been in and done their duty, had buried the dead—who lived there—and had gone back to talking—outside—about other things . . . only her ancient psalter, left in the middle of the bed, right in the middle of the pillow, served as a reminder of the sort of preoccupation of the departed, that is to say, of the special nature of her presence, in that bare little place.

The chaos in Naji's room was like a stage set . . . a needless chaos, for sure, except that it demonstrated the nature of his commitment to coming back. Everything in it represented an open declaration, bore the message that Naji was determined to come back soon . . . the actor was trying hard to escape from his role, for the very intensity with which he screamed showed his lack of conviction and betrayed his deep despair, therefore neither his pajamas, nor his lighter, nor the shirts heaped up on the bed, nor the socks left on the little desk, nor the comb on the chair, nor even the open door of the wardrobe were convincing signs that he would come back to a place that he had chanced to leave. A place he had left in a hurry. It hurt Khalil more to see the excessive chaos, and the deliberate mess made him more acutely aware of the length of time that had passed since the house became empty.

One thing Khalil kept trying to ignore, as he wandered through the rooms and passages, was that thing that screams out the betrayal of the presence of the absent one. Khalil stopped over the coffee tray and began examining it thoroughly. Its brilliant spots used to draw the field of vision of those who were now absent like a magnet and spread it, it made flesh the halo of those who were now invisible, like in science fantasy films.

They drank the coffee and left. They left the dregs in the cups . . . the coffee was still warm when they left . . . perhaps they intended not to wash them so that . . . so that their hands would stay sticking to them . . . so that they would stay, like a talisman, to repel evil from the new inhabitants and so that the cups would sense that they would meet again, they left them as a token of faith in continuity and as a warm welcome for the nervous newcomers . . . they left them so they would say to the newcomers: we are very alike . . . the love between us is a thing beyond love . . . and you will flee . . . and the circles that the movement of our flight traces will cross, like the movement of the flight of bumble bees in the rites of storm and mating . . .

The coffee in the cups was dry and very sticky . . . the coffee in the pot was covered with a light layer of blue cotton mold and was stuck fast to the pitted brass of the tray.

The coffee pot and the cups were ready for whoever might come to the house.

The coffee pot and the cups knew that devout Isabelle and her handsome son Naji would not return.

Khalil thought a while, before he closed the door on his way out to buy a bundle of nylon with which to block the windows whose mouths gaped onto the street.

3

What had Khalil's room lost, exactly, after Naji left the apartment upstairs?

What has changed now that Naji is not living there but has become an occasional visitor? . . . and remains so . . . Naji still visits Khalil on an almost regular basis. In fact, he visits Khalil's room more often than he used to in the days when they were still living in the house.

It's just that Khalil had come to know the time of the visit in advance and . . . it's just that when Naji did not come Khalil knew it was because he was far away, although he never abandoned the hope that he might suddenly come in . . . a small, secret passage linked Khalil's room with Madame Isabelle's apartment, like an artery between the two places, but Khalil never attempted to guess what the liquid was that moved secretly between the two, that gave rise to a certain similarity and that joined what had seemed to be utterly sundered.

Khalil's room was as it had always been. Nothing had changed at all . . . perhaps it was the body living in it that had changed . . . it had become heavier, weightier, more firmly attached to what was behind

the door . . . when he knew that Naji was coming, when he expected him
to visit, Khalil's joy was mingled with a sense of defeat, of deceit and
confusion that he could not quite put his finger on . . . perhaps he guessed
that the visits would gradually become fewer and further between or stop
altogether, perhaps he feared the responsibility that visiting imposed upon
Naji given the many dangers of crossing the Green Line to Khalil's room
as Naji, Khalil believes, is like a cocky little bantam who has no mother to
teach him anything . . .

Khalil gets ready for Naji's visit with forced gaiety . . . he tidies his
room knowing that Naji does not care, that he pays no attention . . .
he buys fresh coffee then sits down, idle, waiting . . . and when Naji
is late, the flame of anticipation begins to die down until Khalil almost wishes, from the bottom of his heart, that Naji will not come . . .
that he will no longer come at all . . . that he will be cut off from this
area of sudden changes . . . that he will cease to . . .

The visit does not add to Khalil's heart, it cuts from it . . . whenever Naji comes as he says he will he is absent a second before and
absent again a second after. He used to say, frankly, that it was a
waste of time, before the visit and after it, and his visits were always
brief, stretching out time before and after them, making it empty,
gaping, slack.

Khalil was disgusted with himself for waiting like this, disgusted at
his self-pity and disgusted at the way he behaved like a plump divorcee . . . a divorcee who sits, white, squat, and pudgy on a stone that
has witnessed the beloved, who waits on a white egg, on the white
stone of witness . . . who waits for a sick man to return so she might
embrace him and say, have you seen, it is I who love you more . . . because
I have waited for you here, not eating, not drinking, taking pleasure in
nothing until you come back . . . until you come back, sick, so I will cure
you, so you can drown in your desperate illness under the light of my
eyes . . . I have waited for you, cut off, in suspense, like a kindly crow to
bury you with these two faithful hands that used to push away your de-
ranged lovers . . . all my life I have bottled up my love and emptied it,
divided it up from inside and out, waiting for you to return to a grave
over which I will crow for you with the finest my throat can give, things
I have not crowed to a man lest he sully their purity . . . I will crow songs
of love for you that you, who have known women, have not heard because

I alone kept tears for you which I brought up and which bred like rabbits, I will set them free for you and shed them on your grave as tears should be shed for you . . .

Khalil was absorbed in the body of the plump divorcee, in wishing that the world would close its door on Naji. He said to himself, I'm like Naji's divorcee, who still hides her passion and begs for the friendship of whomever she desires to brush a stray hair from her shoulder with his finger, after he has put it into the kernel of her soul and made it explode . . . what an apt comparison!

For us to arrange to meet is a sign of our agreement not to meet at all . . . how can we meet people who do not push open the door and drop in whenever they like . . . who sniff our dank and putrid air and find our distant eyes, full of tears, or suspicion, or hatred. How can we meet people who have stopped cutting short what they have to say because they know we know the rest, or because the rest will inevitably come, although they believed that their efforts, that the amount they talked, that their careful preparations might fill the little suckers that suck at the time that bodies share, at the shared smells that coagulate in the atmosphere and hang heavy in the air.

When the smell of Naji's cigarettes vanishes the place is empty, not of the smell but of him, and when the room is cleaned, of the visible and invisible traces he leaves behind him, it is cleaned of the weight of his eyes . . . and of his words . . .

When Naji began coming to visit me he began talking more about the past, telling me tales, telling me stories . . . I sit, as if I were at the cinema, or that's how it seems to me . . . whenever he speaks, whenever I feel that he is absent and fails to fill the place up . . . whenever I hear him, whenever his eyes stop piercing me and he escapes me . . . he must feel all this, he must make his mind up on his way back to the passage not to "cross over" to me again . . . he only comes back to atone for his ideas, he comes back to say they're nothing but illusions and that he's here because he likes to see me and, of course, that the Green Line that runs through Beirut doesn't exist for him. He comes to say that he won't confess to what is happening, that he comes back, like anyone from anywhere in the world would, of course, come back, to visit his house, his place, at a time in his life when he's on the move or traveling around.

Naji was late . . .

When Naji is late, everything that Khalil had thought about before he was late comes back, just empty words, something to do to pass the time . . .

When Naji is late, Khalil feels cheated by the splendor of the ideas, their brilliant sparkle is dulled . . . Khalil dissolves in emptiness, becomes like a hinge with a single pin which trembles and braces itself against the door, seems as if his body is split in two: one half says "he's coming" and one half says "he's not" while his mind stands in the middle torn between the two, empty and piled high, abstracted and overladen like Ibn el Amin in the story of King Solomon . . .

Someone in this situation feels tired and weak only after he has made up his mind one way or the other . . . Khalil, like a generous mother, came to prefer Naji not to come . . . period . . .

Then . . . in the twinkling of an eye, "he's coming" becomes: a dire necessity . . .

When the sun is high in the sky, to us it is a sign that the city is on its way back. That is, because the way we reckon our days has come apart from the way that time is generally reckoned by the sun, to us it is a sign of what looks, when the sun is sinking into the sea in other, far off places, like noon. The city begins to gather up its belongings and people get ready to go back to the places where, at night, they sleep . . . which does not necessarily mean their houses . . . this has made our city's dictionary hard to understand, for an expression such as "people go back to their houses" is no longer spontaneous and self-explanatory . . . the expression "the children eat what their mother cooked for them" no longer means what the listener might logically suppose . . .

When the sun is high in the sky the markets are packed with latecomers. Those who have a stall get their cardboard boxes ready to take their wares off the sidewalks, the school buses come bouncing back through the hustle of the few roads that are open, and the vegetable carts drop their prices so as to shed their loads quickly . . . as the moment draws close. The darkness of what we know as night settles, while people begin to listen out for the moment . . . the metaphoric night settles in, as their inner sense of hearing waits for the revelations of this new night and their ears busily begin to gather up the echoes of the day that is done, so that their heads will be able to respond quickly to the dangers and surprises that the night of afternoon brings, as well as those of the dark night that follows . . .

So, since the sun was high in the city sky and Naji would not be coming today, Khalil decided to leave the abyss of his room.

Khalil asked himself over and over again: why did Claude, Nayif's wife, brush her hair in the sitting room, right where we were and not in the bedroom? And why did she keep combing her hair that way, as if she were there on her own . . . in that confident, careless way . . . although she looked out from under her hair every now and then to comment on what was being said, without interrupting the flow of her movement.

Since Khalil had met Claude, when he was convinced she was a sullen woman . . . since Nayif introduced her to his friends, in the first flush of love and enthusiasm, there was something heavy like the dregs of wine, something distant in her which Khalil called sullenness, for want of a better word . . . she was very pale, she paid no attention to her appearance and, unlike the girls at their college, she was not vapid . . . she spoke little, to the point that Nayif's friends presumed she did not speak much Arabic. Nayif was in no hurry to make the facts clear because he was proud of her French, even though he used to tell her off and tease her for her slight accent . . . the second time they met her, Hamza said, "Where did you get this Armenian from?", and Nayif replied, laughing happily, "She's from the French Faculty of Letters," then added, "Watch out for her, you know, she can't stop her runaway tongue and she swears like a trooper." When Hamza said, "She's not very beautiful, send her back where she comes from," Khalil did not say anything although he thought Claude more beautiful than the girls at college . . .

Claude became less beautiful when she began living with Nayif in his room and less beautiful still when she lost her cool, when it did occur to her to speak and curse, and less and less still when Nayif married her and she did not turn into a little wife . . .

When Khalil knocked on Nayif's door he didn't know he was having a party . . . he was not really longing to see Nayif or his little house which, like all his college friends' houses, was full of old furniture they had bought from the Basta area, which had the regulation rocking chair in the corner of the little sitting room and the tasteless posters on the dividing doors . . . Khalil felt nothing tied Nayif and his house to his old room, where he used to visit him near college. He felt the house belonged to Claude, not for her to live in or have children in but to play in . . . to buy things contrary to her parents' taste, like the sofa in the sitting room, or things that suited her ideas about the relationship between the city and its ancient peasant heritage, for Nayif was still in his "peasant" phase and had not yet distanced himself enough from it to justify this nostalgic craving of his for the raffia mat, the earthenware plates, the coal flatirons . . . electricity had not reached his bare village until after the line of a mustache was drawn on his lip . . . Nayif's raw enthusiasm and his evident simplicity used to embarrass Khalil, when he rushed to put out a few scant dishes on the table as Claude, wearing a thin shirt with her thighs bare, perused a book, absent although present, ignoring them until she made a remark to show that they were less cultured than they should be because of their wretched childhood, or less radical than they should be because of their lack of sensitivity to the wretchedness of other people . . . or even just asked Nayif to take the garbage out . . .

Nayif raised his glass to Khalil, determined to bring him out of his thick silence so that he could get something out of the festive atmosphere . . . then he began to laugh out loud at what the blond foreign journalist was saying, although he didn't seem to be saying anything of any particular use . . . the foreign journalist was rocking back and forth on the rocking chair and whenever he asked a short or a smart question of the others, Claude started cursing the father of his nation in pure Arabic and Nayif started to calm her down giving a long and elaborate reply as the foreign journalist shook his head and rocked to and fro on the chair. Nayif's ability to speak the journalist's language was not helping him at all . . . he turned to Claude and she aimed a few expressions his way, which she followed up with a few words of abuse for the journalist as she brushed her hair even faster . . . then fell silent again . . .

The one who was following Claude in a different way, Khalil noticed, was Said, who was the senior man in Nayif's political party and a son of the same village, which was now crouched in a hostile area . . . although Said was not the center of the circle, as he usually preferred to be, as he assumes that the "loss" of his village is enough to make others pay attention to him and indulge him like a bridegroom, nonetheless the presence of the foreign journalist put him in second place, with which Said was pleased this time, out of respect for Nayif and the party's ideas . . .

The party's ideas were confusing, Khalil reckoned, they so provoked the surprise of the blond guest, who began to act as if he were hearing about a primitive tribe, learning about their unique ways of life for the first time . . . he kept saying "amazing," "unbelievable," especially about what he called the amount of "action" in the strange city. He said with manifest envy, "It's as if you were living on the mouth of a volcano," so Nayif raised the tone of his voice and plunged deeper and deeper, feeding the guest stories upon stories and tempting him to more until, in the end, he asked him, "Why don't you stay and live here?" The foreign journalist replied, his eyes red from maudlin tears which might have been genuine tears of regret, "We aren't allowed to . . ."

The foreign journalist was so overwhelmed at this point that he cut short the evening and asked Said to take him to his hotel . . . Claude said to Nayif, let him sleep here, but Said hastened to call his body-guard Hussein, who was waiting in the entrance downstairs, on the entryphone and said, "Take him home and come back quickly, we have work to do."

Said started paying attention to Claude again after the foreign journalist had left, while Nayif remarked on the intelligent way they re-corded matters and how ignorant and inadequate our media are . . . Claude changed the cassette and put on another one, also by Umm Kalsoum, but with old songs and a slower rhythm and she sat on the ground facing Khalil. She cast the hairbrush aside and began to eat a piece of carrot . . . turning her thin body in on itself . . .

Perhaps this is in reply to Said, thought Khalil, she's fed up with him, or . . . she wants to annoy him by ignoring him so she's sat down facing me . . . Said began commenting on the words of Umm Kalsoum's songs and explaining why he thought that they used to induce a reactionary inertia, which we have now gone beyond, and no one replied . . . he came closer to Khalil and began to make conversa-tion with him while Nayif threw the cigarette ends into a plastic bag and took the plates and empty glasses out to the kitchen . . . Claude said to Said that the best thing for him, given that he disagreed with

Umm Kalsoum's words, would be to bring his wife along when he went to parties and then the conversation seemed to become layered with hidden meanings . . .

When Said replied, in a somewhat plaintive way, that his wife preferred the television, Claude said, then bring your mistress, then went on to say that he looked on women as a substitute for his missing member . . . she said this as if to close the subject. Said tried to carry on with "the subject of women" so as to draw out the conversation, but Claude went up to Khalil and asked him why he didn't sometimes come over, although it did not seem that she was waiting for a reply, then she said that she was dead tired and went away to sleep.

We're in a real corner, said Nayif, after he sat down next to Khalil, and we should get out of this downward spiral because the country can't take it any more . . . we can't take it, he said, and turned to Khalil as if he were doing him a favor and letting him in on the conversation the easy way, but Khalil did not understand what exactly was intended and, when the silence hung in the air, he felt awkward and said, I should go back. Said protested that the house was nearby, that Hussein must be on the way and it was still only nine o'clock. He's pretending he doesn't care that Claude's left . . . thought Khalil . . .

Why don't you work with us at the paper? Nayif asked Khalil . . . lots of people have left work and gone away because of the collapse of the Lebanese pound . . . Khalil did not understand what the connection was but he replied that he didn't think he was up to working in journalism since, in all honesty, he didn't understand what was going on around him . . . who understands everything, my friend . . . you read a lot, you're educated I know . . . a knowledge of what's going on in the way that you mean it is something that comes from living with it daily, you breathe it in with the air at the newspaper. Come on, they need writers now . . . I'll vouch for everything, he's a nice, kind man . . .

Khalil didn't wait for Said to take him home in his car . . .

The streets were so empty on the way to his room even the rats seemed familiar, unconcerned by the sound of footsteps near them, even the deliberately high steps that Khalil took, stamping his feet on the ground hoping that perhaps this might scare them away . . .

The nights on these streets were thick with packs of dogs, so many that one might fear the city was stricken with rabies or what an excess of dogs might cause in the way of public health problems or plagues . . .

They were big dogs, a little like wolves in the way they looked, in the tense way they touched each other and worked along the street, in the way the city ceased moving and seemed to be totally still . . . the dogs from the "markets" and all the empty, burned-out places must have come back as real wolves, thought Khalil, and when he raised his head to the sky and saw the round moon tarnished by black clouds and indigo, the deep barking filled him with foreboding and he said . . . you'll become a wolf . . .

4

Naji didn't come yesterday so as to surprise me today because he loves to play games . . . Khalil opened his old cupboard and laid out the shirts he had just ironed . . . he rubbed the blackened joints with oil and kept opening and closing the door to get rid of the squeaking noise . . . he stood, thinking what to wear in this unpredictable weather and remembered his blue trousers which he had forgotten at the cleaners. He felt the money in his pocket and went out, carrying the string shopping bag with the metal handles.

For days Khalil had not gone to the vegetable market, that is, not since the mined car had exploded on the road leading to the place where the market stalls were, not for fear of another explosion since, if a second explosion did not follow a few minutes after the first, in other words at the moment when people were gathered to help, then the area was relatively safe and so allowed itself to be more serene since, it seemed, it had paid its share and it was time for others to take their turn . . . Khalil had not gone because the electricity had been continually cut off and it was more economical for him to buy a few vegetables from the nearby shop, which was more expensive, than to buy bags of vegetables that would only pile up and go rotten in the useless little refrigerator . . . he had also not gone because he had to be careful with what little money he did have, after his one pupil had moved away from the area . . . most probably, Khalil was putting off going down that street in order to give time to the souls that had passed away unexpectedly—as if they had died of surprise and not of being blown apart—to give them time to realize what had happened, to become reconciled to it and to depart the air.

After the explosion the street seemed to have healed over . . . the explosion had made a gap, a huge, empty hole. It sucked in things and people but, after a very short time and by virtue of its own strength, it blocked itself up again, the sewage found its level and flowed as usual . . . until the street after the explosion was even more meek and peaceful, like a believer after he has said his prayers, like a believer who has passed the test of patience sent by the Lord, whose prayers have been answered and who, compensated, is able to relax . . .

For long years the sky of the city has been cleft in two . . . a higher breeze blows, under which walk those who are concerned with matters of politics, who make the effort to read the newspapers, to discuss and analyze events, to wait for the results of the analysis and for those results to be stored . . . and a lower breeze, from a sky less blue, for people who have no connection with what goes on above . . . who do not understand and do not wait . . . who do not know when conferences will be held, nor elections, nor even the names of the ministers. For them, political matters are completely confused and they have ceased to keep up with them. These are usually the people who move the most, they are the sullen ones who do not care and do not ask questions . . .

Khalil slips among these people easily . . . he takes refuge in the places where they are to be found in the markets and the streets, he tries to be more like them when he feels he is on the verge of a bitter delusion like the one that is creeping stealthily into his head now as he walks through the place where the explosion was . . . the delusion entered through the water: if the water was cut off, then there must be, in the corners, on the edges of the sidewalks, in the piles of rubbish and vegetables, some remnants of . . . little remnants that the hasty brooms and the scant hosepipes had not picked up . . . Khalil's breathing grew shallow and his hands started to sweat on the metal handle, but he walked faster as if, if he lingered, something might hold him in this place . . . forever . . .

Khalil stopped in front of Flippers, gathering his courage which was beginning to desert him. A tomato rolled from his bag but he did not go after it . . . now I'm far away from the circle of sewage that the blue, sparkling water ran over . . . the dogs did not disappear in the day . . . they began to pass, sleepy and slow, by Khalil's legs . . . but in the day they were more like dogs, they pretended to be friendly and they did not bark . . . they pretended to be friendly to humankind like *jinn* which, in the light, take on shapes more acceptable to the ways and imagination of people . . . in the day, their bodies are driven away from the points of their weakness to come back as vagabond dogs . . . some spotted with mange, some with festering wounds, some broken limbs, gouged-out eyes, or tattered ears . . . their mouths lust for prey and scraps of rubbish cling to the yellow froth on their lips . . . and they mingle with the people of the place. They mingle and grow many upon its face . . . it's just that other creatures disappear completely . . . completely, like motes of dust from ancient times, like the sparrows, for example . . .

A young armed man came out of Flippers and looked scornfully at pale Khalil and his bag, which looked like a housewife's shopping bag. Khalil held onto the bag and kept walking, trying to take firm strides, knowing the young man was looking at him . . . and he did not forget to pass by the cleaners . . .

The Egyptian assistant said no blue trousers in your name here . . . and began asking him some of the details in a weary way, like someone who is trying to get rid of a cheap swindler . . . Khalil asked him to call the owner of the shop, Abou Mohammed, who came out to the front carrying a cup of tea, his eyes red from sleeping late . . . Abou Mohammed replied tersely that there were no trousers, neither blue nor red, if the boy didn't find them among the heaps of clothes . . . the Egyptian boy shook his head as if to say: and now what will you do?

Khalil closed the door of his room behind him and sat on his bed, breathing in the familiar air deeply . . . he did not go to the cupboard for he was absolutely certain. He put his hand to his head and felt deeply ashamed of his friends who were rowdy at demonstrations and speeches . . . they used to repeat the word "boot" as the first Christian martyrs used to repeat the word "lion" . . . they were so against the boot that Khalil began to wonder into what rage, what despair and emptiness would they fall if their clement fates had not granted them the word "boot." Khalil saw, by the light that spilled in crudely through his single window, a boot on the ground, a large, shining boot with a smell like a father's neck, or the smell of soup on cold evenings . . .

Khalil began to roll out the rounds of dough . . . he lit the gas oven and turned over the little aluminum tray he kept specially for bread since loaves had begun to get scarce in the shops and the line of people waiting in front of the bakeries had begun to get longer . . . he cooked two loaves then covered the remaining balls of dough with a damp cloth . . . the smell of fresh bread filled his room. He chopped a small onion and put it in the frying pan with a little oil . . . he fetched two eggs from the fridge and began looking in his bag for a ripe, red tomato. He turned down the flame after he had stirred the onion, then began emptying out the contents of his bag and washing the vegetables in the plastic bowl. He took the bowl and poured the water into the bucket by the lavatory for the next time he used it . . .

All our filth washes away from us, we keep it contained in our houses . . . but we find a way to dispose of it, no matter how dear water is . . . and all of it goes to the sea.

Khalil thought a little . . . the sea. It all goes to the sea . . . all the days that wash over the city flow to the sea . . . over the years the days had become many. All that the war had left behind it, all that it had destroyed and burned and broken . . . to the sea. The war . . . to . . . the sea. These words floated between what he had thought of as simply dry land and waters . . . it was clear to him that the sea was: full. Overflowing with things from the city, with its decaying limbs . . .

Then the sea returns them to us as vapors and rains . . . then they come back and . . . we clean with them and water our plants . . . and they . . .

Khalil looked, appalled, at his vegetables which glistened with the suet of the city and threw them into the trash. He turned off the gas ring and stood in front of his single window . . .

Where can we go with all we have seen and . . . heard and . . . known? . . .

Where can the city go to get away from this sea?

It was Naji's sister who called Khalil: he had never heard her voice before . . . he thought there must be some mistake, a crossed line perhaps, or maybe someone had taken advantage of Madame Isabelle's being away for so long and stolen her line . . . something had happened at the house . . . he had happened to drop in, wanting to see Naji's room, to tidy it and, he had an idea in his head, to take a shirt from the pile thrown on the bed . . . and wear it . . . or to take a book from the study.

He was confused and bewildered when the telephone rang . . . he had seen her once, Naji's little sister, and he had never heard her voice . . . she had come in a new car to go out somewhere with her mother and brother and then left alone, hurriedly, glancing around her nervously.

She didn't sound, from her voice, as if she were Madame Isabelle's daughter . . . her voice was altogether unlike other women's voices. It was firm and clipped, as if it were made of metal rods set in sharp, angular, broken lines and fixed, firmly, in place with screws and joints . . . her mother's voice was more like fine bracelets, or dough sweetened with butter and sugar . . . and aniseed.

Khalil was deeply confused and embarrassed when she introduced herself and cannot remember how he explained his being in the house at that moment . . . she left long pauses between her words, irregular pauses, as if she were trying to pluck up courage or . . . to give him the time to think it through, to take in what she was saying . . . she began talking about the things in the house and Khalil tried to find them in the corners and drawers and to say "yes" . . . she asked him, as a good boss might, to wrap up this . . . put away that . . . arrange these . . . box up those . . . then she said that they were very fond of him and they knew how fond he was of them, as he repeated "yes" . . . then she said Mommy says hello, of course. When he asked after her health . . . she left a long pause and then, in a voice that sounded, this time, like her mother's, she said, Khalil . . . Naji is dead.

5

It was a really festive day at the newspaper . . . not like the feast days we are used to.

The usual feasts, for which we prepare and which are over before they have begun . . . which we get ready, which we get ourselves ready for until we fall over ahead of the moment we have been waiting for. The exasperation, the effort of keeping up the momentum of what is over before it has started, quickly spreads, so one always feels immensely frustrated by so much feigned surprise and artificial spontaneity . . .

But the feast at the newspaper, stripped bare of all this, made a little inroad into the prohibited joy zone . . . the fact that the electricity was cut off meant that the light in the offices and on the stairs were limited to a back-up supply. As the bombing and counter-bombing grew more intense, the newspaper seemed more and more like a huge, buzzing hive. The telexes, the phones, the coming and going of the photographers, some of whom were coming back with minor wounds, made the atmosphere of constant alert and the elements of astonishment and surprise greater. Friends of the newspaper flocked in claiming that they knew what was going on and that they needed to make a few calls . . . weaving and turning together, in a circling dance against solitude, against everything outside the newspaper, that is to say against the realm of death that lies outside, or rather, a circling dance to regulate it, to work with it, which allows you to feel as if you are above it, isolated, pure and . . . a saint.

The random bombing was not altogether random . . . everyone knows the newspaper will not be bombed for there are rules, there is method in all mayhem . . . those who work there do not behave as though this were a well-known fact, but rather delight in being part of the rule and ignoring it, adopting postures that suggest that the random attack may also affect the newspaper, but . . . but that they, they, pay no attention for the matter in hand is greater, and more serious, than worrying about oneself as an individual or as an organization . . . much greater . . .

This is what Khalil thought, who was hanging around at the newspaper, in Nayif's office, when the bombing took him by surprise . . . he was watching the feast-zone as if, due to the hidden pain in his stomach, he were standing on the sidelines. They were calculating the rate at which bombs were falling per minute, and seemed pleased whenever the number rose . . . they rushed between the offices courting one another, even those between whom hostilities and bad feeling existed were smiling and patting one another on the back . . . as if they were congratulating each other, for the newspaper was working flat out, everyone deserved more than their wages and, for being there, for their loyalty and devotion to keeping the newspaper together, they deserved the highest commendation.

The high-ranking executives left their offices. Brotherhood and humility were widespread. Grudges were forgotten as people rallied—which betrays the importance of camaraderie—in front of an office table on which were spread, on top of the newspapers, some loaves and cheese and grilled kebabs which one of the workers in the local investigations office had organized, ensuring success in his career by coming up with swift solutions to sticky problems, no matter how intractable they seemed . . . all this made them feel young, a feeling they had bade farewell in the sea of small things that they had, for the best, renounced, but for which a small part of them still yearned . . . they became young again as they abandoned formalities and ate together, smoked the packets of cigarettes that had become the public property of those who were distressed on account of their hair, which was beginning to turn white, and on account of their hands, which were clutching at straws like the deputies of the local barons who seize what little power they can.

The juniors were finding an opportunity, in this lifting of formalities, to forge links and strengthen their connections . . . and improve their chances of promotion.

Everything was provided at the newspaper, which was safer than houses . . . sometimes, they abandoned themselves completely to the game of sacrifice, of "journalism," and dragged a foreign colleague in from his troubled hotel to their lair, or failed to sleep or shave or wash, although there were plenty of sofas and water in the offices, as such eventualities had been accounted for. Even after the bombing ended and the roads home were opened again, they hesitated to leave the place where the feast had been, like stubborn, greedy children.

Everything was provided, even women . . . women who had no professional link with the newspaper . . . they just came in order to find themselves caught in the newspaper at that time, because they were alone and because they knew that this outburst, this paroxysm, this overboiling would make the young men at their most emotionally ready and at their least demanding and hesitant . . . of this they were so certain that they found the time to bring their perfumes and cosmetics, everything they needed to make the most of themselves, things they used in secret in order to maintain the required standard of apparent spontaneity and "existentialism." In order to take the high probability of death as a pretext to get rid of the last remnants of their mothers' moral teachings, in order to show the capacity of their hearts, in circumstances such as these, to embrace the sorrows of the young men, with the passing of the dull certainties of peacetime . . . they prepared coffee and tea, offered their cigarettes around, and ate with everyone else . . . then they stretched out with studied carelessness in sad surrender, in the dark corners where the light does not reach, where nobody goes. The next day, they read the newspapers—and they do not usually read them—with the pleasure of one who knows more about the profession than he seems to, of one who has participated, from a hidden corner but a safe one, in making history, who has stood at the helm of the public event . . . then they sat on the desks swinging their legs with the confidence of one who has managed to gain some special importance that is unavailable to most . . . like the intrepid soldier who basks in the reflected glory of his victorious general.

Khalil had gone out to see Nayif because his room had closed itself to him, like a shop emptied of its wares, or a warehouse that is to be redecorated and turned to another use. The room had covered itself over so well that Khalil could not pierce it with the needle of his eye, let alone get his foot in . . . he even locked the door with the key when he left, as if he were leaving for some time, although he did not know which way to turn his wandering feet . . . until he came to the newspaper building and said, I'll drop in on Nayif . . . and he stayed in the office for three days and nights, during which Suheilah—the least pretty, the one paying the most attention to the quiet ones who seemed not to be celebrating very enthusiastically—tried to bestow the warmth of her company upon him and embrace his loneliness, for she knew he was lonely because of the harshness of circumstances and the smell of prowling death. But, in the face of his obstinate, conceited disinterest, she took to passing in front of him with the tray of sandwiches and ignoring him, not going up to him until the tray was empty when she would say:

—Oh . . . you . . . we forgot about you . . .

Before the feast's flame was extinguished there was a real blaze . . . one of the switchboard operators lost her little boy during the bombing . . . she was carrying him out of his room, which was in a dangerous place, but a bullet hit him at the door. She called one of her colleagues in the newspaper and said she was going to commit suicide . . . and a few minutes later she did . . . she was called Azzah . . . Azzah's name and then her story shot through the newspaper like a burning, brilliant shooting star and her picture, along with the words of the saddened and angry people—including the editors—who paid their last respects covered pages that would have been dull, boring, and insipid, were it not for innocent Azzah and her innocent son . . .

But every party must come to an end . . . the clouds of the bombing scattered from the city and the dreary sun of inaction stripped the newspaper bare . . . Suheilah and her companions went . . . the workers left the building and the cleaners set to sweeping the rooms and corridors clean of the crumbs of the uproar that had been and gone . . . Khalil did not know why he stayed sheltering at the newspaper until that time . . . as if he wanted to make completely certain of what he had seen during the past three days . . . and you make certain of nothing until you see how it comes to pass and comes to an end.

Perhaps the dregs of the feast will stretch a little further for the others . . . they will go out to places where they will be asked how this happened and then they will be delighted to tell the story, to remember a little of the happiness and they will exaggerate their sense of having made a useful contribution in front of their wives and families and friends, the circle of their rays will spread wider . . . they are not cut off from things around them, solitary like Khalil . . .

Khalil went out of the building and began to walk towards his room . . . there were few people in the road, the lucky ones were sweeping up the glass . . . most people were outside looking at the houses from the streets . . . most of them were silent, dumbstruck, looking closely but without surprise and some had raised their hands to shield their eyes from the sun . . . a woman with wild hair and bare feet was weeping out loud as she pointed to her home on an upper floor, no one paid her any attention . . . only a boy standing near her was looking at the place she was pointing to . . . "Perhaps he's her son," thought Khalil . . .

Khalil went slowly on his way . . . the only noise to break the silence of the street where he walked was an occasional ambulance siren . . . some of those who watched the ambulance pass had their mouths open in what looked like a grin as if they were saying over and over again, "we're not in it . . . we're not in it . . . we're not in it . . ."

The bombing had only stopped . . . a few hours ago, so Khalil was deeply astonished to see pictures of the new young men on the walls of all the buildings . . . how did they find the time to prepare the posters and pictures and spread them all over the walls . . . the pictures were, perhaps, stuck onto ready-made notices, prepared in advance in the offices of the parties and organizations . . . printed and run off in underground presses, in secure places. There is only a head between identifying the corpse and the poster, as if there were no time to lose . . . churned out at high speed to win more strategic points, more of the corners most exposed to the gaze of the street . . .

The fresh heads coming out of the walls still looked exactly like the ones that had just been buried, or were on their way to being so . . . death had not yet done its work . . . the original faces were still alive, the pictures all but spoke, for enough time had not yet passed to raise them to the divine world of martyrdom . . .

The pictures used to be posted up to immortalize the young men, that is, to encourage others to die . . . to dramatize their departure from the world in such a way that others might remember them with respect. Their pictures were posted up as a spur to the conscience, to make the living city rush to join the idea for the sake of which they had gone, while the picture remained. But the headlong pace had become so swift that no sooner had the picture been up for the appropriate number of days for passers-by to see than another picture came to cover it and to cover the one it was covering itself . . . why the hurry, then, why the insistence on occupying the most important places . . . Khalil wondered . . . perhaps it's because they still paste them up for the dull and indifferent to see, for those whose ardor is dampened . . . or, more likely, they still paste them up so they can compete among themselves over who has more people on their side, our lot or yours? Who is more beautiful and who has the better place in the street, our boys or yours, that is, who is more influential and powerful here, the thought of our martyrs or the thought of yours? Frankly, who is smarter and stronger, the leader of our sect or the leader of yours and, then, who has the city or a plan to take the entire city, us or you? . . .

All the parties and organizations used to prepare lists of their martyrs' names every season on programs that were remarkably like the promotional leaflets of tourism companies and hotels. The souls of the martyrs, the suns or stars decorating the chest of the party or the organization, are published on the map of Beirut or the map of Lebanon as torches or closed fists or red anemones along with some suitable verses by poets committed to the cause . . . then the Lebanese pound fell and the dollar rose and they began to sacrifice the value of the paper to the cost of the most effective ammunition and arms . . . the living costs of the young men also became exorbitant so they were obliged to raise their wages and, at the same time, to increase the reparations of the martyrs, each faction fearing that the other would beat it in the price race and so the market was struck, but things settled down and prices appeared to become uniform, although there were some exceptions since some of the offices paid in dollars to give

41

their future martyrs some feeling of stability in the face of life's violent upheavals.

As Khalil strolled to the street that leads to his house the clamor in his head faded and died.

He hesitated a little, then asked himself . . . where to now? . . . the only way is back . . . and then there was the sight of his one-eyed window in the distance, less terrifying than the souls hanging in the limbo of the street.

Khalil walked now in the street, now in limbo. Although he knew he was of the living, the vibrations in the street managed to draw his exhausted head towards them the whole evening. The vibrations grew stronger, until they made Khalil feel like someone who dreams he is about to fall from a high place. Fall and fly . . . from standing in the street, Khalil flies again. When a fear like this fear pounded in his head, Khalil deliberately used to use his mind to discipline it as if it were a game. He would begin to repeat short phrases in rapid succession in a determined, emphatic, inner voice like in radio plays . . . he would say: this is a joke . . . this is a joke . . . papers stuck to the wall . . . and . . . a few steps and I'll get there . . . and . . . the sun is splendid this morning . . . and sometimes he would not manage to finish the last phrase . . . as if the words "this morning" hung in the air and began to be repeated on their own without his intending it . . . they would carry on being repeated until they undid the knot of his mind and threw him to the other side . . .

The first "this morning" begins radiant and golden . . . the second "this morning" becomes closer to the actual morning in which Khalil walks and it becomes dimly light . . . the following "this mornings" enter the morning that is on the street and are absorbed in a dark, nocturnal indigo like a slight headache . . . and the final ones burst between his legs, like a balloon full of stale water, to spatter the morning with its true color, the color of limbo . . .

Limbo is a place . . . the dead stay in this place when they leave their bodies . . . they do but one dismal thing and that is to wait . . . wait for judgment . . . wait for a light or an angel or a god to appear to them to pass judgment on them and send them to heaven or hell . . . but waiting here is not like waiting there. There, waiting is not measured as we are used to measuring it . . . we do not reckon our waiting by the hour or by the turning of night and day or by the changing moons or by the tide's ebb and flow, these things are to amuse ourselves, to fill up the waiting . . . there, the dead wait with no tools to shape the shapeless waiting . . . we wait, here, for example, standing in front of the oven door; we imagine the loaf, we taste it, but there, there are no bodies to stand and sit . . . the real pity is that the body is not yet completely lost because it has not died . . . it still breathes . . . if you were to tie a plastic bag up over the body the sides of the bag would steam up as if that flesh were breathing, although it lies still . . . the memory of their bodies which now hang on the street walls tortures the dead in limbo, for they have not yet made the most of the time of transition nor have they yet learned how to go on without these bodies of theirs . . . yet these bodies have started another life, completely independent of that which lingers in the graves, which settles in preparation for the final surrender to rest and peace . . . another life begins for the body in the picture, which unsettles the body in the grave, worries the soul which waits, disturbed, in limbo . . . the souls are stirred by the glances, the movement, the clamor of the street, they recall the train stations and the humiliating wait, for what is absolutely certain is that no train will come . . . this kind of waiting is quite unsuitable for the dead, it tortures them . . . the only happy souls among them are the souls of small children and babes in arms whose lives were not yet burdened by the weight of acts requiring divine judgment and the secret of their happiness lies in the fact that they have no memory of trains and that there are no pictures of them in the streets to disturb their graves . . .

Khalil had reached his room . . .

The room seemed as if it had been empty for years . . . it had an evil air . . . evil, Khalil said. As if another room had eaten the first, ravished it, like in the story of Leila and the Wolf, as if it had taken on its shape, sat in its place, playing friendly and familiar for not a thing had changed or changed place . . . Khalil was filled with doubts . . . some voices raised in disagreement reached his ears and, taking this as a pretext, he said: what's that?! . . . I'll just go to the front door and see what's going on, then I'll come back . . . as if he were saying: I'll give my room the chance to get back to itself . . .

The noise was the shouting of boys and young men, some had beards and were leading a demonstration. It was a hazardous morning demonstration . . . as if the people who had promised to take part in it had broken their word, it was made up of the unemployed, boys with nothing to do since the places where they used to play were becoming more and more piled up with rubble and rubbish, which lingered in the houses longer than it should.

The first two rows, in their divided confusion, were the most cohesive . . . a little way behind them walked the younger ones who were looking so hard to both sides of the street and at the balconies that they seemed to be walking horizontally . . . some ran into their friends and asked them to join in, their seriousness mingled with cheerful promise as if something more fun would happen once the demonstration was over . . . others knit their brows from time to time, kicking at those who failed to repeat the slogans when one of those walking in the front two rows left his place to go to the middle, to keep them in line and rally their cries. The ones from the front got angry and reproached those in the middle, but did not risk advancing all the way to the back . . . the back rows were way out of line . . . they did not even chant the slogans together . . . among these boys at the back . . . among them was a boy who was teasing his friend using foul and uncouth language . . . one of the boys paused in his place awhile . . . letting the demonstration pass, then took a running leap at his companion's back, knocking him to the ground . . . their noisy good humor abated when a signal reached the back from the middle rows that they should be serious and orderly . . . they seemed to sense from them that one of the organizers from the first two rows was coming.

The truth was that the demonstrators were not receiving the support that plays a large part in determining how orderly a demonstration is, the support that comes, usually, from those who watch on their balconies, from the shopkeepers who close their doors, from the silent women on the street . . . it would be easy to say that this demonstration suffered from a lack of any support, indeed it was all but ruined whenever a mother turned from a balcony or shop to reproach her son and call him, unable to hide her nervousness, to help her with a few things . . .

This is a demonstration against Israel, Abou Ahmad said to Khalil in the doorway of the building . . . how are you, my son, praise be to God you got back safe . . . this demonstration is against Israel . . . he repeated, as he brushed the white dust from his forearms . . . I felt as heavy as a bull for twenty-four hours when we lost the war and Nasser gave his speech. My voice was hoarse and my eyes were bulging for a month . . . I believed, if you don't mind my saying, that I'd never get my manhood back . . . this demonstration against Israel . . . none of these boys has ever set foot on its soil . . .

Abou Ahmad went out onto the sidewalk and called to two boys from the back of the demonstration . . . do me a favor and make yourselves a bit of cash . . . the boys fell in behind him. He turned to Khalil and said, in a voice that was almost reproachful . . . praise be to God that the family's in the south . . . the apartment's like a hollow zucchini . . . the rocket went spinning right through it. I'll just try to fix the front door . . . and lock it up . . .

Abou Ahmad turned towards the drawer and began to go up the stairs while he made polite conversation with the two boys . . . Khalil noticed the muscles of his thighs standing out under his white underpants . . . Abou Ahmad never used to go out of his house, not even to the shop nearby, without being dressed in the full elegance of his gray uniform . . . he was a police corporal, still known as "the gendarme" . . . his buttons, his buckles, his shoes were immaculately polished and his hair, likewise, was always sleekly oiled into place. Khalil never mistakes his footfall in the entrance of the building, that decisive rhythm which always traces instantly in his mind's eye the slim hips and the straight, broad shoulders, which calls to mind the smell of the old *eau de cologne* 114, so suggestive of cleanliness and white skin, which always lingers after Abou Ahmad.

The room looked as it had before, despite Khalil's efforts to clean it and restore it to order, so as to get a grip on it again . . . it seemed as if some spirit had stolen into the room, perhaps through the broken window, and possessed it.

But Khalil changed the glass and polished it, he turned on the radio as he was doing the cleaning and washing his sheets so as to suggest to himself that he was back for good . . . yet still, he did not feel normal . . . that evil thing that Khalil had felt the moment he came in stayed in the room for days . . . he saw it going out of its place as if it wanted to catch up with the street, or with the apartments that had been hit, that will not be coming back . . . as if it had split away from him, taking its belongings with it, or as if the room's good spirit had suffocated under the pile of its sisters which he had not reached and its evil spirit had awoken to roam and frolic through the buildings of the street . . . as if the evil spirits of the apartments had won out over the good spirits and taken their place everywhere . . . as if the war of the spirits of the apartments were running parallel to the war of the armed in the streets.

This delusion really worried Khalil . . . as soon as he fell asleep, it filled his eyelids. He even bought a piece of dark, indigo cloth . . . he made a crease the length of its width and stitched it with a firm thread then put a metal wire in the crease whose ends he wound around two nails at either edge of the window. He drew his curtain and the street vanished from his eyes . . . it's become a real barrier, Khalil said and, although he promised himself a peaceful sleep, he woke up after a few hours not knowing how to pass the time until morning came . . .

6

Everything Khalil did during that month was nothing but a chain of swoons, that is to say nothing but confused, if persistent, attempts to forget that Naji had been killed, to try to escape the day he heard the black news. Khalil seemed to have set aside one part of himself, isolated it completely, to have sent away the other parts to overpower it, to have called upon them all to forget it, to put it out of mind for the moment . . . perhaps to prepare a place for it . . . to draw the vivid, colored circles of the target where it must, in the end, explode . . .

Khalil's body, which knew he could not bear to stifle his memories like this, seemed to respond . . . it yielded to the preparation, for Khalil's appetite had increased in recent times, which he seemed to attribute to his late nights and the sleepless hours spent waiting for the morning . . . his sleeplessness did not tire him much, nor even weaken his body. It was a cold, pleasant sleeplessness not brought on by disturbing delusions or tormenting images except for those related to the spirit of the room and the movement of the rats and cats in the streets, which were more entertaining than demanding . . . apart from this, time went by peacefully, at its slow pace. Khalil spent the time staring at the ceiling, or reading quietly, or drinking tea and listening to the radio.

When it rained, Khalil used to burrow under the covers with what seemed like real pleasure. He imagined the rainy nights to be nights whose steps had grown light and whose hours flew like the notes of simple, old melodies . . .

Khalil was surprised at how long Nayif stayed . . . he began to wonder what was making him stay so late, for it was Nayif who was so busy he had not found the time to visit for years . . .

After he had run out of things to say a number of times, Nayif suddenly said, as if the time for confrontation had come: can I stay the night with you . . . I don't want to go home . . . and I don't want anyone to know about this . . .

That's why—thought Khalil—he didn't have to talk so much, he could have asked me straight out . . . he doesn't realize that I don't mind if I only come into his mind when he needs me . . . perhaps he thinks that I should be delighted, now, since he wants me to think I'm the only one he trusts to talk to about his personal life . . .

Khalil gave Nayif a big smile to thank him for his trust and asked him if he was hungry. Nayif said he was nearly dying of hunger . . . to make the atmosphere of trust between us stronger, thought Khalil . . . and, since he was not convinced that Nayif was as hungry as he claimed to be, he decided not to open a new box of cheese and made do with frying three eggs instead.

Nayif got up to help him, to make more of the friendly atmosphere. Khalil let him . . . Nayif began heating loaves of bread on the gas and cutting up the tomatoes and onions . . . he did so envying Khalil out loud for his bachelor life and the freedom it gives a young man to do as he pleases, when he pleases . . .

But while he was eating, Nayif began to feign levity, sidestepping the subject of Claude, cautiously getting close to the reason for his staying at Khalil's place . . . as if the intimate atmosphere were making him talk about the subject . . . he thinks it's his duty—thought Khalil—this man who's always busy with a thousand trivial things at once ... who always seems to have more on his hands than he can manage. A feeling something like compassion for Nayif came over him, Nayif who was spattering himself with the mud around his confessions about women and men, about marriage and the institution and freedom ...

Khalil sincerely wanted to spare him all this effort, so he asked him about the newspaper ... Nayif repeated his invitation to Khalil to work there, then asked him about what he was reading these days ... now he's dragging me to my ground, trying to praise me by letting me know he's confident that I'm a man of culture, well-read, someone it's worth talking to about his special subject ... he must feel sorry for me because I'm out of work, he might even offer me some money, tomorrow morning, before he leaves ...

Khalil stood looking around the room, making it obvious that he was getting ready to go to sleep ... knowing that Nayif would refuse, he said you sleep on my bed and I'll sleep in the blankets on the floor ... Nayif said I'll sleep on the blankets and Khalil did not protest but said very well, as you wish ...

Nayif made a pile of blankets on the floor, spread the sheet on top of them and began to take off his clothes ... Khalil felt embarrassed when Nayif sat opposite him in his short, tight underpants and began to smoke a cigarette ...

Nayif said ... why don't you get a mattress from your friend's apartment up there? ... Naji ... don't you have the key to the apartment? Khalil felt his stomach contract sharply and, feeling suddenly cold, knew that the blood had drained from his head and that he was now pale as the dead ... he wished that Nayif would disappear, right now. He got up from his bed ... I'll put out the light, he said, then the electricity was cut off before he reached the lightswitch ... Khalil breathed a sigh of relief but Nayif asked for a candle. By the flame of the lighter he found the candle on the table where the gas ring stood, lit it and stuck it in the middle of the ashtray ...

He's not going to sleep—thought Khalil—and what's more, he wants ... to talk ...

—I know he was your friend ... a close friend ... I understand how sorry you feel for him, how lonely you feel without him ... but who among us has not lost someone dear in this damned war ...

since it happened, you . . . no one sees you . . . I mean your lingering in this house, your aversion to going out . . . I feel for you . . . but this is no use, Khalil . . . the man has gone . . .

Khalil had not known that Nayif, who was usually kind and friendly, could be so aggressive, so tasteless and insensitive . . . it seemed to him that Nayif had become of the evil stuff of the room and that he, Khalil, was a guest, a stranger to them both . . . like those foreign travelers who, in the old days, used to come to a house whose owners, their heads stuffed so full with the values of hospitality, were forbidden to find them tiresome . . . they offered food and shelter and good conversation only in return for a promise which those travelers would keep with entertaining stories, fantastic tales from distant countries, tales they made up, tales to open up the heavy sky of night . . . but Khalil was a guest accused of staying without keeping his promises . . .

So Nayif went on . . .

—I know how difficult it is.

The light of the candle isn't as dim as he says it is, Nayif must be able to see how pale my face is . . . it must give him more pleasure, make him feel he's needed and being really helpful . . . he sees himself as a surgeon, tying a tourniquet to stop a bad hemorrhage . . .

—I know how difficult it is, especially when we lose someone innocent . . . the important thing is that we believe him to be innocent . . . what makes our loss difficult is that we can't stop thinking about his innocence . . . what did he have to do with it, we say . . . we can't easily accept the death of an innocent sacrifice . . . in the old days, perhaps even now, like in my village, for example, they didn't accept the loss of someone they considered a sacrifice until they had avenged his death. That is to say until they had made others feel the burden of loss. So, you see, they didn't kill the killer . . . they killed one of his relatives . . . they turned their eyes from the runaway killer and chose someone innocent instead, as a victim like their victim.

He chooses me for these complex analyses of his . . . he's trying to ape what he thinks of as my active mentality . . . how happy he is . . . he's sure to get more into it . . .

—They didn't visit the grave . . . they didn't hang his bloodied clothes from the house, they didn't shave their beards. They didn't walk in the streets, nor did they accept mourners until after they had avenged him. After that, the dead man was considered to have died and mourning his death became official . . .

But . . . how innocent was the innocent, in reality . . . sometimes we nurture fancies in our heads, fancies that we need . . . but Khalil, listen to me carefully . . . you're Naji's friend, you know the truth but don't believe too much that he was a victim . . . that he had nothing to do with anything . . . didn't you ever ask yourself why they killed him, why they chose him rather than someone else? didn't you wonder for example why he had so many errands to run across the Green Line? . . . many other people apart from him cross daily from here to there and from there to here . . . they live in one area and work in the other . . . many of them are the Christians who haven't left the area and most are those who have kept coming here day after day . . . so why Naji? well? why Naji . . .

Khalil saw Naji raise his collar and look at the drizzling sky, regretting not having taken the umbrella from Madame Isabelle . . . walking a little faster, for it was quite far from one checkpoint to the other and, if the rain got heavier, the people who were walking would be soaked through for there was no roof, nor even a spreading tree, to keep off the heavy downpour . . . Khalil saw people walking put their plastic bags or cardboard boxes over their heads and some of them beginning to run . . . but Naji was not so afraid of getting wet . . . Naji picked up a little boy who had stumbled running after his mother . . . he smiles at her as he lengthens his stride, and she comments on how bad the weather is.

—Listen Khalil . . . Naji was an agent . . . I know . . . it was never any use warning him, even threatening him . . . he used to come a lot . . . sometimes he didn't drop in on you . . . I know . . . he used to carry important information that harmed people here . . . then he didn't stop at anything . . . he threatened them with their hostages over there. Twenty will be torn limb from limb if you touch one hair of my head . . . then they used to let him leave on condition he didn't come back . . . in the last stage, this is not confirmed in any case, they suspected that he was the one who boobytrapped the car on the New Road and he had to be . . . got rid of.

The next day Khalil awoke around noon . . . he had slept like a child, a deep, peaceful sleep. He got up feeling wide awake and refreshed, which he had not felt for many days ... he began to tidy his room, so he put the blankets on his bed after he had smoothed out the sheets ... then he gathered the plates on the sink ... he was surprised to find water gushing out of the tap when he turned it on ... he fetched his washing and put it to soak in the big bucket, and began to clean the bathroom which Nayif had turned upside down ... on the edge of the little mirror above the basin he found 3000 lire—as he had expected—and stuffed the notes into the jacket pocket of his pajamas and carried on working ... he went out of the bathroom and opened the curtain in his room, where the sun fell through the window onto the floor like a punctured ball.

He crushed two cloves of garlic, squeezed a bitter lemon over them, then opened a tin of brown beans: he warmed them up and poured them onto the plate ... he beheaded the red tomato and sprinkled on some salt. He opened the last jar of pickled cucumbers ... he took one out and put it on the little plate ... he said to himself, I forgot the olives, I should change the water which has grown a skin of mold because I didn't use coarse salt ... Khalil sat down to eat, watching the window ... he switched on the radio and listened to the news ... he put the dishes in the sink and filled the copper coffee pot with water ... he turned off the tap and began to throw up violently as if he wanted to bring his guts up out of his mouth ...

The first time I saw Nayif was in the courtyard at college. I couldn't take my eyes off him ... he was very shy, like me ... and like me, he was diffident and pretended not to care ... what really made him stand out was the collar of the white shirt he wore, with the sleeves cut short at home to suit the season for it was still hot at the beginning of autumn. His shirt collar was narrower than the wide collars that were in vogue at that time ... and it was buttoned up, which was also unusual at that time when young men used to wear colorful, flowery shirts open down to the navel. His narrow, white collar was buttoned up ... he wore black trousers with wide legs ... he looked as if he had just been sent away from a party after the people there had stripped him of half his clothes then thrown him out for being incorrectly dressed ... watching him took me out of my isolation a little and I liked him when he began training for the role of the unshockable, staring openly at the bare legs of the girls and smiling.

After we became friends, he invited me to his house in Moussaitbeh where I had lunch with him and met his parents. His mother was a fat, jolly woman; quick to anger, she would curse and swear using foul words as if they were everyday language . . . he would happily reply in the same language. He cursed his mother, shouted and slammed the door behind him, unconcerned that he left me plunged into a confusion the like of which I had never experienced in my life before . . . she sat down facing me, completely calm, and asked me about my family . . . it was not long before Nayif returned pushing a wheelchair in which a young man was sitting who he introduced to me as his close friend: Nassib . . .

After that, Nassib became our friend . . . he had his sacred times, when we would take him to the restaurant nearby or to the cinema . . . one of us would carry him while the other would deal with the chair . . . we used to play chess with him and sometimes we would drink coffee and chat to his spinster sister who made a living as a seamstress . . . we would tell her jokes while she prepared hot cheese pastries for us . . . when he wanted to punish his mother, Nayif used to borrow money from Nassib . . . Nassib used to lend us carefully folded banknotes which he would take from a leather wallet with tattered edges . . . except for his wallet, everything he owned looked like new, as if he had just bought it . . . Nayif's house was very small, and always full of guests, relatives from the village far away, so he often used to sleep at Nassib's house . . .

Once he came round looking very worried and when I asked him why he said, sadly: what will happen to Nassib? he's so intelligent . . . suppose his sister were to die one day . . . what girl would be happy with him. He's paralyzed, you know what I mean . . . no girl no matter how old or ugly . . . if you don't give women what their lower half wants they won't be happy . . . they don't care about anything else . . . do you know that Nassib understands music? . . . he's artistic and sensitive . . . what do you think? . . . his life is . . . hard.

I said to Nayif . . . Nassib still has us . . . we won't leave him, you and I . . . he soon looked happy again . . . he had been carrying a heavy burden and I had lifted it from his shoulders. He said: of course, my friend . . .

After Nayif joined the Party, he socialized less with his friends. He stopped being with us all the time . . . perhaps Hamza's biting scorn frightened him most, even if he seemed easygoing and friendly . . .

After a while he began to miss lectures and skip college . . . he took to greeting other young men with a handshake, like a man . . . behaving more formally with them. He began to pay more attention to his clothes and to girls, he began to fail in the end of year examinations and to look with apparent scorn at those who were successful . . . he began to meet only the new students and the new girls . . . then he grew his beard and began to take part in demonstrations and after that, he moved up to the front row where he linked arms with men older than him . . . he used to carry thick books and magazines around under his arm although Hamza swore he never read a word of them . . . he no longer invited me to go to see Nassib . . .

I still love Nayif . . . a lot.

—Why do you live in this area when you're a Christian?

—Because you don't get your sense of belonging only from the sect into which you're born.

—Wouldn't your struggle have more meaning and be more useful on the other side where ignorance, misguided ideas, and sectarianism leave people no room to turn?

—They'd kill me there and I'd be no use at all . . . I can't put up any resistance to the sort of terrorism that they use.

—You're speaking as if you'd be on your own although you often say that a lot of Christians have chosen to live here.

—Not enough to resist.

—But there are enough to resist a monster like Israel.

—It's a civil war. I wouldn't kill people from my country in the way that I might kill Israelis. I don't want to wipe them out.

—But your party has some strongholds that take part in the random bombings.

—We retaliate to silence them . . . my being here ensures that a democratic atmosphere exists, in which my party can express itself.

—Is that really necessary? . . . what about the secret struggle?

—It seems you want to divide things up according to sectarian logic: you want those who struggle for here, to be here and those who struggle for there, to be there . . . I mean, you seem to want to have two countries.

—But the reality of what's happening says it is two countries.

—No, I'm a Christian and I'm staying here. I'm putting my opposition down for the record.

—To make you more important, to draw a circle of light around yourself, to be treated like a hero so a picture of your village can hang in the sitting room, so you can stand in front of the guests, you're just longing to be in a place that you can't be.

—No. I reject sectarianism, whatever the rationale for it. I'm standing by my beliefs, no matter what the price.

—The price your little brother paid, your little brother who left the army, you told him so often that the army should go to Sarfand where the Israelis had attacked, so he was killed with the armed wing of your party in Chiyah. The price is that you take liberties and your value on the market rises, you profit whenever the number of Christians here drops and revel in the chaos like bandits in the forest.

—Chaos is what made me live in humble poverty, chaos assassinated my companions, and chaos kidnapped and killed my neighbor Mahmoud because he is a Muslim . . .

—But for you to say I know . . . and I am innocent and Naji was an agent . . .

—Khalil, you're sick. This country is not two countries. I'm not important and Naji is an agent.

—Yes, Nayif, I'm sick. This country is not two countries and you aren't important and Naji . . .

Khalil thought that a hypothetical argument like this was proof of mental deficiency . . . and that Nayif must be right. I really need Nayif . . . Nayif is the one I love because we are so alike, he's the one who comes when I didn't realize that I needed him. He comes to help me to bury the dead.

But who is dead? Khalil had to answer this question, to know what had happened before Naji died . . . the least that the family of the departed could do is to know what they were grieving for and who they would bury . . . even his own family looks at the dead man with eyes full of doubt, for the corpse never quite convincingly resembles its dead owner . . . between fits of weeping, their eyes keep going back to look at him and the women touch him. They do so not because they find his departure difficult to come to terms with but because the corpse bears only a passing resemblance to its living owner, just enough to leave a crack through which doubt can creep in and out . . . they are so confused that they no longer call him by his name but say "the corpse" instead . . . so that speaking of the dead man comes to be in the neuter . . . they say it's been moved . . . it's arrived . . . it's been buried . . . it's risen . . . and when his family mourn him publicly, they avert their eyes from the man in the shroud and turn to their memories . . . they weep as he walks and moves and laughs and talks . . . when their gaze falls on his corpse again, they look again. At that time, they avoid mentioning unpleasant things, they seem to say: it hasn't changed . . . it looks like sleep not death . . . the skin is still soft and pale . . . it doesn't smell foul, it smells like incense, like wild flowers . . .

Words that make you remember a thing that was particular to its owner . . . although a thing far from his pure soul . . . his corpse. But his keys, his clothes, his car, his bed are more intimate things, with a stronger effect on those who remember, these things conjure "it" up more powerfully . . .

There is even some consolation to be found in the corpse's presence among the family of the departed, it gives them the chance to put off, to prepare for the feeling of his total and final loss . . . for here he is in an empty form, to be present in an artificial way that barely comes close to the presence of the absent man's photograph . . . he is here to record the event without stirring up its real dust, without recording the heavy night that follows it . . . he is here to put it down for history . . . the month, the day, the hour, the wearing of mourning, the wailing . . . he is here to make sure it happens, to give vent to its echoing explosion and to postpone its slow descent which will gnaw at the nights of their sorrow like a loathsome worm, waiting until it is surrounded by forgetfulness as it slowly dries its eggs . . . not once when they remember his death and weep for him, not once, is his corpse present . . . it is only present to remind them of the acceptable, domesticated form of death. As if to remind them who was present to console them, who was late, and who was in a hurry to leave . . . who cried a lot, who came to enjoy the wake, and who did not come . . . that is to say, the presence of the corpse makes them remember what seems to be their diversion from death, their forgetting of the dead man himself . . .

Khalil did not have Naji's corpse and, after Nayif had been, he no longer had anything of that which had gone before the corpse . . . a long wand stirred the warm cauldron of his memory, turning it into a bubbling mixture of base elements, a witches' brew . . .

What should he prepare for Naji's death? Should he fold him away carefully in drawers and cupboards with bags of dried lavender so that he can take them and spread them out when he weeps tears of grief in remembrance of a dear friend, the first tree on the edge of the road to old age? Or should he pour his death into pots and pans and bowls . . . in which to cool it down until he feels bored, until his heart is hungry, so he can eat the friendship that is no more and salt away the experience for many future relationships . . . or should he prepare a hatchet for Naji with which to split death open whenever it grows a finger's breadth above the earth of the grave, to wipe out the enormous naïveté, like an idiot, then sit like a useless woodcutter who does not know how to turn his dead pieces of wood into charcoal, into embers that heat the blazing fire of rancor and wasted longing for a man who was beautiful, innocent, distant, who was like as a twin and who used to broil children on the New Road with hexogen and TNT . . .

Do I know so very little about him? . . . is he that other man, whose evil appetites awake at night and make him go, like that, to kill in cold blood and come back to me the next day smiling, handsome and meeker than a sacrificial lamb? When the moon waxed full in the darkness of the sky, did he used to go out to the arid wastelands and howl like a hungry wolf, his fangs glinting in the night, in search of hot, fresh entrails? Or did he used to scream like an eagle soaring on the breeze of still nights over the soil of desecrated graves? . . . or was he a killer like the hit-men in American films . . . wearing soft leather gloves, turning up the collar of his overcoat, winking and raising an eyebrow as he laughs at our stupidity and strolls out to the empty street . . . with an arsenic pill between his white, white teeth which he bites on when he falls into the clutches of the enemy and who, when he goes home, takes leave of his cronies far from the street where he lives, then slips into his room and takes off the hired killer's clothes, hides them under the floorboards and scatters the clothes that we know to be his on his bed in what is obviously a deliberate mess . . . then opens a secret drawer and takes out something like a radio, or invisible ink and . . .

Did Madame Isabelle know about all this, did she help him and cover up for him with the cunning of her gray hair, wound up in its wise woman's coil . . . was she really his mother? Was she really an old woman or, after she bolted the door shut from the inside, did she take off her wig and peel away the leather mask before she and Naji spent scarlet nights together, which the bombing made more furious . . . laughing like vampires . . . playing their bloodstained, satanic games until the first rays of dawn . . .

Khalil was enjoying letting his thoughts run on like this because like a game, like playing, he did not find it tiring so it was impossible to take it seriously . . . he had chosen the images that he wanted to see and he said to himself, I'm doing it on purpose because I don't want to believe it, I'm choosing to imagine things that are patently silly, unreal, extreme, ridiculous because I don't want to listen to Nayif . . . maybe because I can't bear to . . .

Nayif's eyes turned to Khalil again . . . he found it hard to breathe . . . he stood in the middle of his room doing nothing at all . . . rage was welling up inside him, rising like water on the point of . . . for the first time for a long time, he thought of visiting one of his relatives . . . the face of his father who had been dead for years came to him, racked with coughing on the doorstep of their house in the village . . . he turned to the door and thought . . . the time has come for me to stop putting it off. Before he opened the door he suddenly felt deeply frustrated and asked himself: but . . . what am I putting off . . . Naji's death, or his reality? . . . either way it's a terrible loss . . . but I tend to believe that Nayif's telling the truth . . . he's honest . . . and he closed the door behind him.

Khalil sprang lightly up the steps but, as he put the key in the lock, when he pushed the door open wide and heard the familiar creaking hinge, he felt heavy. He went in, closing the door behind him.

Madame Isabelle's apartment had lost its war, had finally become haunted. It had been taken over by those damned spirits forever . . . the apartment seemed a lot smaller than Khalil remembered it, although it was emptier . . . the windows, covered with nylon instead of glass, blocked out the light coming in but, at the same time, they made the apartment look more like the street outside. The layer of gray dust, which covered the things in the apartment and stopped the light that did come in from being reflected off them, did the same.

The breath of the people who lived there had gone, gone from the dry air, disappeared without trace . . . even their things which, with a little effort, Khalil could remember them using, could remember them living with, now seemed empty, neutral, and barren as ordinary things. Now there was a real gap between them and their owners . . . like the gap between someone in pain and his tooth, which has been pulled . . . a little confusion at first, then an awkward stiffness, followed by distant withdrawal . . .

But I haven't gone into the bedroom yet, thought Khalil . . . a disgusting, pungent smell was coming out of the kitchen . . . decaying things . . . rotten pickles or food that should be thrown away . . . Khalil turned to the kitchen . . . his stomach heaved and he held his nose . . . he opened the refrigerator and, unable to stand the sight or smell, quickly closed it. Before he went out, he saw that the sink was running with a black, bubbling, syrupy liquid . . .

He closed the kitchen door and stood panting, his eyes watering . . . on the floor, on the threshold of the kitchen, there were a lot of dead cockroaches lying on their backs . . . these spirits leave nothing alive except the worms and whatever is lower than worms . . .

Khalil rushed back to the sitting room where the smell was less overpowering . . . the boxes were still by the entrance, his sister had not come to take the things she had asked him to pack up, perhaps she was afraid of coming, perhaps her husband had forbidden her to come or perhaps something important had come up that had stopped her ... it occurred to Khalil that Madame Isabelle might have died because . . . she could not bear it . . .

He picked up the receiver after he had blown on it a few times to get rid of the dust . . . the dial tone came, long and high. Khalil put down the receiver, took a leather wallet out of his jacket, and took a folded piece of paper from one of its pockets. He opened it out and began to dial the number . . . he was surprised when he heard a voice on the other end.

Khalil sat down on the edge of Naji's bed spontaneously as if Naji were near him, in the room . . . he began staring in front of him without seeing anything . . . the news went into his head . . . like a dog, prowling where it pleases, squatting down where it sees fit, not bound by the circle of the direct conscious. What Khalil sees and hears, without taking it in, settles, slow and elusive, in the circle of his thoughts. He stayed where he was for a while, on the bed for several long minutes staring at the drawer of the little table right by the bed . . . it occurred to him to move a little so he opened the drawer and began to turn over the things in it . . . there were a lot of papers, rusty keys, beautiful little empty leather boxes, and there were some photographs . . . Khalil spread out the pictures and pulled out one . . . it was an old, black and white photograph of Madame Isabelle with some women . . . she could not have yet reached forty and her face was lit up by her smile, which had not changed a lot . . . her black hair was very like the gray hair that Khalil knew so well except for that white streak coiled up high on her forehead, which seemed like a joke . . . the women sitting together around her seemed very calm and composed and Khalil guessed, from the clear light in the background, that it must have been sometime before noon . . . the large sofa on which Madame Isabelle was sitting with one of the women was still shining new but the cloth of the little benches was different . . . the women were smiling for the photographer, gentle and calm except for the one sitting next to Madame Isabelle who seemed naughtier than the others, as if at the last moment she had suppressed a laugh that was on the point of bursting out . . . he paused a while to look at this last, familiar face until he remembered the lonely old spinster on the fifth floor, who had died at the beginning of the civil war, for whom Madame Isabelle had wept a lot and taken it upon herself to make all the arrangements for her burial. She was a well-known seamstress, as far as he remembered, to whom only a few women went, women of her own age who covered their withered faces with white powder . . . Khalil had been a newcomer to the building in those days . . . he had moved there from his uncle's house, which was full of children, after he found a teaching job at a small private school during his first year at university.

Khalil took another picture out of the drawer . . . it was in color, on thick paper . . . one of those polaroid photographs. It was very small and dark . . . it was of Naji with a girl next to him, by the seaside with the fading red sunset behind them. There was a strong breeze that blew Naji's long hair across part of his laughing face, so nothing showed except his open mouth. The girl's long, flying hair was all blown over to her left shoulder. Revealing her face and her neck. She was not laughing, nor was she even smiling. She was beautiful. She had raised one of her legs to rest it on the metal railing on which she was leaning . . . she had a short skirt and her legs were long, still, and brightly lit, whereas Naji's body was drowning in the gloom in his dark clothes. Khalil looked more closely at the picture, at the girl's face, making certain she was not smiling, nor even laughing. He began trying to reconstruct the original colors . . . her lips seemed to be pink and her eyes intensely black . . . her eyebrows were thick, joined above the nose, and she was looking directly into Naji's eyes. Gazing into his face . . . as if she were saying to him, about Naji: he's unbearable . . . unbearable . . . I'll go back home . . . but it seemed Khalil had made her pause a little, made her stop to see what he wants . . . Khalil thought he wanted something from her, but he could not work out what it was as fast as she was asking him . . . then she seemed to slow down and stop again, a little longer this time, giving him a real opportunity. Khalil said: well . . . it occurs to me to tell you about myself, now, now that we have talked about so many things . . . I find this intimacy between us confusing. I mean, I've never yet desired any woman at all, and I haven't gone to the doctor . . . I don't remember if I told you about the district president's daughter in the village. That clean little girl with long blonde hair who I used to love, I used to cry tears of exasperation whenever I saw her passing in front of our house near the square with her mother . . . after they left the village I never desired any girl, any woman . . . sometimes I used to think about Madame Isabelle's body. About what was under her clothes and I was seized by the desire to take her in my arms but my member would have nothing to do with it . . . I mean . . . you understand . . . I used to want to see her naked, I used to feel intrigued, a kind of longing . . . I used to hang around the house when my aunt used to visit us . . . she'd take off her scarf and her high heels . . . but generally, women only arouse a dull curiosity in me which turns into a sort of fear when I get close to their bodies . . . their bodies are more complex than I can bear or rather than I can imagine . . . they seem impossible to reach . . . but you . . . I want to touch your legs, I'd love to run my hands over them, from the ankle up . . . slowly . . . slowly . . . to the top. To put my lips to the crease in the back of your knee while my hand moves up your thigh, my cold hand on your hot thigh, you wouldn't move because you're in the photograph. I'd stay like that for a long time . . . a long time and then I'd tell you how much I love you, how many empty years I've sat waiting for you, my heart like a rotten egg hopelessly trying to hide its stinking inside . . . my body like a molted broom which sits, ignored, in a corner gathering dust and sticky dirt and getting shorter. You will give off a smell like the smell of women, which calls me with its rough, sacred, animal voice in the thick forest . . . the smell walks and I follow, humble, intoxicated, proud, frantic, keeping a grip on my entire body in the narrow space which gets denser and smaller and more precisely marked out . . . I control my speed, I move faster, my steps, my dry head gets lighter. Then you get up . . .

Khalil no longer saw anything in the photograph, only small, dark perpetually vibrating waves for, having stared so long at a small dark space, his eyes were filled with tears. He put down the picture and put out the lamp, then threw himself across the bed, on top of Naji's clothes which were still piled up on it. He felt a sudden chill rising from his feet. He took the edges of the bedcover in both hands and tugged them, with the clothes that were on top of them, over himself . . . he began to stare at the ceiling and the dog saw fit to come out into the smooth white space, into the circle of light: Nayif loves me so much he thought he should make me hate him so I can forget him . . . Naji was killed by a sniper's bullet, he was shot down before he reached the Green Line . . . Madame Isabelle said that the bullet reached him from their side . . . that he fell while he was still in the eastern quarter . . . that they brought him to her . . . that she buried him . . . and that she is going to Saudi Arabia.

Khalil . . . I'm going to die . . .

7

A month or more after Naji died, after he was killed by a sniper from the eastern quarter of the capital, Khalil developed a lighter touch and handled the things around him better during the daytime, that is to say, he became more able to withdraw, to isolate himself, and the more he managed to do so the happier he was, and the more certain of his legs which were becoming stronger and better able to scale the mountain ... the high mountain, even though it was not so very high, its tapering peak capped with a dusting of snow ... its foot drowning in green meadows where the pure, fresh breeze fills the lungs, purges the blood, purifies the imagination, and keeps the demands of the body to the bare minimum ... that mountain that looks like the mountains on boxes of fresh cheese. It was as if Khalil's being alone were his one solace and the sister of his days, since he completely neglected all other futile activity ... whenever he came to eat less and thus needed less money, he used to cover the distance and rise towards the peak, he used to reckon his longing to sit there in terms of the little white handkerchiefs that he would wave at the city that lay waiting below and that, by virtue of the height, would vanish under its smoky clouds and vaporous smells which would turn to cotton wool changing shape with the light wind showing Khalil a sheep, then a balloon, then an enormous elephant walking . . . and so he amuses himself . . .

All this does not mean to say that Khalil had cut himself off from people altogether . . . he used to leave a margin open to them, a hallway from which he would see them and talk to them and love them, but he did not let them into his storytelling, his laughter, and his sorrow, he did not sit them down nor invite them to eat, nor did he make them sleep by his bed nor entertain them with his memories, nor rejoice nor get angry nor be sad because of them, nor did he put himself out to talk to them about himself, or about anything . . . he would see them for a little while in the hallway of his eyes then close the door and retreat inside.

He did not make a conscious decision to do this . . . it was as if other people understood or, rather, as if circumstances favored him and the opportunity that he craved arose, and he took it.

But the nights were something else . . . when the sun went down it seemed to take down with it the small pleasure that Khalil did have, to the other tropic of our beautiful, blue globe.

Khalil, although he was happy during the day, found himself unable to fill time at night . . . in the day, time filled itself . . . Khalil did nothing to make the daytime pass for he did not feel it necessary . . . only at night, Khalil began to wonder about what he might do to take his head by surprise to empty it, like that, suddenly, so that he might seek something to fill it . . . not his head, exactly, perhaps his body, or perhaps the room . . . in the day it seemed full of warm waters, a womb in which Khalil swam, breathing in the cosmic harmony that the light radiates, soaking it up into his very nature as if it were an extension of his slender body, as if when the light fades something pulls the plug and drains those waters away, leaving the room dry, thirsty, sucking on another time that resembles external time. Time that has to be filled.

Khalil's skin, which had become more and more pale and sallow, perhaps because he stayed out of the sun, lost its ruddy blush and took on a leafy shade of green . . . moving so little, staying in one, small place had made his life more like that of a plant . . . by day, pure oxygen and by night, carbon dioxide which muddied space with its disturbed breathing.

Time after time Khalil used to switch on the radio at night . . . a small, orange plastic radio which used to get dirty quickly and which, during his frequent, methodical night-time bouts of cleaning, he used to clean with a large piece of cotton wool soaked in white spirit, wiping the radio very carefully, poking the ends of the cotton wool into the corners and crevices with a matchstick . . . once, as he was cleaning it, he began to listen by chance . . . he was surprised to hear talking, which he was not used to hearing on the radio, then he found that the button had moved to FM, where it had not moved before.

There were many small stations like this one. Wherever you turned the needle, familiar voices were talking . . . familiar? not altogether, but there was something in them that reassured Khalil, that made him listen . . . listen in a special way . . . not because he particularly wanted to or because he was particularly interested, but . . .

He used to take the little metal tray and sit next to the radio for hours, picking over lentils or rice for the soup he had at dawn, his only meal. Or, he would sit next to the radio unraveling old woolen sweaters then wrapping the crinkled threads around a thick book to smooth them out, in the hope that he might knit them up again as soon as he went shopping and bought the right needles. Women, who tame external time, in their wisdom know that knitting, stitch after stitch, row upon row, is what guarantees that the thread of the days is drawn out as grains of worry are drawn out from troubled souls.

Khalil came to know the FM people because, like him, they stayed up all night which means that, like him, they did not work or go out in the daytime except the way that he works or goes out . . . like him, they were in touch with one another without knowing each other, from their jagged little mountains that looked like his mountain. The FM people were people who lived in the city below. Outside it. In its internal night. People like him, who knew neither how to get into its days nor into its streets. They talked without speaking . . . they talked to the broadcaster who kept on talking, who said nothing at all . . . who only filled the ear with an empty, emptying human feeling. The broadcaster greeted the people. The people greeted him . . . he told them jokes, he played them songs that, longing for the cosmic emptiness that reigns in distant galaxies, were like them. They talked to him on the telephone and they talked to each other through him. They sent each other polite messages full of fine emotions, transparent as sheets of gelatine, emotions that crossed the night outside as hidden vibrations beyond the hearing even of dogs. There was never any news on the sentimental FM broadcasts nor any mention of anything particular to the city's daytime existence . . . the broadcaster laughed a lot, laughed between words and phrases . . . he did not prepare his show or read from a script but worked on the telephone with individuals, in the network . . . it was like a network . . . a network of people who speak, using false names, to a broadcaster whose name is also false even if it is his real name. They speak in this evasive, figurative language because they play with the dream of metaphor and live it . . . the dream of unfastening the buttons, at night, of stripping yourself and your city and your meanings down to pure metaphor. Metaphor that strikes at the heart of the original.

Nothing makes the listener listen to the FM programs, nothing at all, and the broadcaster is a point of connection, like a priest entrusted with the great secret, the telephone number. If he were dragged off by armed men to a cellar and beaten and tortured, if they pulled out his fingernails he would not give the telephone number to anyone . . . this goes without saying. Ronnie wants to get in touch with Gloria, who was sad yesterday when she talked on the subject of "do you believe in luck," directing what she was saying at Danny . . . only the priest knows Gloria's number because she herself gave it to him to give to Danny who had perhaps not been in touch because he had forgotten it or lost his phone book. Gloria or Fatimah know Danny or Mahmoud but thousands of other listeners do not know each other and they know neither Gloria nor Danny . . . but Gloria and Danny become their heroes, the center of the net that they weave around their time for nights on end. Around their city. When the priest calls Gloria, she is awake and he asks, Gloria were you sad yesterday and what are you doing now? She says she is listening to the broadcast and makes a request for a song which she dedicates to Ronnie to thank him for his concern and to assure him that it is only a passing cloud and that at any time of day or night—some things make you happy and some things make you sad—she asks him if he has finished mending his car, which was on his mind, she asks him to take care of his health because it is the most precious thing in the world . . . she dedicates the latest song by

Wardah el Jazayeriyeh to the listeners and the broadcaster . . .

They are people, but they are not real. Only their voices are real and this was what gave Khalil pleasure . . . voices that existed in corridors. For the pleasure of benign corridors, voices that had no wish to come in at all . . . real voices, empty and false, they were the real voices of a city like this . . . the real city, people like me exist, then, they are real and they talk on FM . . . they aren't like the sewer rats that lead another life underground in the cities . . . they are the real city and those, those who are above them are the lie, so the city has not ceased to be, so given the choice between Nayif and Danny my heart chooses without hesitation: Danny is the real friend . . .

So Khalil stretched the telephone wire into his room and put the phone on the little table by his bed . . . he spent long nights thinking about calling the station numbers that the broadcaster kept repeating but he did not . . . he preferred them to get in touch with him . . . he waited a long time and they did not get in touch . . . how would they know that this was his number and not the number of one of the people up there who would curse and shout, not understanding at all why they had been woken up after midnight, citizens taken up in the days of the city, who sacrifice the night to restore the strength that they will offer the city the next morning, like donkeys carrying the waters of the sea to a hole on the shore for the sake of a lovely orange carrot in the evening. How would they understand.

Mervat was very hard on Rafat, who had called to say what he thought about honesty. She asked him not to make generalizations based on his personal experience and said that if there was a girl who had broken his heart it did not mean that all girls were liars, but she assured him—not from personal experience—that young men were devious and lied to girls because it was in their interest to do so, to avoid getting married or to persuade the girl to give them what they wanted . . . then she apologized for being so sharp, but said she could be nothing if not frank . . . and she dedicated a song to him and the listeners.

Rafat called again to reply . . . his voice was low and he spoke slowly, not because he was embarrassed but because he had difficulty breathing . . . Khalil thought that Rafat sounded very sad and stoned, and he began to listen closely. Rafat started talking about the beauty of girls and how their beauty was not suited to their ways . . . of putting things off or escaping . . . then playing with people's feelings . . . he said that he believed Mervat but that he . . . he was different . . . because he had really loved his girlfriend and he had been honest with her . . . he said that she had very long, soft hair and he left it up to the broadcaster to choose a song, which he dedicated to the listeners . . . the broadcaster did the right thing in choosing "Why Did You Cut Your Long Hair" to lift the gloomy atmosphere that was not right for the program, but Khalil found his eyes drowning in tears . . . and he began to think about Rafat . . .

The broadcaster asked Khalil what he wanted to say . . . he said he wanted to be friends with Rafat and the broadcaster began asking him questions . . . Khalil found himself replying that he agreed with Rafat, he said what he thought about honesty and dedicated a passage from Abd el Halim Hafez's "Lovely and Lying" to the listeners . . . this made Khalil happy, it brought the smile back to his face and, after a few minutes, he went back to winding the woolen threads around the book, while the lentil soup bubbled on the low flame, scenting the air with the aroma of cooking.

Khalil was running in a cropped meadow in a place something like the green in his village. The touch of his feet on the ground sent him bounding, flying for yards and yards across the meadow, which stretched out endlessly before him. Although he did not have long legs, they sent him light and far like a heavy balloon and he laughed like the Egyptian actress Mervat Amin, his long, shining chestnut hair flying out behind him . . . Rafat was laughing and flying too, but could not catch up with him . . . he was laughing and asking Khalil to slow down a bit, not to keep on tormenting him. Khali-i-i-l, Rafat was calling, in a delicious, inviting, melodic voice that made him want to flirt and leap . . . and laugh even more.

Khalil leaned back against the thick tree trunk while Rafat began to carve on a green olive branch a dark red heart, where the letters K and R shone out with a particular, oily sheen. Rafat came close to Khalil and pushed back a long strand of hair that was fluttering across his face. Khalil looked shyly at his legs . . . he saw they were the legs of the girl next to Naji in the instant photograph and he was more sure that he was beautiful and ready for love. Rafat brought his hand down to Khalil's neck, where the hair grows thick and, panting loudly, brought his eyes and lips close to his face. Khalil's head rose violently and hit the tree. He put his hand up to his face, feeling the fiery slap, then saw Naji looking at him, his eyes red, his face distorted in anger. Naji stood facing him for seconds that seemed like minutes, looking intently into his face, close to his face. Khalil was trembling, but not out of fear. Naji took hold of Khalil's collar and tugged at it, pulling the buttons off his shirt as he tore it open down to the navel. Naji took a step backwards and smoothed down his hair with his hand, then slowly came close again, stretching out his strong hand to pull Khalil's leather belt undone . . .

Khalil found himself standing next to his bed for— perhaps—minutes . . . every opening in his small body had let forth every drop of its special waters . . . he was drowning in his cold sweat and his pajama bottoms were clinging between his thighs . . . a watery blob of mucus was sliding down the saliva that ran from his mouth, running down in threads from his chin to the jacket of his pajamas which was open, showing his shoulder and part of his arm . . . only his eyes were dry, so he sat and wept a flood of tears until the sun had filled his room completely.

III

1

Whenever the sound of the bombs and rockets exploding got really bad they used to put their heads down between their shoulders and call on God to spare them, invoking His protection. Then they would tell off the children, who were quick to go back to playing their games, even if these were limited to the length of the silence between one blaze of fire and another . . . it was as if the children, who were the only ones over whom power could be exercised, bore the brunt of people's feelings of powerlessness in the face of what was going on outside, for people were no longer able to bear their neutrality, or the fact that they were able to go out, heedless of the living fear or unaware of the high probability of their death . . . the children wanted to live life and enjoy it so they ignored this, between bouts of nervous diarrhea, and their eyes would no sooner meet the eyes of other children than they would agree that their gathering would be like an invincible feast. They stick to their mothers, but only for a few moments. They begin to demand things, they get more hungry and thirsty than usual, perhaps they do this to bring their families back from being scattered in fear, to bring back the secure image they hold of their families, far removed from the stain of madness that flashes in the eyes of the adults, to make their mother like the mother they knew at home again, who used to serve their food or look at their faces a little before they fell asleep, so that their fathers do not betray them and go out into the street, into the night outside.

Khalil did not stay long in his room. He took his blanket and closed the door behind him. He ran across the entrance and leapt quickly up the few stairs to the landing on the second floor. The machine-gun fire and the echo of the explosions were getting close. Any exploding bullet making a hole in his wall, which gave its back to the street, meant his certain death . . . before, he used to take shelter in his little bathroom, lighting a candle that he would put on the shelf by the mirror. He would put down the seatcover and begin to read, or work at one of his many handicrafts . . . Khalil really felt safe because he believed that he owned his body and knew it backwards . . . or that he had got to know it honestly and possessed it like an introverted boy, enigmatic and dull, but he possessed it in any case. The similarity of his body to other peoples' bodies . . . to Naji's body in particular, restored his sense of security and took the edge off his anxiety. Of course this similarity did not lie in their being the same shape, but in the way they did things together. It was something like brotherliness . . . when they skulk in their houses, people feel the need to come out into the street. Believing they simply feel bored, they go out to take a stroll, for a walk . . . really, they are anxious to get a grip on their bodies since they don't know what might become of them, for they fear their bodies may escape. That they may turn into wolves, for example. That in their isolation they may be turned into some sort of monstrosities, into vagabond beasts of prey . . . so they take their bodies for a walk as you might take a dog. They tie them to their hands and walk them among other people's bodies to make sure of the resemblance, to remind themselves of their limbs, to see them reflected in the way that other bodies, balanced or unbalanced, behave . . . to make sure that our bodies stay supple, that we keep control over them, we walk in the street. We say: look, body of mine, see how like you these bodies are. How at ease and beautifully made, how supple and responsive they are, how well-behaved . . . so we never go out in the clothes we wear when we are alone, that is, in our wild skins, but we spruce ourselves up, we comb our hair so as to help others by showing that as we care so much for our possessions, so we have every right to ask that these possessions of ours acknowledge who is master and look like the others.

After Naji was killed, Khalil's body no longer had a brother or a close match, so it began to get confused, the surface of his inhibitions was split open and his suspicious dreams invaded him, they unfastened the ties by which he kept a grip on many intricate and ambiguous matters, the least of which were his erotic dreams which used to shake him like a violent storm. They would batter him with their sharp little hatchets and, after he woke up, he would struggle to gather up the fragments and rack his brain to analyze them, which helped a lot but did not completely wipe out his feeling of anxiety, especially since he did not have much faith in psychiatry or in what was in the many books he owned ... Khalil knew that a fear of blood to the point of faintness, having short legs, a slight build, straight chestnut hair and large eyes, all these do not make a man a hermaphrodite, or effeminate, or make him any less masculine, or ... queer ... he knew that the temporary breakdown that he was suffering was only a psychological crisis that the mad world outside had imposed upon him ... he knew that there were certainly more female hormones in him than there should naturally be, for they protected him from committing the crime of the act, so it was only a passing crisis, it would come to an end ... he definitely desired women but, at this moment in time, he did not feel particularly susceptible to any particular woman. Khalil's efforts end in a short, broken phrase in which he says to himself, to no avail: "Naji is dead."

So Khalil, when the bombing grew heavier, no longer used to stay alone in his room.

The children dozed on the landing. Then they slept ... the sound of the explosions made them blink a little and curl up where they lay on their mothers' chests and around their fathers' necks. When the adults became tired, their fear left them and the wisdom of peace, which says that fear drives out sleep, seemed naive. Sleepiness drives out everything: war and the shaking earth have their own, certain wisdom. Even the bride, a newcomer to the building, felt drowsy and abandoned the larded, powder-puff femininity that she had brought with her from home: the loose hair, the dark rouge, the long, long nails and the transparent, rose-pink nightdress which she let peep out from under the velvet dressing gown . . . she even left her pink satin slippers with the lace and fur and shiny ribbons leaning on their high heels by the wall, since people were too sleepy to notice them. Her slippers had provoked stifled indignation among the women; one of her neighbors had remarked in a whisper that the slippers had come straight out of the box to celebrate the bombing and that they would be a fat lot of use for running and leaping up the stairs . . . their indignation was not innocent, for that night the mothers had found nothing in their pot of sorrows to equal the spices that the newcomer sprinkled over the men. And then, they did not believe her when she writhed and moaned and whimpered pretending to be scared, but although it did not convince them it might convince their men. Abou Ahmad, who lingered around the house without his family, seemed the most disapproving of the bride. She made his eyes turn red and he began to heap curses mercilessly upon all the armed men killing each other outside, everywhere, knowing that the bridegroom was one of them . . . it was as if he wanted to provoke her to talk, to answer back, so he could look at her mouth a little longer, at the opening of the rose-pink shirt where it was rumpled over her ample chest . . . but she did nothing, seeming at the same time unperturbed by his abusive words . . . or as if she understood and was encouraging his rapture.

They were all tired, all drowsy because the fighting had gone on longer than usual this time and, although it was nearly three in the morning, the bombing was still going strong . . . Abou Ahmad, his eyes red, said this was no ordinary bombing and that this time, there were invasions. Things would not calm down until one of the sides had taken firm control of the road; then he added, addressing his words to everyone: we might stay here for two or three days . . . or more . . . they'll calm down a bit in a while . . . then leave everything where it is, get milk for the children and some bread and cushions, and listen to me. None of you is to risk your life by sleeping in your bed.

Everyone knew, from the hidden network of communication, from the code that they used to use with the armed men on the street, that Abou Ahmad was right. Then one of the neighbors, relying on the retired policeman's greater wisdom, asked Abou Ahmad whether he believed the building had been hit directly, hoping to hear the conclusive reply from his mouth: that is, that it is Abou Ahmad's apartment which has been hit and not his own, for his is the most exposed to the street and another bomb would not make it any more of a wreck than it is already . . . everyone would find something to justify his hope that his neighbor's apartment was the one that had been damaged.

After a couple of days, people came out of their buildings onto the quiet street. They moved slowly, calmly, as if they were going for a walk and had still not quite decided exactly where to go, seeming indifferent to the houses behind them that had been hit . . . but some stopped for a few moments in front of a broken balcony which made them feel more like laughter than reproof. The wall overlooking the street was collapsing, its stones all gone, while the open refrigerator, complete with plates and vegetables, hung, propped up by a split stone and the dishes, arrayed on the shelf over the sink, as well as some of the pickles, stayed as they were, as if they had not even heard the sound of the rocket that had sheared the wall. The pot on the stove seemed ready to serve, for it was lunchtime. Only the housewife's apron was out of place, raised like a small blue flag from an iron bar that stuck out of the wall in the corner.

When people coming out into the street saw the large, freshly-painted barrels that blocked off one of the alleyways, they knew that the star of a new leader had been born during the past two nights in this very alley, so those people whose cars had been set ablaze felt less stricken by grief for, whenever the alleys are blocked off and people are forbidden to use them, the street narrows and people who have cars worry more about how to park them in the few remaining spaces, or about how likely it is that they might sell them off quickly for a reasonable price.

2

Since his father's younger brother and his family had moved from the village and come to live in Madame Isabelle's house, Khalil had become less isolated and more prepared to approach people . . . perhaps it was the vitality of the large family that made him rise a little to the surface of the liquids of his room, that made him open the curtain and come and go, or go up to his uncle's house and come back to his room, more often.

That is what Khalil believed and, when he doubted the purity of his intentions in his explanation of the changes that were coming over him, he used to put it down to Zahrah. The truth was that the family, which came from a village far, far away, was completely exhausted by the suffering and the dangers to which it had been exposed on the road, under fire from Israeli planes, for they had been forced to sleep in the open and walk long on rough paths, in order to avoid the many roadblocks, before they reached the capital. That arrival was a source of great confusion for them, as they knew that the city streets were not safe at all and that the city nights were haunted by strange demons; however, it was a city less complicated than they expected for Khalil was quick to deliver them Madame Isabelle's apartment, after he had piled up some things in Naji's room and asked them not to use it.

When they went around the apartment, terrified, peering in the corners and at the ceiling as if looking for things or people that did not know why they were there, Khalil felt cheerful, as some hope of driving out the evil spirit of the apartment had come back and, given that there were so many of them, it seemed highly likely that the apartment might become a home again and look more like it used to look before.

Zahrah used to come bounding downstairs in her plastic flipflops and knock shyly on his door to ask him to eat with them, and he used to accept every time. He would sit facing his uncle and they would always eat whatever was on the big tray with the same appetite, but Zahrah did not sit with them. She stayed nearby, leaping to the kitchen whenever one of them asked for something, but she often used to get it wrong and fetch something they did not need. Her father would shake his head in mock despair, then burst out laughing at her and when her mother asked her to eat, she would answer, furiously: I don't want to. Khalil thought it a shame that her solid, plump legs and skinny waist were so mismatched and although he thought she had beautiful eyes, they were nowhere near enough to make her large, blowzy face that of a beautiful girl. Only from the rump to the neck was she well-proportioned and exciting, with her small, jutting breasts.

Khalil was happy when he sensed Zahrah's infatuation for him . . . he thought all the time about this infatuation of hers, about how she busied herself cleaning and tidying when he was there and never sat still, how she lost her appetite, became a little awkward and rubbed her left eye whenever he looked at her or spoke to her . . . Khalil loved the fact that Zahrah loved him . . . it was as if she loved him from inside of him. Or as if he, he and Zahrah, both loved Khalil. He was perpetually daydreaming about what her infatuation for him did to her. How, when he was not there, Zahrah would lie sighing, limp and listless, how she would strain her ears to catch the sound of his footfall by the door, how she would touch his empty glass or coffee cup before she put it in the sink, how she would stay up late in her bed dreaming about him, by some chance, touching her face or her shoulder and confessing his crazy love which kept him awake at nights, then how her burning hands, which had become Khalil's hands, would pass over her body.

The place was always littered with Zahrah's tapes of singers whom Khalil had heard on the FM broadcasts but whose names he was unable to remember. The sad thing was that the chaos of his uncle's large family and what he thought of as their vitality, the way they made the place busy, only succeeded in dragging the apartment into the realm of the house, that is, to the spirit of Madame Isabelle's home . . . the things that filled its every corner were distinguished only by their utter and direct utility, as if it were impossible to sit in the apartment without some urgent task like eating or sleeping or going to the lavatory or washing, as if it were a place of work not of quiet, or repose, or reflection, or . . . a place to live in . . . the way things passed through it, the way there was no place in it for anything useless or impractical, the apartment was like the post office . . . it was even clean in that fast, functional way, that is to say, not really clean . . . the other lamp, the dining room lamp, fell into disuse of its own accord because the light from the lamp in the sitting room was enough to see by. Some things moved, as if by themselves, from the kitchen or the bedrooms to the sitting room because it was more "practical." The apartment was, then, no longer a home because its internal time was time in a hurry . . . an upstart, not settled and quiet and reconciled to itself. The feeling of the family that they were temporary was not enough to make them scatter its time and mince it in that way, which made Khalil feel sad and made him more positive that Zahrah's infatuation would not be one to bring any responsibility to bear upon him because it was certainly the passing infatuation of a passing girl, and this gave him more relish with which to savor the effect he imagined it was having on her.

All the space that Madame Isabelle's apartment and his uncle's family occupied in Khalil's head was a space struck by artificiality and ambiguity. The intimacy of the large family, with its cooking, with its anecdotes about relatives, the summoning up of its past prosperity, Zahrah's infatuation and Khalil's infatuation with her infatuation and the raptures of his imagination, his coming out from the pit of his supposed isolation, his concern with the apartment and with the passage of time in it, which did not bring back its original spirit. All this paled into ridiculous nonsense the moment Khalil saw Youssef. The moment he saw him.

Youssef was younger than Zahrah. He did not stay around the house much for he was passionately in love with the city, he used to go out to it all the time even if, most of the time, he did not go beyond the corner where Flippers was at the end of the street. Youssef, heedless with his new experiences and busy with children of his own age, was breaking Khalil's heart . . . shattering it like thick, glass dishes flung to the ground . . . there was something in Khalil's stomach dead set, as if physically, against Youssef's seeing that thing which, were the old Youssef to see it, would make him drop dead.

Whenever Khalil saw Youssef he would be stricken and feel faint, he used to say over and over again in his heart, or in his stomach, "oh my God, oh my God," especially when they first arrived.

Youssef was tall and he was thin, thin in a particular way that suggested hardness and concealed strength, not weakness or saplessness. His skin was a subdued brown, the brown of earthenware coming out of the kiln, an ancient, burnished brown like the skin of a pharaoh's slave, like the wood of an ancient icon whose picture you might find in a book. His fingers seemed as if they had never touched a firm body, as if they had come straight from the water in which dried peaches had been soaked. His face, when Khalil looked a little longer at his face, his face that left in the throat the taste of a bite of green quince leaves, which, despite the sweet waters he saw lapping in Youssef's eyes, made Khalil feel an intense thirst playing in his gullet like a maddened bee. Youssef's honey was poisonous and the fruit of his body was bruised and blue from the inside, inviting, like a vast chasm on the edge of which we stand, dying of desire yet fearing to dash ourselves against its distant rocks which are cloaked in the vapors of the chasm's span.

Youssef was so beautiful he made the Renaissance sculptors seem like fools, with their white, pumped up, lean bodies threaded with veins like the bodies of happy cattle. Shapes, mass, closer to the shape and mass of beautiful animals because they come, complete, out of themselves, the sculptor leaves nothing to them to keep for themselves, nothing to keep hidden from the curious eyes that look at them. A man with no soul, like a weightlifter in a sports magazine.

81

The saint in the icon drawn precisely in liquid gold or the mask of a pharaonic mummy colored with fine needles give what they want to, of the face alone. That is, both give a door through which you may enter the other face that you need, through which you may enter the beauty in it that is particular to you. They ask you to watch, to linger for a time, the time your eyes take to get ready before the icon and the mummy become open to you.

Youssef's face was a mask for him like the mask of the icon and the mummy . . . you would not be able to tell easily or quickly how beautiful Youssef is: first, you have to see how cold, how hard, how distant, how impossible to reach he is. And he is more intensely real and impossible when he is not there. He has the effect of a distant bombing that has already passed when the noise reaches you, when whoever is to be hit and killed has been hit and killed while you know, you get tense, you start back like a confused donkey, Khalil sees himself in front of Youssef like a donkey, far from its mother, from the field, from other donkeys, alone and afraid and hungry and naïve while in the corner of his big, black empty eye a fly lays its eggs.

Khalil hated to see Youssef, and he loved to see him . . . a lot. When Zahrah invited him to eat with them it used to free him of the burden of initiative and he would go up, his knees trembling lest Youssef be there or lest he not be there. The city had come to seem almost calm and the bombing in the streets was less heavy. That bombing, which Khalil craved like one who craves a swift death because it would have stopped Youssef from dying and would have fixed him in time and space, he had had to bear that happening already, and once was enough.

Some nights, some evenings there was bombing. He would stay in his room until his uncle or Zahrah called him to take shelter on the landing. In the beginning, he used to sit between them, on the fine line between his good intentions and temptation, but he soon calmed down and his anxiety turned to lifeless inertia. Zahrah would be overjoyed with the bombing but Khalil did not manage to be overjoyed by her joy, he was unable to draw her to him when Youssef was there, while Youssef was restless in his narrow space. He seemed very agitated, always on the ready as if he intended to go out suddenly onto the street. When he asked what was going on Khalil would give terse, muttering replies from which Youssef understood that there was no scope for elaborate explanation now, for the answers were immensely complicated. However much Khalil avoided looking into Youssef's eyes, they kept coming to him like flying pollen from trees, like those microscopic thorns that the Indian fig sends out with every puff of wind. Whenever Youssef got into his chest too much Khalil used to put his cold hand on his knotted stomach and keep pressing until the knot turned into pure pain and Khalil wished that the bombing would end, if there was any chance that it would not last forever.

When Khalil went back to his room he would make haste to do the things he was wont to do after the bombings . . . cleaning the room, washing the sheets and clothes but with more enthusiasm, more neurotically and with less satisfaction with the results. He felt something like despair when he reached the happy, peaceful state that he used to reach after cleaning . . . it did less and less good to summon up Zahrah's infatuation with him, until he realized that he was completely entangled in his love for Youssef and that his withered body, connected by a cord to Youssef's body, was letting a diabolical hemorrhage which filled him and overflowed inside him like the waters of a volcano. He used to sit, confused and vacant, for hours at a time. Sometimes, he would think of leaving his room and going far away but he found no place to go. He would think that he should do a lot of things so that he could come back exhausted and sleep. He would think of not accepting their invitations to eat or stay up late, of excusing himself with pretexts which they would interpret as his not wishing to impose upon them, as an excessive fineness of feeling, or as a flight from Zahrah's infatuation, which they must have discovered, motivated by high morals . . . but Youssef, who was always on the move, would sometimes drop in on him in his room although he did not stay for long because he was shy of what he imagined to be Khalil's high culture and experience of life in the city . . . he finished his swift visit by announcing that he was going to go up to the house and inviting Khalil to come to watch television . . . Khalil quickly catches up with him. But one of Youssef's friends is calling him and he goes downstairs within a few minutes of Khalil's coming, excusing himself, as Khalil drowns in hot waters and the feeling he has inside, like a soaked tomcat, turns to intense hatred for Zahrah the blush of whose cheeks betrays how delighted she is to see him, he becomes extremely sensitive to and disgusted by the dreadful smell that her armpits exhale, making him certain that two legs of that size, hands as red as that with such thick, animal skin cannot belong to a creature with a soul. He thinks of her as an old, rotten fish, its eyes covered with a thick film, which still swims around only to send out more rancid smells. On evenings such as this Khalil used to look long at Zahrah for he had nothing left to do then but to torture himself.

When he went back he used to stand in the middle of his room, his body small but feeling heavy and useless. He would twist his head and mouth into dry sobs and before leaning back against the chair or the wall he would say over and over again: oh my God . . . I'm dying of love.

3

When the rich used to get too unsettled by the many check-points in the streets at night, they used to hire out an ambu-lance from one of the hospitals to take them to nightclubs, which continued to operate in the same way, inviting rising singers with a talent for provoking laughter and ridicule from the audience. These talents were the favorite with the late-night clientele because they were as far as they could be from being serious, they did not make them feel sad or call upon them to sigh, or think deeply. They cleared the way, with their enormous humility, for every man or woman to hope that they had a presence equal to the singer's presence and to become, consequently, the hero of the evening, the funniest, the noisiest, and the most devastating on the dance floor.

This is the "love of life" that the western and Arab newspapers talk about ... Khalil thought, as he started off again ... people in our country love life in a way that surprises the scholars who, whenever they speak of us, express their surprise at this formidable ability of ours to love life ... so much that some of those countries have managed to get hold of videotapes, from their correspondents, of those evenings where the dance floor is raised and everyone dances on the tables to the melody of songs that have nothing to do with, not one of them, with the tunes that the singer is desperately trying to bring to their ears . . .

Viewers around the world may be much more surprised to see us spending our evenings this way than by the sight of people patching over the holes in the houses and their walls, or the spectacle of people swimming over a surface of several dozen yards of blazing Green Line, or the sight of the tomato growing on the old sand barriers which one of the boys, whose wide black eyes pulse with love for life, plucks.

Khalil began to remember incredible scenes from one of those parties that was shown on television during a series of shows put on with the aim of raising the people's morale. He began to remember it and, as if reproaching himself, remembered that it was boring, that it made you want to choke, that it was unbearable, and that it made you feel artificial, it had nothing to do with people. These are people, the people, thousands upon thousands of miles of nerves and coronary arteries. People who look like you whether you like it or not, people to whom you flee whenever you are struck by a touch of madness and megalomania, people whom you implore to take you into the tender embrace of their multitude. People with more feeling than you, you Khalil who are so sensitive, because they are real people. Human beings who weep, who fear the bombing, who dream of infatuation, but who dance.

The television should manage to raise the people's morale, for here it is raising mine. I'm heading for a late night out, it's worth my being a little smart and looking a bit lively. Khalil began to smooth down his clothes as he walked, inviting himself to become absorbed in the party on the television screen. But the tape running in his head kept stopping to rewind whenever it got to the singer, with the puffy features, the face waxy with sweat, and the lard of powders whose colors had run, as she wailed as if she were giving birth, until the party went out of his head and he said in a barely audible voice: here are people that God created this way . . . that's the way I am, a boring man, with a hole in my brain . . .

They were pesticides, gnat repellents, those ones that work by electricity, when we are blessed with a flood of electric current, those ones that burn and send out choking smoke, they still succeed by and large in getting rid of those insects, through the wide open windows, which then gather to make a low, buzzing noise in the stagnant, muffled air of the streets. Nayif's house was in a quarter far, far from being popular for, despite Nayif's relentless enthusiasm for the people, he takes great pains to avoid the popular quarters for it so happens that they are the "baronates," as he used to say, that is, the crowd there belong to a single sect, while those quarters that are not popular still keep, even to a lesser extent, a mixture of creeds and sects which, to Nayif, justifies his nationalist activity . . . Khalil thought about Abou Artin, the owner of the store that sold musical instruments, which turned into a *ful* and *falafel* store after it was plundered several times and Abou Artin bought its contents several times over before he became quite certain that the country had chosen the music it wanted to play and he went to live in Antelias . . . Khalil thought about his face, always red, always on the point of apologizing, giving off something like shyness or embarrassment, or perhaps it was red from drinking *arak*. Then Khalil thought about Nayif's Dutch neighbor who used to ask for hashish from Claude in a loud voice, who used to have a laugh with everyone, before she was afflicted with "Rita's hysteria," as Claude called it . . . Rita who had many lovers and colored sandals, who told many jokes, who used to get more enthusiastic than was called for whenever she won at cards in the shelter or on the landing and began to address the people in Japanese, that first Rita disappeared for a while and the Dutch woman found her sleeping and waking in front of a shrine to the Virgin Mary which she had set up in a corner of her bedroom . . . Rita wept incessant tears of humility in front of the picture, which was lit up by an oil lamp, she stayed kneeling in front of it for weeks asking the Virgin to appear again to dictate the message that she had promised to dictate to her. But weeping and prayers did nothing to wipe clean the sins of the forsaken saint, and her incredibly handsome and elegant husband sent her to his mother's house in the village far away while he abandoned commerce, as one who abandons a pit of sins, to become the leader of an armed faction loyal to one of the neighboring states to prove that which was never refuted, that belonging does not mean belonging to a sect but rather to a country, and the neighbors and people close to him were obliged finally to forget the matter of the Virgin's appearance . . .

Only the Dutch neighbor could not swallow the story . . . even after everyone else had forgotten it she kept clattering on about what Claude called "Rita's fit" then "Rita's hysteria," for the Dutch woman kept on asking what was the matter with Rita, because she wanted to understand. One day the Dutch woman came to say goodbye to Claude because Faraj, her husband, had decided to send her with her two sons to Holland because that was better for them and because it would take some of the weight off Faraj, who was sick with illusions, because that would clear the way for his secretary, Leila, to get the house in order the way she wanted, then because that gave her an opportunity to get her shattered nerves cured by recognized specialists . . . all that in one sentence, while the little blonde one held her hand. Then she kissed Claude hastily and made her promise to write long letters to Rita because she had got hold of the address . . . and she went, leaving Claude plunged deeper in her constitutional sullenness.

Although Nayif's house was not in a popular quarter at all, still, clouds of little gnats hit Khalil in the face and he began to snort to get out what might have got up his nose, holding his nostrils, which were blocked by the thick smells rising from the heaps of garbage. He stayed on the alert as he walked, keeping his eyes well open to see where he was putting his feet for he was loath to step on a dawdling cockroach and hear the crunching sound of it being crushed underfoot over the noise of the generators, which purred in the entrances of buildings and their balconies. These insects, the rats and stray cats have become so familiar with people and houses that the invitation rising, to approach and be brotherly, seems like the dawning of a new age in which the intelligence of those creatures is discovered, in which it becomes clear how human behavior has come to be like their behavior, how people are forgetting the way they used to cling proudly to cleanliness in olden times, spraying with insecticides, burning garbage, hiding their filth in an apparent attempt to conceal their sins and ignore them . . . how they are more confident now of the darkness and damp places below . . . how a true love of life is the opposite of this manmade pride which convulsively built its artificial fancies only a short time ago. The craven rat begins to pass close to the foot of his brother man, slowly, with no fear nor any sense that he is less, he may gaze into his face a while before winking to his companion to catch up with him and go onto the streets in which he has come to have real domain.

Rats are clever creatures, thought Khalil, if a rat wants to carry a piece of soap, or an egg, for example, he wraps himself right around it, with all four legs, then turns over on his back so that the soap or the egg is on top of him, shielding it with his body, then his partner joins in to play his role and drags him by the tail to the table . . . intelligence is looking to the future and planning for it, intelligence is using tools . . . rats have it all . . . except they breed in a frightening way . . . Nature, who is responsible for keeping the balance on this earth, still does her work most efficiently . . . the evidently intelligent creatures, that is to say, people, become less as a result of war and likewise, their mental activity becomes less, their intelligence, so Nature substitutes a number, a species, with other creatures . . . in any case people had become sure that there was something that was coming to live with them in their houses. All of them knew and they had become a great deal more tolerant than the people before them . . . even the rats that walked through the sitting room there used to stop for seconds at a time, or start to play in front of his uncle's family if their slippers and shoes were out of hands' reach . . . under those skies of verdigris, swollen by the hot dusty *khamsin* wind that blew in from the desert, was a woman washing down the metal edge of her balcony while the water fell onto the barrels filled with concrete that blocked off the sidewalk, opposite the window of the hardware shop, sending up a drizzling spray . . . Khalil shook the water from his shoulders and his hair and strolled behind the concrete blockade to the entrance of the building while he thought about that lonely woman who still believed that it was within her power to rinse away, to struggle against all that the street blows onto her balcony and into her eyes . . .

The foreigner was there, dominating Claude's attention, but this time he did not dominate the atmosphere of the evening altogether as he had done the previous time and Nizar, who had decided to come back to the city after the long years in Paris, was not eager to fill his place. He felt that there were not enough incentives or that the welcome of his friends was not as emotional as he had expected, he wondered if they were accusing him for his absence but he felt that they felt superior to him for having stayed with their city in its dark days, that they were indulging themselves with the indulgence that was due to them, flirting like the faithful, virtuous wife who does not turn her back on her husband just because he is suffering from a bout of impotence.

Claude fetched a leather-covered notebook and began to take down the addresses that the foreigner enthusiastically dictated to her . . . Claude will leave you Nayif, said Abd el Nabi. She's sentencing me to death, Nayif replied . . . if you weren't so busy being darkly handsome you'd have heard something that neither you nor your friend would have liked, Claude said, so stop harassing me . . .

Abd el Nabi was expressing his surprise that any Lebanese could leave Beirut, for he is an "eternal lover," as he used to call himself, saying that there was no pleasure in life for him unless he passed once every year through Beirut, this mistress who has made him the weakest of men, unfit for love in any part of the world. Claude was quick to interrupt, to stop him from going further. But when he began sobbing about Beirut, she shouted, Abd el Nabi, don't try to convince me that what I see under your trousers has become like a deflated balloon. I'm not strong enough to live with a picture like that in my head. For me to become impotent, said Abd el Nabi laughing, that's one thing. If it were to happen, God forbid, this would be something about which there was no doubt or which would be hard to believe. But for me to believe that Beirut, with its exceptional charm, is finished, has died, that its sparkle has faded . . . every time I come back to see if it's true but my thirst is not quenched. I leave, more confused, more lost, more doubtful . . . all of us young people, from any country you like, are lost without our star which was, and still is, the pivot of our hearts . . . oh world, understand us, without the star we are like orphans. But Nadim, Nayif's colleague at the newspaper who seemed to share Abd el Nabi's feelings most closely, said . . . when are you leaving us this time, Abd el Nabi? Now. Right now, Abd el Nabi replied . . . you have become unbearable . . . if you've come to doubt as well, then mine is a great loss . . . but Nayif cried out, what are you saying, my friend . . . Abd el Nabi said, many have left. Take Claude for example, how happy she is to leave . . . but Nizar came back, said Nayif, proud of his friend, while Nizar shook his head in modest disavowal. It's an unbelievable thing. Year after year after year . . . its coasts, its streets,

its cafés . . . this time I'm going to say something you might find painful.
You do not write, you have stopped, I believe, writing poetry and painting, you do not paint . . . sometimes, I confess, after what has happened
and what is happening to you in Beirut I wish I were Lebanese . . . what's
going on here may be the explosion of the age and you, creative people,
are in the middle of it . . . what are you doing? I don't understand . . .
what's going on is an artist's dream come true . . . the Arabs write about
what is going on more than you and you . . . with all the turmoil and
harbingers there have been, you seem to be still reeling from the shock, as
if you didn't understand or . . . you don't want to understand . . . as if all
those harbingers . . .

Slow down, said Claude . . . what do you mean by the word harbinger? The man here, and she pointed to the foreigner, it also concerns him to understand . . . after Nizar had explained to her what
harbinger meant she said that it was an ugly word and stopped trans-
lating for the foreigner, interrupting him halfway. He looked more
lost and seemed to mete out his smiles more carefully.

Abd el Nabi, having managed to lighten the atmosphere drew it to
him and carried on, fervently. He to whom Beirut did not confess
remained in the dark, falling, not taking his chance . . . we used to
come to her to be . . .

How old are you Abd el Nabi, are you over fifteen? No . . . less . . .
why don't you get married and have a baby . . . find yourself a wife
from your village and . . . but Abd el Nabi ignored this and went on:
the cafeteria at the Faculty of Law, the cafeteria at the Faculty of
Education, the Dolce Vita, the Horse Shoe, the theaters, even the
market . . . I cannot forget . . . you leave as if you were betraying me,
as if you were betraying a whole generation . . . myself, I feel that I
lose the ones who leave . . . you throttle it with your going away . . .
you do not deserve Beirut . . . I find only a few these days. This may
be my last visit, friends . . . Abd el Nabi uttered these last words with
high drama, then looked around to find out what the reaction to
them was. Nayif shook his head sadly, while the others did not stir
from their dull lethargy . . . is the matter one to be taken so lightly,
Nayif? there are only a few left . . . who . . . what do you think, Nayif?
it concerns you . . . your wife will leave the country for good, as I
believe, or for ten years . . . who will stay? tell me . . . who does not

have the price of the ticket, said Claude, who deals in arms or in . . . oh and by the way . . . why don't you pay the cost of literary and journalistic articles and contributions to your magazines as you used to do before the lire fell . . . you've begun to say twenty dollars is enough for them, for those who—as long as they dominate us and make us understand that they are lords of culture—allow us to find no recognition outside their cliques, as you used to say, those Lebanese who read in foreign languages, who only translate in their spare time so that we're always behind them in keeping up with the times. Now you take malicious delight in each other's misfortunes, Abd el Nabi . . . you hire the Lebanese for pennies to humiliate them . . . all your talk and your sorry songs are nothing but stupid malice. If you get off our backs, Abd el Nabi, you and your shit mistress Beirut . . . you'll reach fifty. Forget about love, get married and have children and you'll solve your problems and ours at the same time . . .

The tension increased, for Claude had lifted the weight of the atmosphere and the boredom of those who were there . . . and the foreigner was more on his guard, while his smile vanished.

Nayif said, with the calm for which he was known when he was speaking to Claude: it has become necessary for you to leave the country quickly, Claude, because you have begun to behave like an hysteric . . . you know Abd el Nabi very well, and you know that he's not been able to go back to his country for a long time. He is in exile because he is still strongly opposed to the regime in his country, which does not accept any form of opposition . . .

So let him stop being in opposition where there's no system at all . . . where there's nothing at all . . . interrupted Claude . . . he can't sleep at night if he isn't singing the praises of the martyrs . . . of the rose of blood, of the fist raised in the face of this and that and freedom and the destruction of . . . bonds and frameworks . . . tell me, brother, why is exile forbidden to me, then . . . let him destroy things and blow them up, let him be a martyr in his country . . . my God, what a joke. What must I do, me, to Abd el Nabi to make him stop blaming me, stop telling me off for getting out of here. What can I do to him so that he will stop, even for a little while, committing slow suicide because he feels sorry for us . . . my God, what a cheek this is, if he wants to talk let him go and talk to you in the newspaper,

I don't want to listen to him . . . what are you waiting for, Abd el Nabi, get up and go . . . come back when you're in a better mood.

For the first time, Claude's perpetual pallor and that inveterate sullenness left her. Her face was deep red and the small veins on her throat were pronounced . . . it is the first time I have seen her making an effort like this although she is the only woman here, the uncontested heroine of the evening . . . even so, her mood grew worse. Abd el Nabi said: well, Claude . . . I understand . . . you're all tired . . . may God help you all . . . who could put up with all that. Now he wants to take pity on me . . . said Claude, after she had recovered her calm, then she said, I want you to stop speaking to me now, if you want to stay in the house. OK, Abd el Nabi?! Nadim . . . go and pour a little gas into the generator tank. You'll find the gas can by the refrigerator. On your way, get some more bread. Khalil . . . turn over the cassette. I'm going to bed. Nayif, don't forget to put the garbage out.

Everybody chuckled when Abd el Nabi began to heap his famous dirty jokes upon them. He said a warm goodbye to everyone and left, refusing to spend the night at Nayif's, claiming, with a wink out of the corner of his eye, that there was someone waiting for him. After a while, Nadim said: my God, they love Beirut . . . then, the man was right when he said we don't do anything . . . that we don't write, we don't paint . . . we're just as he said, it's no exaggeration. We don't understand what is going on, exactly. How? Nayif said, with what seemed like reproach for his not toeing the party line.

Nizar leaned over to Khalil and whispered: since the relationship between them came to an end and Abd el Nabi's visits are further and further between, Claude has become very hostile, as if she hates him because she can't enjoy him . . . you seem surprised Khalil . . . no, your news reaches us as if we were here among you . . . what makes her more tense are words like exile and vagabondage and nostalgia because they were what drew her in the flower of her youth . . . it's as if she's regretting it.

Tell us . . . tell us, you man of Paris, what's the matter with you, you're not talking, you've made Abd el Nabi steal the limelight from you, said Nayif, evidently merry that the evening had picked up again although his eyes were red. Did nostalgia bring you back?

They stay up late as if they were imprisoned with each other, thought

93

Khalil, who sensed that everyone wished to leave, and that they were promising themselves that this evening would be the last.

After that Nizar went on to explain the difference between himself and Abd el Nabi. Khalil said to himself: now we have to feel sorry for ourselves, that is, for Nizar.

Nizar said, we leave the country, but the country stays where it is. There's no particular pattern to our leaving. Abd el Nabi leaves his country and clearly feels that he takes its heart with him—the essence is with him, while the country is left behind, empty, redundant. It's a conviction he passes on to others. We flee the country, afraid of making the same, huge mistake over again and we make more mistakes there, we do things there that we wouldn't do here so we don't come back. It's a funny thing that you pay no attention to. When I was there I worked for Abd el Nabi's organization, which I wouldn't dream of doing here, not for people like him. Can you believe it?

Nayif said: is that why you came back? Nizar hesitated, then said: more or less. I couldn't find work. The competition was too intense. And I'm a social mule.

They had dismissed him from the organization where he worked . . . all the obedience, the flexibility, the culture that he had struggled to grow and prune so that it lost its wildness was no use to him . . . they did without him, without his smart moves and in his place they hired someone who was less intelligent and who provoked less anxiety, someone who was more obedient and who stuck more to the party line of the magazine, someone who was a lot more stupid than him because he was much more easygoing . . . perhaps one of those exiles from his "sister-enemy country with a rotten regime" which had to be brought down to keep things going happily along, perhaps someone who had a beautiful wife who put an artificial flower in her hair and laughed for the people who stay out late at parties . . . thought Khalil, cutting through the clouds of gnats.

But the man who was a social mule went back to Paris two months after that evening, after he received a letter from his French girlfriend in which she forgave him for everything that had happened and promised him marriage and French nationality and work in her uncle's business, who kept saying how much he loved him. His beloved foot only had to touch the ground of Orly airport and she was waiting for him even though the plane was late and her tears watered the bunch of wild flowers, which were beginning to wilt, on her arm . . .

As for the foreigner, he had appeared on television one night looking drawn and, although his dream had come true, of being at the heart of the action and the heart of the volcano of the exploding world where there was absolutely no place for being morose, particularly since he filled the world and preyed on people's minds by being kidnapped from in front of the guarded door of the newspaper where Nayif worked, he was still not as fulfilled as he had dreamed of being. This time he was patently more tired of those who dictated the recorded message to him than he was afraid of them.

On his way back from the party Khalil passed underneath the balcony of the woman who was doggedly resisting the dirt that came up from the street . . . it was after midnight . . . he raised his head to where the flowerpots were still dripping water and his eyes found her, she was standing on a high chair and was busy polishing the glass, busy with the irresistible love of life.

4

At that party Khalil heard a lot of talk, more than he could remember. He felt his head had been filled right up to the brim and decided not to accept Nayif's repeated invitations to pass by him in the newspaper because there was something important that he must talk to him about . . . but talking, talk, particularly the sort that Khalil knew all too well, the sort that digs into the ear as if it is being forced in . . . Khalil found it impossible to listen to that sort of talk and he stayed in his room with throbbing pains in his stomach . . . they were only feeble excuses to arouse Youssef's pity for someone who is suffering, cut off from the world, and who deserves, if not his compassion, then a visit or a question every now and then.

Khalil's being cleansed of the desire to talk became an embarrassing matter, seeming more like a protest, sulking displeasure, an aversion to those who do talk, hence, he who does not put out his hand to the dish of words to take part, to salt and share the bread, is by definition an idle listener or an arrogant protester. In the past they used to talk a lot, with the appetite of someone who has just discovered the magic of speech . . . like someone who sits in a green meadow under a gentle sun in a mild breeze, the phrases would pour forth like a little stream watering the tender young plants, making the trees grow and flower and the fruits ripen in a few moments. They began with the pleasure of talking about the existence of God after reading some books, the succulent seed of whose pages had reached their distant villages, then, bit by bit, as faithless waters do, the little stream had grown around them until it covered their slender legs and each rose up to his own little hill, each suffering the exile, the alienation of those who understand what is going on but in any case, they kept on talking, talking in a way that began to seem like a solo recital . . . then suddenly, the treacherous waters began to rise and rise and the torrent started, the number of people who were dying in the war kept growing until it divided the unity of the solo singers, even if it did not reduce the rate at which the flood was rising. There were some who joined in the combat and acted on their words and they were a minority . . . as for the rest, some found the path of psychological crises and nervous breakdowns easier and forgave themselves, and others saw an escape from the sin of talking in making written confessions and so were included in the lesser amnesty of writing. People deliberately forgot each others' faults while the martyrs, stone who were tempted to listen more than they should, persevered in their martyrdom as if driven by some malice within that had seduced them and that did not allow forgiveness. They forgot each other's faults but deep hatred reigned in their hearts for each was true to himself and, if he happened to see one of those friends of his, he remembered his despised self and was certain how much his friend resembled his own self, he found no way out of despising this thing that was so similar to him and he loathed it, out of self-pity—and all's fair where self-defense is concerned—even inventing new colorings and delights through gambling, or infidelity, or dancing to pop music which unfortunately, in a word, is a waste of time, and they lost a lot of time.

The surprising thing, Khalil thought, is that they've changed the vessels that they speak through but they haven't turned up their noses at speaking completely, they long for it, they feel nostalgia for their past which, by necessity, is an innocent past.

The women, those lucky creatures, do not talk . . . they warble and they sing . . . they do not form sentences with thoughts, therefore they do not attempt to form histories when they talk. The cannon does not roar, what does roar is the thought that created the cannon . . .

The women do not like to discuss subjects. They skip lightly from one thing to the next like butterflies . . . they say useful things, their talk is that with which to buy bread and fry eggs and do the laundry and fix the faucet . . . they say things that make you laugh or send you off to sleep. Their talk is that sort which, if it went out into the street, would soon go back to the house . . . they talk for hours without harming a fly. Hours on the telephone neither about orders nor plans, hours at the bakery but the bread is ready and with it, delicious herb bread . . . talk that, at worst, might make one of them fight with her daughter-in-law but which would not spark off a war in the street . . . it was talk for nothing, talk through the smoke of the water-pipe, talk that owns nothing and, when it wants to be, is clear, invites you to a bed with low lights in the market or in the bedroom, while the husband is resigned to putting the world in boring order because he is so persistent, makes such a lot of noise and is so sluggish. The women do not need money, what they need are things such as food and drink and sleep and kindness and dresses and jewelry . . . so they do not inherit much and they do not wrangle with great thoughts . . . they feel they can be of use in keeping petty things in order, which is confined to their houses or their jobs which are attached to their houses and so they have no sense that they are lacking in any way, or that they are of no use, nor do they have any sense of the necessity or importance of large ideas which keep the world in order. The world of the women is ordered and acceptable, and what it does sometimes need is confined to a few little bits of mending.

My uncle's wife sits on the ground, in the middle of the sitting room, hollowing out zucchini and talking with women from the village who had found their way to her . . . all that they say about politics is that they do not understand what troubles the soul . . . they weep when they remember one of the dead and laugh about the unusual things that happened during the mourning ceremony or the burial . . . they come to stories about sex, whispering, and boast of nothing but the prowess of their husbands, of how much their husbands love them, and of how honorable their husbands are, honor that cannot be bargained over . . . they complain in a pampered way about their declining health and they like to appear younger than their age. They talk about the best cooking and about the children's projects, the titles of which are the only thing that they understand . . . Youssef wants to study what his cousin Khalil told him about, "puten"—by which she meant computing—then she laughed, putting her hand over her mouth, while his uncle, although he used to repeatedly confess his inadequacy still, with dogged determination born of a sense of duty, wanted to talk about politics . . . he would express opinions that he had strongly opposed with a neighbor of his, over which he had got so worked up that he stabbed his opponent's arguments to death and threw them to the ground . . . he even draws out the listener to oppose him in the hope of doing just that . . . but it always ends up with him cursing politics and the leaders who have brought us to such a state of affairs . . .

When my uncle's wife was young, learning from her mother how to cook and how to wash her little brothers' faces and dreaming of Abd el Wahhab, my uncle was clinging onto the tie-cord of his short trousers, leaping in the air a few yards in front of the little demonstration shrieking until his voice was hoarse:

My brother in Baghdad
Let the bullet ring,
My brother in Jordan
Let the bullet sing,
My brother in Hejaz
Nationalize the gas,
My brother in Aures
We want unity pure
Of which we can be sure.

Those were the days, my uncle says, sighing with nostalgia before he goes on: Nasser, oh Jamal Abd el Nasser, we nationalized the canal, long live the Arab nation and death to feudalism . . . politics was delicious then . . .

The real pleasure in the demonstration, thought Khalil, lay in the occupation of the asphalt . . . in stopping all movement in the little square and, in particular, in winning back the place that the daily increasing number of cars did their utmost to occupy, scorning the pedestrians and forcing them into the narrow passages and between the shop stalls . . . cars that used to go far away, to Nabatiyeh and beyond, to Chiyah, for Beirut was then Chiyah, to the cinemas of Chiyah and the girls with their bare heads and the boastful people who only occasionally came back to visit the village . . .

There were so few visitors that the buses that used to come from far off had names, like "Rabihah" and "Ghazaleh" and "Leila Mourad" . . . and Khalil's sulking uncle waited for the demonstration so that he could occupy the asphalt, stop the conceited wheels from turning and take revenge.

Whenever he demonstrated he would twist his mustache and not do as his mother told him to do to help her, he would make ready for masculinity with greater enthusiasm. He who demonstrates understands politics, and no one understands politics but men.

Khalil was not particularly bothered about politics but he did used to talk a little about it, in an attempt to understand and to enter into the community of men. They always believed that he was younger than themselves and were patient with him. Khalil was more inclined to literature and reading in general but everything those days pointed out how necessary politics was, so he began to ask questions, to listen and to stay up late. The community—that blessing—was fooled by his questions, they believed that there was more to his questions than met the eye and that they were not as innocent or simple as they seemed. As much as he needed the community, the new family, the community needed him and young men like him, village boys who studied diligently, boys with faces that spoke of clear conscience and honesty.

But the talk that began, even with Khalil, would get on to colored hot air balloons and go sky high and, before long, begin to fall like dead flies on the table after what happened to Mohammed Haddad about which his friends expressed nothing but a deep, transient sorrow and then kept talking.

That was before the angry and resentful ones began to discover the series of great mistakes. Mohammed Haddad talked and argued like the sheikh of a dervish order, he was a blazing torch of activity which burns night and day . . . at the height of the war Mohammed Haddad said: friends, now show us the words, the words that have been said. Let each man now cling to what he says, like he used to cling to his mother's skirt. The fighting is fierce and the enemy is known. He went down to the market-place on the Green Line and began this verbal bombardment but his little sister died by their sniping neighbor's bullet and, when Mohammed Haddad came back to the young men, he talked a lot less. One day he said: I've got something new to say to you this time. I'm going to the south to fight the Israelis, and he went, without looking back. After a while Khalil heard that his little brother, who was crippled by polio, had blown himself up in a pickup truck in the middle of an Israeli patrol while his sister was suffering a difficult birth in an Israeli hospital where her husband worked for a dollar wage. On her way back to her family's house, which had been blown away to dust, his paternal uncle's fundamentalist son, who had offered to marry her but whom she had refused, overtook her and shot her in the head, felling her a few yards from the lane where the house was, her and her baby.

One day Elias came and said: we can find no trace of Mohammed Haddad, have any of you heard anything about him? Nayif said, they say he's got a dose of daydreams and idiocy. Months passed before Nayif told Khalil that Jacqueline Geagea had contacted him from Basharri, seventy miles from the Green Line in the eastern quarter. She said that she had seen Mohammed Haddad walking on Cedar Road in Chebat at about five o'clock in the afternoon in two foot of snow or more. She went up to him and identified him. He was pale and not dressed for the icy weather, on his way up on foot just as night was about to fall. She realized that he had completely lost his mind. She asked him to stay with her and he thanked her politely, saying that he had to go on . . . Jacqueline was very worried about him and insisted that he come back with her, hoping to take him the next day to Tripoli where he had friends, but he turned down her invitation and went on his way . . .

Mohammed Haddad went on his way walking the path that he had chosen. Everyone said: he couldn't bear it . . . some fall along the way, that's to be expected . . . Mohammed Haddad went on his way falling, in the snow, at an altitude of 5,500 feet from the surface, above the capital of talk, seventy miles from his friends and from the Green

Line, a hundred and fifty miles away, in the opposite direction, from Israel . . . but Khalil decided that he would not understand and that he, Khalil, would return, because he was, in any case, not man enough to walk that path . . .

Khalil lost the warmth of the group before the group lost itself or created new groups. But every day he learned more and so was happier to be in a group, even if he was a hanger-on. For you to listen to their voices and their jokes as if they came from your mouth . . . for one of them to drop in on you to have a bath and wash his socks and eat and sleep and tease out the cotton of your time. To tell you jokes about his mother and his aunts as if they were women from one of the old ballads, women whom you love like your own mother and your own aunts. To tell you, laughing, what makes him shy and what he dreams of, to act the lad and lie because you know and because you can tell things . . . to cast aside his family in favor of you . . . when you leave the group you are truly orphaned, you lose your chosen family, the family that you begot because you have become a man. Your friend is your last father and you forget the first, you put him in a corner of your childhood memories, to make room to fashion your new loved ones, who stand in their underpants combing their hair over your bathroom sink.

Something else made Khalil feel distant from his friends . . . the light way they spoke about girls and the amount they used his room for the purpose of love, which made him feel disgusted, confused, and deeply embarrassed.

Because his friends made him feel so sad, Khalil began to encourage Youssef to join one of the local organizations, or was it because supplies were so short that only those who wore speckled camouflage jackets could get hold of them?

Khalil felt embarrassed whenever the gas or bread upstairs ran out. His uncle's wife used to manage to get hold of flour which she would roll out and bake on an aluminum tray, but flour was scarce and the gas ran out and she began to complain to him as if encouraging him to sort things out, since he was the one who knew how the city and the quarter worked. Those days, Khalil used to boil potatoes and vegetables and say that they stopped his stomach from hurting.

One day, Youssef came home with two bundles of bread and threw them onto the table in the middle of the room, then sat down smiling. His happy mother rushed up to him and asked him who had given him the bread and he replied, tersely: a friend of mine, a young man from around here.

Now I've become a man and I can't ignore things, Youssef said to Khalil. My father can't get things together . . . they're good fellows and man can't live alone, it's as if my father stood accused of being feeble or juvenile. What do you think?

However hard Khalil tried to win Youssef over by playing the wise man who has all the answers for a friend who has fallen in love with questions, however he tried to make claims on his time for a few minutes in which Youssef's face dictated his views, this question deserved serious thought.

This is your personal choice, Khalil said, drowning in confusion up to his red ears. Is there anything wrong in it, Youssef went on . . . in wanting to make sure that the needs of the house are met and to take a salary at the end of the month. I have to wear a uniform and have weapons training for a couple of days, and do a bit of guard duty from time to time . . .

Perhaps it's in his interest, thought Khalil, everyone has his group and Youssef only has my wretchedness and brokenness, the misery of my silence in front of him and if not that, then the warmth of the friends he has chosen, so let Youssef test him and get out of it when it occurs to him to come back, because there's no forcing anyone.

I'll keep it from my father, Youssef said. In any case, my father's going to the Emirates soon, with Abou Hani, to do some construction work because the pay's good. I won't tell my father or my mother. Why, asked Khalil? Because everyone condemns the armed men. They think they're just thugs who're in it for the killing and the plunder, but what does that have to do with me . . . you can stay who you are, wherever you are . . . anyway, there's no getting out of it now. What about your studies? asked Khalil . . . I can't afford the first instalment of the fees . . . I'll go to the institute that you told me about next year, I'll have got together a little money. Next year, things may have quietened down and there won't be any need for the organizations. What if they asked you to take part in some fighting? asked Khalil, who was obviously disturbed . . . What fighting?! They don't fight.

There isn't any fighting now in any case and if there was, I'd give up the uniform and go back home. I'm not ashamed if it becomes a matter of life and death.

I don't think they're immoral, they're young men like me and you, they're just poor, said Youssef. They're fanatical about their sects, their ideas . . . said Khalil . . . No, their ideas are like everyone's ideas . . . or to be more precise, they don't have any particular ideas . . . and as for their fanaticism, what's it got to do with me . . . He's right, thought Khalil . . . he might as well take the opportunity to be like people his own age and make his own bad memories, he might as well enjoy their company as long as he likes and then disown them later, he'll get tired of them and grow up, there's no escaping that . . . if not, what do I have to offer him?

Khalil said nothing, so Youssef got up to get the tea ready, happy that his confession was convincing and happy with Khalil's reaction, which was not at all negative. Khalil began to look at Youssef's neck and at his slender body from behind.

5

Youssef began to go out a lot. He began to come back to the house only occasionally and stayed only a short time but long enough for Khalil to notice how much the shyness had left his face and the way he moved his body, which was no longer confused and stumbling but had begun to grow and fill the air around him with a relaxed companionability. He began to stretch out on the bed on the floor, spreading his feet apart, closing his wide eyes, making himself absent from those present, busy with that relaxed manner of his and the effective way he managed to actually close himself off from what was happening around him . . . he came to talk but little, even with Khalil, and that was confined to exchanging greetings in the manner of men who know how to fill the time that they have, the time in which they deserve to enjoy being withdrawn, now that his father had traveled to the Emirates.

He has grown up, said Khalil. He's absorbed in his external time while I'm waiting at the other end of the tunnel, clutching the egg of my dreams like an old hen . . . waiting until he knows, until he gets bored and comes back so we can be closer and can sit like two widows exchanging stale sorrow like an old piece of gum while our false teeth clack over little bygone memories which we've recorded over with the misery of our protests.

So much did Khalil long to see Youssef that he used to try to accompany him on this adventure of his. He would select stops on the journey where he could see him. He would see him walking and see him standing and see him sitting sipping tea with them and bowing his head, in his huge military boots . . . see him playing pinball and carrying the hot herb bread and washing the glasses and listening to boring jokes without minding. He would see him looking at their strong thighs, covered in hair, under their colored underpants as they turned over their weapons, laughing about girls.

All that is very tempting, so how can I compete. Khalil began to feel furious with them, with those people who had snatched Youssef away to make use of him and blackmail, those cowards who sent him where they were afraid to go themselves: take the car, Youssef, although he still can't drive, and go to the bakery . . .

Because he is the youngest and the newest to the group, Youssef goes. On the road that is packed with people and cars Youssef knows, as everyone knows, that one is certainly booby-trapped and will explode, and as the panting unease of the street rises its clamor rises, so Youssef is not able to hear the ticking of the timer on the bomb. Youssef walks on the sidewalk which prickles with cars like the teeth of a comb. He chooses one and says that's the one and speeds up so as to get past it. It does not explode. Another one. No. The cars that Youssef has passed fly as the trees fly on both sides of the road when you ride a speeding car. But his heart pounds more violently as his certainty grows that he does not know and guessing is no use . . . now, any one might be the booby-trapped one before you get to it and it never occurs to you that it might explode behind you after you have passed. It is always waiting for you to get to it and when you do, walking loses all direction, as if you were walking sideways or upwards or downwards or backwards . . . it makes absolutely no difference for it is somewhere that you cannot know, and the bakery is in the middle of the chaos of things which may look like the primal, cosmic chaos, before the creator brought order out of it in the first explosion—the "big bang."

The big bang happens to return things to their studied order, to bring back direction as soon as Youssef hears, and the others, the sound of the sublime explosion coming from somewhere far away, far enough away, they sigh deeply and smile glad smiles of relief, seeming to congratulate each other on their safety. It exploded in the other street, we're alright . . . we're all alright here . . . praise God who is merciful and generous, God who—we don't know exactly why we thank Him for our safety, except that His blessings are limitless. The street begins to celebrate. The trader drops his prices a little and is generous with his customers . . . the customer buys more because he is now more certain that he will eat what he has bought tonight and that the food will enter his bloodstream through his digestive system, not be mingled directly with his blood. The air becomes so pure that it cannot tolerate those people who are confused as to which of their loved ones and children may have been passing in the street when it exploded. Those people leave quickly, as if they felt embarrassed for being beset by an anxiety out of keeping with the air of exhilaration, of rejoicing for another day for free, another day for free. They feel themselves to be dull, lacking good taste, like someone who feels sad when the wedding is in full swing, so they leave quickly and quietly to check, to make certain, and their leaving the neighborhood will not bring any emotional emptiness or sense of loss, for most of them will find nothing but joy and delight when they find whoever had gone out, or whoever happened not to be passing when it happened, still alive. Only for a minority, a tiny minority that will not greatly disturb the overall figure, will that night be bitter bread, but bitter.

A car driver stands, appalled, on the sidewalk. He looks at the trunk of his car that has no air, at the rim of the tire and smiles, like a mystic . . . he thinks what he thinks. A few seconds ago, he was blaspheming and pouring sweat out of anger at his lousy luck. His luck at finding his car trunk dented when he had an important appointment to tie up an important deal, where, in the street that was blown up . . . exactly where they said it had blown up. My lousy luck saved my life, he thought of saying . . . if things had gone as they should have I'd be dead, he thought of saying. If it had been a nice, easy day I'd have been ablaze with hexogen, he thought of saying. If my mother hadn't got angry with me after the morning prayer because I beat my wife, my flesh would now be flying around and chirping like little sparrows . . . he thought of saying, the car driver with the dented trunk.

Youssef came back from the bakery. He came home carrying two bundles of bread in his hand and some cake, as a present . . . I said they send him to come back as a punishment to me. When he came back I was certain over and over again of the depth of the pit into which I myself have fallen and from which I cry: Youssef. When I rejoice for his return and my heart sings at his being saved every evening, I sit at night gathering firewood in his face to feed the fire of my sorrow, I cry out to God and offer up sacrifices, I say: the patron saints exist even if God does not exist and I resolve not to let him go out the next day and I say I will dedicate him a song on FM in a girl's name and I sleep coiled up in my bed like a cold viper.

The following morning Khalil would see Youssef going out, walking quickly and laughing. Since he had got his group of friends, Khalil had become more miserable because Youssef began to laugh a lot, and laugh out loud.

But the war that goes on in cities hates laughter . . . detests laughter. The two explosions yesterday did not both happen in the street. In fact there was more than one . . . yesterday there were two, and the two exploded in two cinemas. One in the Beirut cinema in Mazraa and the other in the Hamra cinema in Hamra Street. The cinemas were showing comic films. What a coincidence. No, it was no coincidence . . . war is a serious matter. People die in the streets while there are those who go and pay money and give up their spare time to laugh. It is forbidden to laugh like that. It is forbidden for whichever group of friends to agree, in a particular place, to laugh. Laugh on your own, sob with laughter, burst with your companion. It is a solitary activity which relieves people only to recharge their batteries. But for laughter to become a social activity, that is against the law of a warring community. They want to laugh until they burst? Then let them burst!!

Laughter is beautiful, it makes life more beautiful . . . a jewel here, a bauble there . . . but that it should occur to the warring city to sit on a carpet of laughter . . . let's pull out the rug. Laughter does not go with nationalistic feelings.

Only deep sorrow suits nationalistic feelings. Tragedy. Death. Nationalistic feeling means death. Death. You walk side by side with it, you talk to it, you play cards with it, you iron its clothes, you feed it from your plate, you love it, death.

This is what Khalil saw in the exhibition in the glass hall of the Ministry of Tourism, a pool with many tiers at the top of which was a fountain which sent out a red liquid which flowed over the lower tiers and gushed out. He did not understand . . . he came closer to have a better look. Blood. A pool with a fountain that overflows and makes a sound like blood. He fainted.

What's the matter with him, asked the people who gathered around . . . give him some water to drink. Water. He fainted again. He will not drink. The blood flew from his body as if drained by thousands of powerful suckers and his body did not want to come round.

He stopped eating again and the stomach pains came back to trouble him at night. He said, it's better . . . that my stomach causes me pain, not Youssef.

Death does not accept joking and laughter. Nationalistic sentiment feels pain if it is far from death and history, nothing makes history but death which loathes and despises laughter.

Khalil had two history teachers, he remembers them well, neither of them laughed and they were both in love with nationalistic sentiment and death.

The first was called Mufid. He taught him in the last year of primary school. He had been summoned to their distant village as part of a state plan to develop formal education and spread it, effectively, to all parts of the nation. He was bald and feeble, he wore gold-rimmed spectacles and smoked a brand of cigarettes called "OK." He was very ordered, in a minimal way. Khalil remembers that Mr. Mufid always had hollow cheeks, because he used to puff heavily on his cigarette, the OK did not draw easily and his cheeks would hollow out for seconds at a time . . . he was very strict and did not hesitate to use the cane, he was bitingly scornful of those who failed but with a small significant smile he permitted the clever boys to laugh at them. Mr. Mufid loved significance. Get the significance, he used to say to them as he walked augustly between the rows of pupils, waving his long, thick ruler.

Whenever Mr. Mufid got a little enthusiastic in class, and he usually got a little enthusiastic, the hair on our heads used to stand up and Khalil used to wait for bedtime to come so that he could cry in his bed, out of grief for the raw, fragile peace that weighs heavy on the heart of the nation. Mr. Mufid used to go into elaborate detail about the heroism of the Tyreans and our Phoenician forefathers from the coast, he would often recount the tales about the people of Carthage who defied death and their heroic, martyred leader, as he looked contemptuously at the excited little heads which forgot his hollow cheeks, drowning in the smoke of the OK which rose from the blazing temples filled with the people from the cities the length of the proud, blue coast.

All the way home, Khalil would remain deep in thought, a serious expression on his face. How can I say it, how can I tell my nation how much I love it, how I would die—in any savage war, against any brute enemy—a martyr, like the people of Tyre who closed their city to the great invading conqueror. Who went into their temples in jubilant high spirits and . . . who set light to themselves and burned, so that their ashes would stay free. Khalil used to see them dying, ablaze like great suns. Then stretching out in their white, radiant flesh like angels . . . and he used to cry, for love of his country and sorrow for its misfortunes.

If I was your only son, I mean, if I didn't have any sisters, would you agree to send me with the soldiers to die defending my country? Khalil asked his mother one day. Against who, his mother said, as she tipped the water from the sink onto the dusty courtyard in front of the house. Against the enemy who wants to take away our independence, answered Khalil, whoever that enemy may be. No . . . she said, laughing, as she put the shining plates in a row on the big stone out in the sun . . . I'd tie you by the leg to the iron bedstead. But then the enemy would raze our walls and burn our temples and libraries and parade our corpses and they'd kill me in any case. No, said his mother, they'd kill the men and I'd say to their leader that you were one of my daughters and when he saw you, he'd believe me and go away. You mean I'd live while my country died of disgrace? said Khalil. To hell with your country and every other country, my precious . . . she hugged him. He pulled away from her . . . and she laughed out loud . . .

Khalil wept bitter tears that night . . . he began to find his mother, that ignorant traitor of a mother, embarrassing, he began to feel deeply embarrassed when she passed the school gate on her way to the market and asked after him, or called him over and kissed him in front of the boys in the playground. What is my mother compared to the women of Carthage, who melted down their jewelry and finery, who melted down the copper pots in the kitchen to make weapons, who cut their long, shining hair to plait into ropes for the national fleet which defended the country's honor . . . in any case, she has no jewelry and not much hair, what hair she does have is lank like mine and wouldn't do to plait a washing line. And she laughs a lot . . . I'm so ashamed . . . Khalil came to hate his mother a little, to hate her laughter a lot and he came top of the class in history.

In the first year of secondary school, Mr. Muqbil arrived. He was square and fat with a round, protruding paunch and he, too, had thick glasses, but with a white metal frame. He was serious, dramatic to the point of violence and used to explode in the classroom at the glimmer of a laugh or even a smile, not even a slight curling of the lip was allowed, nor did he resort to scorn himself as, for him, whose time was completely given over to giving the lesson, no one was clever or stupid, there were only the serious and the rabble. It was violent drama that etched its mark on his classes for he used to insist on pronouncing the letter *qaf* in an extravagant, concave way from the lowest part of the throat and this provoked the boys, who did not understand his stern insistence on this point, to stifled laughter which would raise the curtain on the tragic Muqbil, who would start to shout and turn red, convulsing and chastizing and cursing the fates until the banality of everyday life harnessed him to grim reality with the long ring of the bell, when he would cut short his long speeches and go out holding his thick leather briefcase, grumbling, before casting a last, reproachful glance upon the rising generation.

Khalil was tortured by the suffering of Muqbil, Muqbil who knew no cure save to pronounce the letter *qaf* as it should be pronounced, to be so serious that he seemed on the verge of despairing of life, bound by an obstinacy that would not loosen its grip on him unless the borders of the true nation, of Greater Syria, were to suddenly burst apart . . . only then will we smile in bliss, then may we laugh long and

111

loud. Khalil often used to think about what he could possibly do to alleviate Mr. Muqbil's suffering, to make the class pass quietly. He began to feel embarrassed by his friends and began to hide from them, lest Mr. Muqbil see him in the company of the rabble. He wept for joy and pride one evening, or as a protest against the dark days, when Mr. Muqbil patted him on the shoulder, frowning, with tender eyes . . . you're something else, Khalil, you'll be something, mark my words.

When Khalil remembers his words now he thinks he was killed by seriousness, not by the many wings of the party, one of which his sense of drama had made him think of becoming the leader . . . what killed him was his thick spectacles, apart from which Khalil remembered nothing else of the huge body of Mr. Muqbil, who was opposed to laughter.

While history may have whetted his imagination in the last year of primary school or the correct pronunciation of a guttural language in the first year of secondary school, Khalil, pure in this knowledge of his, would sit, laughing out of nationalistic feeling whenever Youssef came back alive.

6

When Youssef was late, Khalil would begin to wait.

Youssef began to be late like Naji used to be late. Khalil began to wait for Youssef like he used to wait for Naji. It did not really occur to him that Youssef might die as Naji had died. He began to walk around his room looking for something to pass the time, to comfort himself and drive thought from his mind.

He began to read. He read again . . . he tempted himself again with being drawn in, losing himself in the pages, forgetting the whole world and all time in the delight of reading.

He began to lay out the ladder of the pages, setting them rung by rung all the way up to the small, high window, freshly painted, lush with flowers and greenery, with a fluttering curtain, like a window on a stage set, where the writer leans, smiling warmly and tenderly at the tired, anxious person climbing the stairs. He feeds him milky leaves and gives him warm letters to drink, then slowly begins to play with his ruffled hair, slowly, until he enters the heart of reading as if he

113

were gently drifting off to sleep and the window rises high and flies, carries the reader far from all earthly trivia, makes his body and his memories light and he swims in air like the waters of the womb while the writer is like the *maitre nageur*, or a conscientious swimming instructor. He gives him his strong, supple forearm and Khalil lays his head on it while the atoms of his body enter the movement of the wave, Khalil is absorbed in reading and the burden of time is greatly lifted.

What does the writer not do to transport you to happiness. With what sweet waters does he provide you so you might have the pleasure of floating and feel comforted. He leaves the kernel of his heart in your hands and effaces himself, saying it's for you, you're free and I am far from you. I'm not putting pressure on you, not with my eye, for how would you know what the look does to a person, nor with my voice, for the voice is the direct ambassador of the soul . . . it's just that I martyr myself in my battle to write the best of what I see and feel and imagine, far from you, without making you feel any of the pain I feel. I give you the cream of my soul which I don't give to my wife or mother. You and your conscience. How can a person make his conscience obey, make it close a book, or jump a page, or even stray from reading. Then, what does the writer gain from all this? Nothing but the happiness of people whom he does not know and does not know when they read him or remember him . . . more than that, he risks that he will not please them at all. That they will curse him and spit upon him and laugh at his conviction that he is the messenger for whom they have waited to redeem the sons of Adam, for there is such a claim in every piece of writing . . . what infinite tortures they must go through, Khalil sometimes used to think . . . but when he reads he does not think. The atoms of his body enter the movement of the wave and he lays his head on the strong, supple forearm of the writer . . . and the hours go by. The hours go by and stay and go until they stop going and Khalil falls from the ladder for some reason, any reason, because he needs to pee, or because there is a power cut, or because he hears footsteps in the entrance to the building, just footsteps.

When Khalil falls from the high ladder of reading he is beset by thoughts as butchers set upon a cow that has fallen as it runs away.

Was it really I who gave him free rein, to choose who and what he wanted, to regret his choice and come back?

Lies.

All this was lies which pushed Khalil to the bottom like a huge cork in a basin of water. The truth is, I'm using him to test things out . . . to see how to go back to the bosom of the group, to see what I'm not able to test for myself because I'm a coward. I push him to see what happens while I hide like a thief behind the wall. I'm using him to test things out so I can pull back and feel my nausea, so I don't have to go out and do dirty work for money. He's my man, the man who takes care of the house which I used to have to take care of myself . . . he's the one I rely on for the things I need every day, which overflow from above to my room and to my belly . . . he's become the pretext behind which I take shelter so I don't step down from my high morals, so I don't have to sell the things in Madame Isabelle's house, he's the obsession which keeps preying on me when I lack the strength to do it.

What do I want from Youssef? Khalil asked himself. What do you want from Youssef, Khalil. Give yourself one, clear answer and you'll feel better. But no one answer was clear, no one, clear answer was convincing and no one, clear, convincing answer made him feel better.

I cling to Youssef like Potiphar's wife, Zuleikha, clung to him.

I walk in front of him, in all directions. I dig a pit for him and cover it with dry grass so he will fall in and, whenever I feel him approaching my pit, I'm certain he will fall in far from me, so I run on to dig another pit.

All that toil because Youssef is beautiful and because I'm a wife of the wrong sex. I push him to all that is vile, all that is rotten and poisonous and I begin to slap my face in despair as I gather my women. I gather my women and slap my face in despair pointing at him while they do not see him and nobody's hand but mine is cut, while the oranges of my lust remain full and round and red. Hundreds of times. Thousands of times I gather my women so they can see and they do not see and they do not know and it is only I who cut my hands. Whenever I touch the hem of his robe I tear it from behind. I've torn it thousands of times from behind but he did not see me nor did he turn around nor has any robe of his been torn.

115

I tore my robe. I tore my robe and screamed, look at the sinner. Look at what Youssef is doing to me. I tore my body and screamed, look. I tore my heart and screamed, look, and no one looked, no one heard. Even Youssef did not look and did not hear. Even my body did not look and did not hear, I fell to pieces, even my heart did not look and did not hear and so it splintered.

I am a wife of the wrong sex as if, in my stupidity, I wait for Youssef to come one day to ask for my hand. To knock at the door in his most splendid raiment and ask me . . . while I blush, shyly, hesitating a little before nodding my head in agreement . . .

I should have studied acting, thought Khalil as he combed his hair in front of the mirror over the basin in the bathroom, the stage is the best place for all my dramas.

I'm going to sort out some work.

On his way to the newspaper Khalil saw Zahrah. He followed her and made sure it was her. She was walking next to a tall young man. Khalil walked a little faster and moved over to the sidewalk opposite so he could see the man's face without their seeing him. Zahrah's face was like Maryam Fakhreddine's face in her youth. She was fluttering her eyelashes and smiling, twisting her thick neck round. The young man, who was talking and laughing, nudged her with his elbow and so she raised her shoulder coyly. Then they paused in front of a shop window and he brought his head close to hers as if he were whispering something in her ear. She moved away from him and gave him a reproachful look, then walked on a little faster . . .

That tall young man must be one of Youssef's friends, now politics has come into the house through the front door and the back . . . look at Zahrah! Look at my fantasies that the girl was head over heels in love with me . . . perhaps she was infatuated, then abandoned hope. Girls are quick to abandon hope and quick to fall in love with someone else. She liked me in the beginning when she came to the capital, then she got to know the city and began to pick and choose. She's grown up too, her horizons have opened up.

They both look like little pigs, pimples covering their pudgy, red faces . . . they must be talking about mankind in the middle of this crowd. About society, about feelings and beauty and pink hearts that

flutter on candied wings. Two pigs who walk, with the revolting secret smells that their vile bodies secrete, amid piles of garbage in the
loathsome vapors and dust and dirt. Amid the din of the electrical
motors and the scalded, oily air, while in their heads they have it that
they are on the shore of a desert island, their legs plunged into the
soft sand while the gentle breeze plays with their hair and the sun
between their heads vanishes in the shape of a purple heart, which
sends out soft music.

Khalil laughed as he thought of telling them that all these blazing
embers are extinguished in one, tiny moment in two disgusting little
parts of their bodies . . .

Even Zahrah doesn't love me, Khalil said to himself as he approached
the turning for the street where the newspaper was.

Khalil was late for the appointment Nayif had given him. As though
he wanted to go but did not want to. Nayif was not behind his desk.
One of the photographers passed. He said hello to Khalil and told
him that Nayif was in a meeting and showed him where to wait: in a
big reception room facing the door of the editor-in-chief's office, where
the meeting was. Khalil sat on a large, leather sofa and began to look
at a huge painting on the wall opposite. There was a big, blue sparrow
swooping over a yellow, burning plain. A symbol of freedom. Next to
the sofa was a large green plant swathed in dust. This is wartime, not
time to be concerned with plants. The earth was dry so Khalil picked
up a glass from the little table in front of him and poured what was
in it onto the stem of the plant. Then Khalil began to look at his
dirty shoes. He thought of wiping them with a tissue that he had in
his pocket but decided that it was not important and that they would
not notice that kind of thing . . . and if they did, they wouldn't think
it disrespectful but would think I'm a busy man, always on the move,
who pays no attention to that kind of silly detail which has nothing
whatsoever to do with revolutionary ideas or struggle or modernity . . .
no, shoes that are carefully wiped, shiny shoes can do their owner a
lot of harm, because they give a powerful impression of a vicious and
reactionary character. Or of double-crossing class intentions, or violent fascist ambitions, or a latent sadistic streak, or . . .

Nayif came out followed by a number of men, who stopped on the
threshold of the door. Khalil stood up, but Nayif did not notice he

was there . . . they carried on talking among themselves in low voices, then came out into the reception room. Nayif noticed Khalil and greeted him with a reproving glance, then took him by the hand to where the group was and introduced them to him and Khalil to them very politely. There were four of them and Khalil caught the titles of three. Nayif simply introduced the fourth one as "the Gentleman," without going on to explain what he did, in the newspaper or outside it. The editor-in-chief made Khalil welcome, as if he had known him for some time or as if he were one of his aged, highranking relatives, gently encouraging him, spinning off a rapid series of jokes and laughing out loud, encouraging the others to laugh. The Gentleman was smiling but did not say anything. Nayif vacillated between swift bursts of laughter and gravity, a gravity that Khalil had not seen in him before . . . but he seemed happy.

Khalil is a fine young man, said the editor-in-chief . . . I must see you, Khalil . . . Whenever you have the time, said Nayif.

Khalil remembered that he had seen the Gentleman's picture in the newspapers, so he smiled at him. A door that Khalil had not seen opened and a young man with blond hair came through it followed by a dark man with a thick mustache. After he had greeted the others, the man said: he died in hospital. Make space for it in tomorrow's issue. Nayif said, frowning: may God never return him and we hope that all Israel's symbols will follow suit. I'll be late catching you up then, said the editor-in-chief and then, pointing to the man with the thick mustache, our Brother and I will sit for a while. Then, turning to Khalil: Khalil, you can start with us from now . . . write a series of articles, then we'll meet . . . what do you think about something meaty on those people so many of whom have been killed . . . a sweeping investigation into their lives, their fortunes, their black history, and how to punish them, what do you think? Khalil shook his head then said, as if against his will, but . . . I wonder: if the people in the south were able to go into Israel through what we call the "cracks in the wall" then why don't the assassinations take place among the ranks of the extremist leaders inside Israel itself? Slightly astonished, they looked at Khalil, who was mortified and regretted having opened his mouth . . . the editor-in-chief laughed: take it easy with us . . . when the younger generation are so radical it makes us feel our age . . . write your investigation. Brother, write what you want and we'll see, said the editor-in-chief, as if he were bidding Khalil goodbye. But the man he had first called Brother stopped Nayif, who was trying to leave. Nayif wants to leave because he's annoyed with me, thought Khalil. He asked him to catch up with the editor-in-chief in his office, then he said: Nayif . . . bring Khalil with you to the party tonight . . .

Everyone went their separate ways. Nayif gave Khalil a look of surprise, mixed with scorn, or pleasure.

They all misunderstood me . . . thought Khalil.

Khalil did not understand why he had asked his stupid question . . . no doubt he had wanted to look intelligent but everyone had understood that he was droning on feebly as if he were saying: you rejoice that the symbol has been killed, shame on you . . . why don't you attack the root . . . that had been an incurable, a degrading stupidity which meant that finding work at the paper, any work, was now in the past tense. Then, he thought, they also may think I'm absolutely exasperated, furious that the man was killed and that's an outright joke, it's ridiculous . . . I'm ridiculous . . . Khalil sat, thinking about what he had really intended to achieve by asking that stupid question. He found no answer except that he felt he had to say something and could not keep his silence . . . he would find another job.

That is why Khalil did not believe that they had really invited him to the party with them until he arrived with Nayif at the house of the editor-in-chief, who greeted them both with the same warmth and made them sit by him. He doesn't look as though he despises me, thought Khalil. He's a tolerant man with a good heart, or he wants to play the man who understands the younger generation, he's one of those who fondly indulge our ignorance, who are generous enough to put up with all our faults because they're part of the future which we bear on our shoulders, so that people won't say that he's backward and that he's just another head of just another organization. The house was large, with plush furniture. It looked like the houses of recently returned emigrés who are enticed back to take leadership in local politics, who consider they have come to deserve it, although the editor-in-chief, according to Nayif, often used to recall his humble origins, taking pride in the fact that he learnt journalism starting from the bottom rung, until he became one of its few lords. When you say the Lebanese press you mean the flagbearer, the institution of the press in the whole Arab east . . . so Nayif used to say, who, Khalil knew, did not like the editor-in-chief very much, perhaps because he thought himself more deserving of that post but was too noble to ingratiate himself the way the others did to get their luxurious offices.

The sitting room was swarming with men and women . . . although people kept bursting out laughing, the women seemed less happy, less enthusiastic perhaps because the conversation was drifting away from the effect of their femininity which they had been cultivating all afternoon so as to stand out, to shine, to make an effect. Perhaps because they were of the age at which to lose time had become something not easily forgivable and, when they were not the center of the evening, time was lost, frittered away, although they were supposed to be used to that.

The editor-in-chief's wife was cheerful, running around, serving everyone and smiling widely as if she wanted to make a place for herself by force. Interrupting loudly here, asking a question there, she makes a remark and laughs, then pushes up the big flower impaled in her hair with glaring, artful coquetry. Every gesture was overstated, as if she wanted to seem younger than the other women, or as if she were accusing them of not giving their husbands enough support. She was doing more than her duty to support her husband and make the party a success. If the party was a success, life was a success, thus she took her part in that with which God had blessed the family, certain that were she not such a strong character, so intelligent and so self-sacrificing, that her husband would not have achieved what he had achieved, suggesting to the important guests that a man who is happy at home can be relied upon in the most difficult matters and will be given all the help he asks for . . . in any case she must have heard, or read in magazines, that the most important and critical stage in the presidential election campaigns in America is the one at which the qualities of a candidate's wife and his family life are considered, most of all because it is she who will be the first lady of America and who, with her tenderness, her understanding, and her self-sacrifice, will take the whole American family under her wing . . .

More than that, thought Khalil . . . she wants to convince herself that the lump in her throat that catches her by surprise, on some nights when she yearns naïvely for the dreams she used to have of a life of radical asceticism and struggle, was only a delusion and that she was bound to become a miserable, unhappy woman always complaining and regretting the promises she made to herself that she has broken.

But the editor-in-chief's wife, after the third glass, began to lose control of the image she wanted to project and something akin to stifled hostility towards her husband started to slip from her. She repeatedly ignored his requests that she bring him a clean glass . . . then she contradicted him with unjustified anger and began to laugh, nervously, mocking men and married life when someone came from the kitchen complaining that he had found no water to drink. Because she was afraid she might explode in his face when he asked for more ice, she began to draw the conversation towards telling jokes that were a little less sparkling than those she had told at the beginning of the party.

The air burst with laughter again until the Gentleman finally abandoned his dignity: imagine, he said as he coughed . . . imagine, after the explosion that tore our friend away today . . . imagine that you knew that the new rationing program gave current for no more than two hours in every twenty-four . . . then he began another coughing fit and the women's voices rose in indignant comment on the power cuts and each began to tell of her daily battles, until the wife of the editor-in-chief silenced them, encouraging the Gentleman to carry on, so he did . . . imagine, the explosion blew up the water main so there's drinking water and sewage all over the place . . . when people get together . . . imagine, if it was time for the current to come back on in the area . . . and, according to the system, the current came back while the wires sunk under the street . . . and the water . . . but it's up to you to imagine . . . when people are gathered together like on the Judgment Day . . . and the . . .

Torrents of laughter poured down while Khalil's legs were numbed with pins and needles. Our neighbor on the first floor, said a woman as she wiped away the kohl smudged like the traces of a bruise around her eyes, our neighbor was spreading out her rug in the sun . . . as she passed the balcony door she noticed that the rug was moving from underneath! She thought it was the wind. She ran to the balcony. A thief had got hold of the rug from the street, so she held onto it and shouted out . . . he was holding onto the bottom saying let go you silly bitch and she was holding onto the top and shouting. Of course no one dared to come out to help when they saw the revolver . . . Laughter . . . Our neighbor was furious, she cursed and swore for days, until her mother-in-law, who had given her the rug, came to visit her and shouted: you silly cow, why didn't you hold on tighter . . .

The laughter tugged from below and Khalil, who imagined he was the neighbor on the first floor, was laughing at his mother-in-law who burst like a balloon she was laughing so hard.

Then the party ended. The Gentleman leaned over to Khalil and said: leave the place you're living, its full of thugs and thieves.

The editor-in-chief's wife leaned over to Khalil and said: we like you although you don't talk very much.

The Brother leaned over to Khalil and said in a soft voice: I want to see you.

Nayif leaned over to Khalil and said, looking sleepy: call me tomorrow.

Laughter . . . thought Khalil as he made tea in his room . . .

This is the place where people laugh more than anywhere else in the world. When the bombing is in full swing the children laugh and the government employees laugh because it's a holiday . . . they eat plenty and well . . . they bring the best videotapes to their parties because they will be staying up late and there is no work or school early next morning.

The women laugh amongst themselves because they will have more opportunity to meet their neighbors and more opportunity to talk endlessly about their health, about insomnia and injustice, about their marital problems and how naughty the children are.

The shopkeeper will laugh because people will be so busy buying so many provisions that they will virtually empty his shelves.

The baker nearby will laugh because people will buy a lot more than they need, he sells a whole week's flour in one day then sits quietly at home without having to pay the wages of his workers all week.

The man who owns the restaurant will laugh because people will resist the feeling of being hemmed in and having to be stuck at home by going out more and they will be more extravagant, because they love life and because death knocks at the door every day.

The man who owns the gas station will laugh because his power will become like the power of the patriarchs of ancient times and people will crowd to win his affection and to kiss his majestic beard. This may lead him or his son to political leadership.

The moneychanger will laugh because the currency conversions will pour in from outside, in sympathy for family and close relations and, when he closes against a flagging dollar, he opens onto his own overwhelming interest, like the Java wave on the Krakatoa dollar . . .

The poet will laugh because he will feel sadder and because someone in his family or sect will be martyred, which will lend him the microphone of the crowds which come, humbly, after they have left him for so long, begging him to lament and warble in that unique voice of his, made for calamities and the power of words and wisdom will return, in the name of the clan, of the tribe, of kin . . .

The foreign correspondents will laugh because it gives them juicy stories to work on, certainly more juicy than their lean salaries.

The journalist will laugh because time will fly by and his newspaper will be completely ready before eleven at night, even the fourth-rate newspapers. The photographers will laugh because their horrible pictures will remind the executives just what the photograph's status is, when they are printed on the most important pages.

The landlord will laugh because the bombing will make hosts of people move to the city. There will be more pressure on the crowded city which will make for so many more new rental agreements and places falling vacant that his ready imagination rejoices, his apartments become like precious pearls and, if they are hit, the tenant repairs them, then the builders and the carpenters and the painters and the smithies and the furniture sellers laugh . . . and the doctors . . . the whole nation laughs. Even the mothers of the dead will laugh because new arrivals will take their children up and keep them company and so make the burden of the mothers' loneliness less.

A country that laughs . . . a country that does not stop laughing because the high power of wars muddies the purity of its bliss. A living people that is opposed to power . . . that does not object to the open sewers which drown the country. That does not protest against bombing or death or humiliation or the lack of water or electricity or flour, because it wants the warring powers to become more deeply embroiled, wants more scorn and accusation and so stays silent, so it can laugh more. So the angels fluttering in their shining, laughing heavens can laugh.

A country that laughs and plays, believing that its power does not laugh and play and that it is making a fool of power.

A strange country.

The powers laugh their own way . . . every power has its way of laughing . . . just like in the countries that prohibit alcohol. They prohibit its import and consumption . . . but these are the countries that are always drunk. The countries that never sober up. The powers drink in their castles, their clubs, their houses, and their apartments and prohibit drinking in the street. The street makes alcohol by its own hand, or it sniffs glue, or the exhaust fumes of rocket fuel, or ether. It may be poisoned or go blind or die, but it drinks. It does more than drink. That is the way we are: so, laughter is prohibited, everyone has his own way of laughing and we are the nation that laughs the most, more than anywhere else in the world.

The armed men, most of whom are distinguished by their impetuous nature and the strength of their hearts, that is, those who will martyr themselves, are the most madly in love with laughter . . . the suicide divisions in the organizations and political parties laugh most of all. Look at their names . . . the Billygoats Division. The Rot Forces. The Grot Forces. The Abou Wotsit Forces . . . a depressed man noticed this . . . he thought he was suffering a loss and was sad, and that he would not laugh. He blocked off the street in front of his little bakery and sold the contents. He called himself Abou Cholera. He bought a few pounds of dynamite and stood in front of the house of the maid with whom he was in love, lit a stick of dynamite and threw it in a hole nearby and shouted come down, Muntaha, or I'll blow the whole world up, and the neighbors shouted from the windows, clutching the glass . . . come down Muntaha . . . then he began to laugh and laugh. Young men meet at his place and talk about the price of light weapons and about politics. He began to tell jokes. Once he told them a joke he had made up: he said: there's a woman who had triplets so she named them after three villages that had been bombed, and bombed again, and again: Kfarfalous and Libaa and Ain el Mir . . . Libaa was fair as the moon, like his wife Muntaha, the mother of his children. Once, during the fighting, he wanted to save one of his men who needed surgery, so he carried him by the legs, for miles, at night and, when he went to put him down from his shoulders he found his legs were all he'd been carrying . . .

A tempestuous festival of laughter. A city thrown onto its back waving its arms and legs like a huge cockroach under a massive joke. Laughter that fate does not give a chance to catch its breath, the chance to draw a little oxygen . . . laughter whose blood is blue and turns black from laughter . . . dies of laughter.

And you, Khalil, drinking your tea coldly,
why are you not laughing?

7

Early in the morning, at dawn, the evil spirits grow still. In the villages they used to say that the demons and the fairies disappear with the first rays of light, in the cities the whispering and crawling of the insects grows still, the drunks fall silent and the pains of the sick grow less, lovers and cheated husbands sleep and, on the battlefields, the fires die down but for a pale smoke that makes the plaintive wailing of the fighters and the wounded who drink the last drops under the romantic dew seem awe-inspiring, or something like a cause for regret.

That was some time ago . . . when the leaders who disputed some land, some borders, or some idea met in fields far from those who did not want to do battle and thrashed each other, until whoever was doomed to win won and the losers and their peoples settled up, paid tribute, and offered their obedience and humility but, after the dead were buried and the wounded gone, after their leaders had stepped down or committed suicide . . . then translations begin and cultures and religions mingle, civilizations are founded and their turrets rise high . . . usually history finds a way to do away with humanity . . . for us, all this is forbidden and war is nothing to do with chaos. What is forbidden is absolutely forbidden.

That is why the street war went on shamelessly until noon, or a little after noon.

The sound of the bombs quietened down. The people who lived in the building went back to their homes. Khalil went down to his room and stretched out on his bed to relieve the numb sensation in his legs. He began bending and stretching them quickly to get the flow of blood going. From the street came the sound of raised voices, calling out to each other playfully.

He went up to the window and, with the curtain, blocked up all the cracks where the light got in. He swept the shards of glass away towards the window with his foot and decided to go to sleep.

I'll sleep long and deep and when I wake up he'll have come back, thought Khalil. Then he heard a loud knock at the door and "Mr. Khalil . . . Mr. Khalil, open the door." When Khalil opened the door the entrance to the building was in darkness.

The corpse was quivering in the gray blanket. It must seem black from the inside, thought Khalil, not raising his eyes from the stretcher. If he could see he'd think he was in a pit . . .

There is no call for all this haste, for these sirens, but the ambulance drivers had grown used to it and no longer thought about what they were carrying or where they were driving, whether they had the dead or the wounded with them, or whether they were on their way to the hospital or leaving it. Then, what is there to make them put up with the crowded roads when they have white flags and warning sirens. The driver and his mate offered each other cigarettes in a slightly exaggerated way, then cautiously offered one to Khalil. They spoke to the center a number of times and the driver began to joke with the girl working the walkie talkie. The driver's mate asked Khalil what relation he was to the young man and Khalil replied that he was a neighbor . . . then he said: I'm his family's neighbor, and fell silent. The ambulance stopped at an armed roadblock. The driver said: a corpse, mate. Then he asked, do you want to search and the young man said no, giving Khalil a hostile, suspicious look. The driver said: their neighbor, he's doing the necessary. The young man said go. God bless. The driver's mate said: how old is he? I don't know exactly, said Khalil, about twenty.

If he hadn't been human he would have stopped us and searched us, the driver said, after a silence, perhaps because he felt uncomfortable. Sometimes they smuggle arms and supplies in ambulances, his companion remarked, and they say they're corpses . . . it didn't happen in the University hospital ambulances, or the Red Cross ambulances. I know, said the driver. Then he braked heavily and got out, shouting and swearing at a friend of his because he had not kept his word and dropped off the bundle of bread that he had promised them. The leather straps stopped the corpse from slipping. Khalil thought then said to himself: I'm calling him the corpse like them. The driver apologized to Khalil and slammed the dented door a few times, until it shut.

The sound of Zahrah and her mother's shrieking rose from the balcony. Khalil got out of the back door of the ambulance and found his hand in the hand of an old man whose face he had known for a long time. We're prepared, the man said and Khalil remembered that he was one of their relatives but he had forgotten his name, old age had changed his features so.

Khalil said to the man, pointing to the ambulance: he's inside. The man said, I think we should go now. Here, things are . . . as you know.

Khalil did not understand what one of the young men was trying to whisper in his ear, but he kept saying: the Gentleman is very sorry. Very sorry, he sends his regards, he didn't know and he'll see you . . . but he's very sorry and hopes that everything will be over and done with quickly because things aren't as they should be, he says that the young men are furious because the young man . . . I mean your relative killed his strongest two men. They were brothers. He hopes that people here will not take it as an excuse to stick together, that is, because of the burial and because things are bad . . . this shrieking . . . the Gentleman sends his regards.

Khalil did not know where the yellow ambulance that had brought him had gone. He noticed that it was evening when the two women,

128

as if suddenly, stopped shrieking. It's as if I hadn't been here all this time, thought Khalil, then he wondered if he had gone out to the cemetery or stayed here since that time, that is, since around noon.

He looked for the old man and did not find him.

The following morning his uncle's wife was in the entrance of the building carrying large bundles and nylon bags. Zahrah was hurrying her two little brothers along and, at the door, the old man was waiting. He came up and said hello to Khalil while Khalil thought that for months and months, since they came to live upstairs, he had not seen his uncle's wife in the entrance . . . this was the first time . . . as she held onto Khalil's arm, she began to cry more and so did Zahrah.

They got into the yellow car, busy with their belongings and did not look at him through the glass windows. After the car had gone a few yards Khalil remembered that the man's name was Abou Qassem and he saw him a lot less old going into their house, with a tray of sweets wrapped up in a leafy green bundle from Nabatiyeh in his hand.

8

It had not been a long time but Khalil convinced himself that it was enough time to go back over what had happened and to believe it. He had seen the corpse. He had not seen it. He had seen it wrapped up inside a gray woolen blanket, quivering, on the stretcher. Held in place by leather straps to stop it from slipping. But that was not enough at all.

Youssef's mother had not seen the corpse either. But people, everyone who knows them will help her to see it, even to touch it with her hand. She will wear black and see people who will confirm to her what has happened and repeat their confirmation. The women will wear black for her, and they will receive her and sit near to her, encouraging her to weep more. At a particular time in the day, for a number of days, she will go accompanied by them to Husseiniyeh. Her daughter will sit there next to her and they will sit in a circle around her. One of them, known for being active, hands out tissues to the women there before anything begins, she will hand out three or four to every woman because the dead man is a young man who was snapped in two. A woman, whom they all know, will go up to a platform that is a couple of steps or more above the rest of them and then sit down, clearing her throat to polish her beautiful voice, to read the condolences from the biography of the great martyrs. She will recite and sing and receive the rest of them at the table of tears and the tears will pour forth and flow over. They will all weep for the dead man and for those they knew who died before him. They will skin their eyes when they hear the mournful sound of the sighing voice, they will invite each other to tears as if to a delicious fruit because they know that the dead man has to die and be buried and that what buries him is not dust, but the water of eyes. They will prop each other up and help each other to stand in line behind the beautiful voice of the woman who recites, like chicks behind a hen . . . the voice of the woman who recites walks along the road of death leaving behind those who have died, waving to them, drawing away from them. The mourning women walk like chicks along the long line of weeping behind their mother, death, to weep for one death which is repeated over and over again. The voice distributes death to people so that they can weep until it comes back and gathers it up into the death of the greatest of martyrs . . . when it merges with this it seems a small death, a trivial death and so it will be forgotten, in the way that minor points and details are forgotten when they catch up with the center of their gravity.

Women, thought Khalil, moaning in envy alone in his room . . . all the wisdom is given to women. Wisdom of life and death and wisdom of what is farthest from it . . . they're in touch with the world, they have a secret communication with it which makes anything that doesn't belong to them nothing but a flurry of dust . . . they weep for the dead man and they bury him because they know this clay and all its fields of gravity, they know the turning of the planets and, if they do not, how is it that their periods stop, regularly, keeping time with the heavenly bodies and the moons and how is it that they have done so for millions of years, like the ebb of the tide and its flow, like the night of the heavens and their light, like the seeds of the earth and its harvest . . .

They tame death, instinctively. They make it dismount and make it sit by them, shyly but with the confidence of mastery. They feed it, they give it coffee to drink and they walk by its side until it becomes like one of the family and they do not hesitate to tell it their little problems as if it were a friendly neighbor picking over lentils with you on the big brass tray.

When it defies them, they pursue it. They do not run away from it. His mother will keep silent for a while during the day out of regard for the men who say that he is a martyr, who stick his pictures on the electricity pylons because he died while he was fighting the enemy . . . what enemy? It does not matter at all, because the men will not comprehend the complicated politics of the city. They see him as a knight of old bringing down an enemy and dying on the battlefield. They are convinced that he is a martyr, they are convinced by the salary that they bring at the end of the month to his mother. His mother keeps silent during the day out of regard for those upon whom God has inflicted inadequacy and a lack of wisdom. As soon as her children sleep and the dark of night falls to her liking she resumes her stubborn pursuit. She begins to wail long before she reaches the grave. She sees him before she gets there because she knows her way to him well. She keeps wailing and weeping and beating her face with the dust from his grave until it comes to pass that she, or it, that is, death, talk about household matters, as if it were a friendly neighbor who sits with you by the same brass tray. She says the hen isn't laying and that she lost the scissors and that she had a fight with her sister-in-law and that a bridegroom came yesterday to ask for Zahrah's hand and that she has received money from the Gulf which she will use to buy oil because the shortage has become acute.

I'm like someone whose dead have been stolen away, Khalil said to himself, regretfully . . . someone whose two dead have been stolen from him, someone who's left on the edge of the desert a few seconds before the murder . . . someone who raises his dead with the tears of his eyes . . . who carves their pictures chip by chip and always, before the desire is ripe, before the mellow season comes, always, before Khalil's buried desire to kill them makes itself clear they kill them and they steal away their corpses, leaving him only the inability to weep for them and the lack of will to bury them, to remind him, always, that he is not man enough to forge his world of dreams and not woman enough to accept.

Khalil's envy grows and grows more intense . . . he is at a loss as to what he could possibly do to see his two dead and bury them. It is no use to him to stretch out on his narrow bed waiting, for he knows that death does not pass in this way, it does not pass if you stretch out waiting, watching it in its emptiness. Time has a belly that has to be filled so that it can keep going like any horse, any tortoise, so with what is Khalil to fill the belly of time?

Khalil did not see Naji's corpse but he invented a corpse for him, he saw it and it went away. It went far away, but how was he to see Youssef's corpse, Youssef who fought like a lion in the street battle until he killed, among the others, two brothers, the boldest and best of the Gentleman's men so their companions caught up with him and killed him in the ambulance, on his way to the hospital when he was only wounded, hit in the shoulder and the leg. Because he was so fierce in the fighting. Because he killed so many of his enemies, the party's enemies and the enemies of his creed . . . Khalil kept telling himself that this is what happened, that Youssef was not killed by surprise when he was out late with his young friends or on one of his turns on guard on the chair in the street in front of the building nearby, where they had their headquarters. They did not take him so much by surprise that he didn't have time to throw down his weapons and his army boots and go home once he found out that it was more than a matter of a bottle of butane gas, more than a salary at the end of the month and more than the short year he had spent to pay the university fees for the following year, there was something serious at stake that made it a matter of life or death. It was not like that . . . he was fighting. Youssef beat me to the farthest of the snares that I had devised for him. The farthest by far. Youssef had been swallowed up and more. Who was the Youssef who was killed? Khalil knew that he would have needed a lot of time, would have needed to rack his brains to stumble upon a corpse killed in an ambulance but he had a strong intuition that the gray blanket that seemed like a pit from the inside was indeed a pit and that Youssef was in it, that he had not got out of it and that he, Khalil, if not all of Youssef's thousand brothers . . . Youssef's own brothers who cast Youssef into the pit . . . and Youssef did not get out of his brothers' pit.

Well, said Khalil, sitting on his bed . . . I'm the one who dug every trap for him, even this one that he beat me to. I threw him into it, I made a mistake and I sat down half expecting him to come back. I made a lot of mistakes before I succeeded, I who opened the back door of the ambulance and rained down the bullets on his body, many bullets which left open, red holes with charred and lacy edges, thirsty, gaping holes. I'm the one who killed Youssef and got away, free, from the poisonous magnetism of his body. I'm the one who's free of him now, I'll say I'm the one who killed him. I'll make my confession like a big watermelon. I'll eat his death, morsel by morsel, until the watermelon is finished. I'll eat his killing, pip by pip, until it's finished. I will weep with regret, for my great sin, for my passion that was snapped in two. I will weep long for him and sob deeply and bitterly as he deserves . . .

But the tears did not come . . .

IV

1

Time is not a steed that eats to keep going.

Time is a sugared doughnut. Little pieces strewn about empty, even, of their soft fragility.

In a city like ours, your life is like a butcher's block. And your time, you stand at the sink rolling your sleeves up over your arms and begin to mince it up into little pieces and eat. Tiny bits which get more minute whenever they are gathered together . . . the more you mince them, the tinier the bits become, until they vanish. Nothing holds your time together and gives it its essence or content except the bombing. The bombing rearranges the city's schedule like the calendar of the fast does in Ramadan. Before the bombing—during the bombing—during the long bombing after the bombing—before the bombing. All sorts of bombing.

Everything is minced into tiny pieces, a puff of dust, except during the bombing. On the radio you hear nothing but fragments of words and songs . . . of long songs, such as Umm Kalsoum sings, you hear—

when the bombing has stopped—nothing but very short snatches, because everyone is in a hurry. When the bombing becomes intense, you can hear these songs from start to finish since the presenters of the live shows are busy with themselves, with their safety, with listening to the news here and there so they give the singers who like to sing long free rein . . . the people who prepare the short programs cannot, for the most part, get to the broadcast transmission centers and the live shows, such as those that cover artistic or social activities or that aspire to broadcast witty interviews with artists, become impossible to put into effect . . . then, the bits of time grow large and round and you hear the sort of thing to which listening time should be devoted.

The auspicious bombing returns primal time to you and restores the city's first coherence. Death is the only spur to the city, for it is death that gathers the city's many little splinters and holds them to itself like iron filings.

Death is the only man in the city. When the city is plunged deep in her seductions and games he twists her arm and, in one swoop, holds it fast towards him and she leans on him and calms down and she begins to breathe regularly.

He gives the city her real flavor which she forgets, when the bombing starts. It is death who is the father of the city, who always reminds her that she must refrain from standing by the window . . . who chides her, holding her back from the dreams that tempt her to play outside the fence, to talk to strangers, that tempt her to the desire to be like the distant world that sends the city its disgusting pictures in magazines, in immoral books, and on television.

When the bombing becomes intense, death sits at his desk. He cleans his spectacles thoroughly before picking up the long ruler and the pen to draw up a plan for the city as befits a great architect. Only those who have some connection go out into its streets: the fighters and the death squads. As for those who have no job, they loiter in his vaults, in his natural places. Things are not confused, the lion does not lie with the lamb, this is one of Nature's catastrophes, one of its bitter peculiarities. There is no place for confusion, no place for you to wonder whether the shoeseller is a blood merchant, or sells plundered electrical goods. Even the petty thieves restrain themselves and take their family life seriously.

Death is the master of clarity and precision but, so precise and clear is he that he rises up from the city like a spirit and is tormented whenever he has to define his features or forms. In his buildings he suffers the torment of one concerned with God's incarnation in man and man's incarnation in God, buildings that perpetually fall a little short, that are always tight across his infinite shoulders.

Death the master is tormented even when the president of the organization's wife talks about him. She gives her military husband support, with her national and civil qualifications, to establish his power and to give it more credibility. My husband's ranks kill because they are always obliged to kill while I cast off my jewelry and dedicate myself to war to be elevated by death to its most sublime form, to martyrdom.

They lose their entrails and their limbs on the asphalt in the heat and rain because they are sensitive and because they are generous, as intelligent people are, because they know that it is better for them to rise to the jewel of martyrdom than to die just for nothing, by mistake, without becoming immortal, they feel my presence, they know that the president does not come near me once during the year he is so busy with their concerns, he does not see his children. I'm here burning up my time and my youth, neglecting my father and my house for their sake, for the sake of the wounded and the orphans and the disabled. Look at our disabled, victims of the enemy, whom the god death returned to us that they might bear witness to our innocence, that we might celebrate them with their eternal mutilations, that we might spit the poisons of anxiety from our weak consciences. Our lovely disabled lean on their sticks, their hands outstretched for our intercession, they are better than you are at making cane chairs and sitting us on them so we can find rest from you. They play with their severed limbs and their plucked out eyes to make us feel happy and to ease our consciences, to encourage us to walk in the path of righteousness. They run around in their wheelchairs, happy as sandboys, urging on the fighters of our organization, crying out for joy and beating drums. They leave their mothers and wives and children to follow the organization which walks on the face of the water.

We shall whet society's appetite. We shall arrange classes for sewing and fitting, workshops for knitting and embroidery, markets to sell stuffed peppers and stews and pickles and preserves. We shall fill sandbags with the gravel from their kidneys, we shall clean the areas around the blockades and wash the pictures of the martyrs with the juices that run from our wounds, we shall polish the glass of the party head-quarters with the waters that run from the corners of their eyes and we shall steep the bullet in mothers' milk so that it shines and glim-mers in the dim light.

We shall put life in order, this whole dirty, short, wretched life, this life that does not deserve to die by a stray bullet but by a bullet shot true for the sake of the order, we shall put life in order along the same lines as death's eternal order, we shall reduce it for the confused and bewildered, we shall reduce it a great deal . . .

Death is tormented but he does not stop to give in to the president of the organization's wife.

Blood . . . Khalil was vomiting up red blood. He was unable to get a hold of his guts or of the president of the organization's wife who began to draw her speech to a close, dancing on the steps of the pool with the fountain that spills over with blood, shouting and slapping her face as she felt his head, aflame with fever.

Then the president of the organization's wife sat behind the roaring Singer machine and when she becomes engrossed in her sewing, many rows of little girls behind their machines appear behind her. Then Youssef goes into the entrance of the place which is bare, except for the big mirror, and begins to walk, light on his feet, spreading out his hands, swaying from the waist like a model. The roar of the machines stops and the little seamstresses catch up with the president of the organization's wife and wind themselves around her, each one holding a very small piece of white cloth in her hand. Then they draw back and hover around the red fountain, leaving a little gap for the presi-dent of the organization's wife and they begin to sing in exquisite, angelic voices like the voices of babies crying.

Then the president of the organization's wife stands up and walks towards Youssef. She puts her hand around his slender waist and be-gins to lift his cotton shirt until she pulls it over his head and turns around and lets loose what she has in her hand and two large, white, outspread wings appear, hanging by many silk threads. Youssef turns around and the president of the organization's wife passes the white silk threads through the holes that the bullets made in his chest so that she can fasten the wings. She holds him in a strong embrace, then twines her hand in his and they begin to walk with broken steps towards the pool as the voices of the girls rise. Youssef goes up the steps of the pool until he reaches the fountain and he sits on the fountain fluttering his white wings until the red liquid gushes from the top of his head without coloring his wings.

The overpowering smell settled in front of the brass basin then moved away a little, a small part of it bore him to warm waters that seemed familiar to him, that he loved and she began to bathe him as she sang and laughed out loud.

His sisters' eyes were fixed upon him, laughing, peering at his little member which was not the way the family had seen it before ... the sound of their calling out *bismillah*, in the name of Allah, surrounded him, rising like warm vapor from her hands and from his round belly below his protruding navel. She anointed his head with perfumed oil then dropped white milk from her large breast in his eyes. One of his sisters clapped whenever she touched his watery skin while the others were warming his round legs with hands that moved to and from the heater, as they laughed among themselves. Was snow falling behind the window or was the milk in his eyes turning everything white? His white robes were moving from her warm, deep lap to the girls' hands like the remains of a saint who has just risen. With the broken snatches of their singing, the girls are gathering the waters of his body, the swaddling clothes that bound him and the hairs of his head, to bury them carefully far from the envy of strangers.

After the cord of his navel fell away he came to be standing in the basin for a little while so she came back and sat him down saying *bismillah* and pulled open the curtain. They were hovering around him, wary lest their laughter make him fall into the water. They kept covering him with the white towels, like one who shrouds his pharaonic desire with liquid gold while the women, like priestesses, handed down the oils to embrocate his pure body. Then she lifts him, in the face of their hunger for him, to her large breast from which warm milk drips into his face before it reaches his mouth so he raises his clenched fist and begins to beat with his fist again and again, asking for more of the smell with which to bathe his happy appetite.

When he began to walk, began to spill the water from the basin, asking them to leave like a petulant princeling, the smell faded so much that the sound of his demands became more rough. Snow was falling behind the curtain and his towels were scattered on a little wooden chair by the basin, bubbling with its white foam, when he began to shout in a voice that sounded like crying and his voice fell into the water. Suddenly the soprano note of the original smell left without him being aware of it, as if by mistake. He discerned something like panic in their eyes. The little girl's cheeks turned red and the other girls burst into stifled laughter. She sent them out like butterflies from the room and said, "That's right, you've become a man and you will bathe yourself."

Laughing, she put her hand to her mouth and said: speak, let me hear your voice. Then she went out with her breasts which, at that moment, disappeared completely and she closed the door on their loss.

When his voice fell and its high wave broke like the glass of a lamp his surprise was so great that it left him no opportunity to realize what it was that he had lost now, for ever. His voice became thick, like a thick wound and his green leaves fell from him in a moment, leaving him a large, dry, brown trunk which will carry him as far as language can to the edge of nothingness, to the isthmus of successive extinctions.

His voice which fell, as if into his light testicles, said to him from below that he was of a certain sex and he was of a certain age and that his sex and his age had begun the outward journey, under the pouring snow, even if he stayed all his life standing in the froth of the basin. With this high cadence that was lost for ever was lost the delight at being outside sex, it abandoned Khalil before he knew which string he would play to compensate for this loss.

Khalil sat on the chair on top of his towels and began to talk to himself in his new voice, so he did not hear its complaints and was unable to catch up with himself, with his sex, in his voice. Whenever he spoke, his complaints fled from him in fear and ran away outside, outside the kingdom in which he knows the women will die. From now on he will not speak in a voice but in a language . . . and he has to know in whose language.

142

All of my voice will be outside my language, my language will be peeled of my voice and it will be stripped, as I was stripped now and I will never, come snow or sunshine, be able to know the person I was and to remember him as he should be remembered.

The little apple that hangs in his throat without being eaten away will change all colors, from now on, to variations on red.

Khalil was very ill. He kept vomiting up water mixed with short, red threads.

No one knocks at the door now so Khalil's body is stretched out, now filling the darkened room, now shrinking until he almost throws it down the lavatory and pulls the chain on it. Now his body drew close until it went almost completely into his stomach and he swallowed it like a viper and now it drew away, slumped and spread out until it almost slipped out through the keyhole, the joints of the window-frame, the mouths of the taps and drains. But he was always thirsty, he swallowed vast quantities of water which immediately escaped in a white froth like cotton wool as if it saw what it feared inside his guts.

He sweated a great deal, determined not to open the window in this hot weather. His skin kept leaking sweat even if only a little, so he took off all his clothes and sat, half sprawled, on his chair and began pondering long on his weak body.

The tortoise has armor. The fish has scales. The hedgehog has spikes. The octopus has suckers and ink. The sheep has horns. The cat has claws. The dog has fangs. How is it that man has nothing in his body to protect him. He is naked, laid so bare that the air will kill him. He no longer has the hair that used to cover him until it disappeared, he has come to walk on his hind legs so his body is more uncovered, more exposed, while the things around him have become more dangerous, more damaging, so how does anyone have the tremendous courage it takes to open the door and go out, to what lies beyond the walls . . . how can he risk opening his window when he knows that the skies over the plains and deserts ripple with bees and wasps and birds with hooked beaks. The soft fragility of his body makes him beneath all other creatures, he is killed carelessly and mindlessly by his enemies. Other animals die only for clear reasons and purposes.

They draw their courage from their clarity, said Khalil as he listened to the sound of the children playing in the street, running around the entrance to the building. He is different, if not, then how to explain the blazing of his lust when he sees the corpses of the men who have been killed in the newspapers, the men whose torsos are always exposed. He feels that excitement that goes directly from his lungs to his loins whenever he sees a corpse with its chest and waist and hip and throat and arms laid bare in the newspaper, for those firm, naked bodies of theirs confirm to him beyond all doubt that they are men, that the sharp flame of their masculinity is what led them to kill. They are so masculine that they make Khalil's pale, pale, still body nothing but a person who feeds his poor, ugly flower between which, between him and his flower, a language had crept one day that stole Khalil's first voice away and did not give him another, a language that did not adopt him. He was still like the son of the washer-woman.

Lies.

Whenever Youssef's face came to him, his whole body became a mouth. He knows now that he is the storyteller and the listener at once, that the oil in the pan splutters and smokes waiting for Khalil to take out his past illusions, his past evasiveness, his equivocation and his fear and eat them, because they are overdone.

What about the women, the women who look like my mother, who look like my sisters, who look like my first voice? Have they died? Did they rain down bullets on them in the ambulance, were they killed like Youssef was killed? Do I know what I know? Can I be certain?

A woman will walk in front of him, with no legs, her torso will move, with no breasts, she will ask him about the house of one of the neighbors and look into his eyes and he will not see her lips, she will put out her hand lifting her hair from her slender, veined neck and he will not see, or he will see, the trace of veins under the skin of two small hands which rub two round thighs with the moist cream while the faucet still drips over the steam of the basin . . . he does not see a navel sunk, like a little grave, in a stretched-out plain of flying flour, round, like the steppes of Russia in the atlas.

All this is sad and would make you cry were Youssef's fluttering body with the white wings not still oozing gelatinous fluids which gather like steps upon which Khalil rises, swaying, rising as if sucked up by his bubbling head, rising as if sucked up by his mouth which neither tells nor kisses, he rises to an embrace, he flies then he is poured down instantly like a thin drizzle over a storming ocean, which falls without ever touching it . . . Khalil rises from his body to Youssef's body, there before his eyes and above him like a difficult and devious saint while the fountain blazes from his every exalted pore and turns like a halo of fire around him, all around him.

Khalil ponders his body again. He does not like his body, his weak, stiff legs, his chest, hollow as a frying pan without a handle, his arms, hanging down the sides of the chair like a pair of molted brooms, his skinny body, undone at the seams like a scarecrow planted in a bare, dry field, a scarecrow that scares nothing but the crows in his distracted eyes.

Poor Khalil. Your poor bed and your poor body, which dangles like a mildewed and broken clock pendulum . . . your poor illness and your poor puke and your poor embarrassment of yourself . . . your poor war.

Poor, sickly Khalil. Poor, lowly Khalil. Poor, puny Khalil.

2

K halil's body no longer went with him anywhere.

It began to refuse and dig in its heels like a stubborn mule, which is why he began to use it rather than work with it.

Khalil used to spend his time lost in thought, sleeping, looking at the wall, listening to the radio, reading. Now the ugliness of his body and the pains in his stomach had begun to eat up his time, time whose concern it was to bring Khalil out of his body, to lighten him of its burden, to bear him to the dream, to the wall, to the radio, to the book. This time was a great pleasure to Khalil because it used to pass far away from him, he was busy with his blessed leisure, with his soft fragility and his great compliancy.

Now, Khalil opens a book and begins to climb the ladder of the pages and the writer, before Khalil reaches the edge of the window, begins to push the ladder from the top and it falls, and Khalil falls from it . . . when he rises to the challenge and tries again he finds the writer threatening quite clearly to use boiling oil to defend his secure fortress. So Khalil closes the book, shrinking and afraid.

When he switches on the radio and begins, little by little, to penetrate the wall of his room his stomach begins to twist his ear like a strict aunt, who switches off the radio and makes him sit in the middle of the room on the cold tiles.

Sometimes, he used to think of going out but his fear used to drive him back from the door at the last moment for he knew that he had no protective armor to protect his ugly body and he had nothing but his body, which he knew was declining rapidly, relentlessly. And, in the end, however ugly and loathsome his body was it was his body that preserved his soul . . . his soul, onto which he clung . . . his soul, nothing other than his life . . . and, even if he did not cling very hard to it he was more of a coward than to lose it, more of a coward than to feel pain, as all those who die feel acute pain, without a doubt.

Sometimes, he used to listen intently to the sound of footsteps in the entrance of the building. He would cock an ear towards the door and begin to watch out of the corner of his eye, expecting to hear a knock which would drag him, by force, to open the door and, by force, the face of someone he loved would look in. Then he knew that there was no face he loved to look in, so he came to be satisfied with the idea of seeing a familiar face. But he stayed, holding his breath, fixed in his place when Nayif came and knocked on the door a number of times. He heard his voice in the entrance asking one of the children if he had seen Khalil going out or coming in. He asked him since when he hadn't seen me then asked the boy to tell me, when he saw me, that my friend Nayif came and that he must see me about something important. Everything Nayif does is always a must.

Why did Khalil not open the door to Nayif? He heard the knocking on the door and heard him talking in a worried voice with the boy and he felt immensely happy. Nayif's voice sounded kind to him, full of the kind familiarity for which he was burning. But he did not open the door . . . perhaps he wanted to find out how determined Nayif was to see him, to ask after him, to find out how much he loved him.

But Nayif came again. Again, Khalil did not open the door but Khalil was not delighted by this second visit because Nayif did not knock persistently enough. When Khalil lifted the hem of the curtain he saw Nayif . . . he looked slightly annoyed. He did not look worried or sad. He got into his car and left without asking about the boy he had spoken to the first time. Why does he not suppose that I am dead here, in this room, that someone has to come and open the door for me so they can bury me. Perhaps his nose had sought wind of the evil smell. And, when he didn't find it, he didn't tear down the door. He went. He comes because he's sulking now since Claude left and he wants someone who has no work to do to lend an ear to the drama of mens' relationship to women and, of course, he finds no one but me.

Nayif should have torn down the door, he should have entered by force, he should have swept me away to his heart and patted me on the head while I wept for joy because he loves me.

After a week, Nayif came back for the third time. Khalil got up and opened the door because he knew that Nayif would not tear it down, he would not pound on the door and he would not ask the boy, even if he met him in the entrance to the building. He got up and opened the door and said to Nayif, after he had sat down heavily . . . the boy told me that you asked after me . . . I was in the village. Of course, said Nayif, I thought as much . . . what are you doing about the water. The water at the newspaper has all dried up. They're buying water by the cistern. The house is unbelievable. I've come to hate sleeping there and the Kurdish woman doesn't come any more. The Kurds have become the richest people in Beirut. They hire Sri Lankans to work in their houses. How are you doing? Managing, said Khalil, who had not had a bath for a long time and who supposed that Nayif would put his long, prickly beard down to his being excessively deep in mourning.

No doubt you use the water in the apartment upstairs, Nayif said. Khalil preferred not to reply and to clear his head of the images of the apartment upstairs, which began to reel through his mind in broken strips.

What does Nayif want?

By the way, Nayif said, the Gentleman asked me to say hello to you. He said that you have a unique personality. I was talking at some length about the past few years so he asked if you two could meet but I put it off because there's some sensitivity about what happened.

What does Nayif want?

Do you want to have a bath, Nayif?

No, said Nayif. I'd like a cup of coffee.

Khalil found that there were no coffee beans on the shelf when the water in the little copper coffeepot had boiled. Nayif went out and came back with a small packet and made the coffee himself . . .

He poured out a cup for himself and forgot to pour one out for Khalil, then he began to comment on the unusual chaos in the room, sounding surprised, surprised in an overstated way. You used to be so neat, my friend . . . we were always so on edge when we came to your place. It's better this way . . . perhaps it's a sign that you're tired of living alone, without women, I mean without a woman, a wife. Mind you, don't think of getting married. It's a dreadful plunge to take, my friend . . . everyone suffers . . . only there are some who won't admit that that's the way it is, just to be contrary. There are so many problems, you can't imagine. It's just that you feel that you have someone imposing on you. So the first thing you feel is hatred. Deep, lurking hatred which takes a lot of time and patience and pretence. But it's unthinkable for anyone who has his head screwed on the right way . . . it's impossible, no matter what you do. It's hell on earth.

What does Nayif want?

Everyone, even the ones who seem to be really compatible, together, as if they have a secret understanding between them. When I saw the Gentleman and his wife I thought they understood one another so well that it was nothing more than that they had discovered everything about each other. They knew each other inside out. The cards were on the table. What do you want and what do I want, no lies, no deception, no ambiguity, no illusions. He's a smart social climber and she's a smart opportunist. They agree about everything. They used to. That perfect edifice which took years and years to make strong and beautiful is in ruins, or near enough. All because his sister left the country and took her mother by the hand and sat her in the living room in front of her sister-in-law, his wife. His sister didn't forget to throw the little bundle in the passageway, and left the country. The day of reckoning came for the Gentleman's wife because she hadn't taken this unforeseen factor into her calculations at all. She began to shake the foundation of the entire edifice and it wasn't built to take the dreadful shocks she gave it . . . now it's the season and work is in full swing . . . the young men all over your quarter suggested a solution to him, I mean the empty apartment upstairs. They said take it as a headquarters for us, an arms depot or something like that. So he thought he'd solve his problem, I mean send the *hajjah*, his mother, to live there, away from his wife. He came to me. I told him I knew nothing about it—by the way, that lot won't be coming back, that's for sure. You should take anything useful and bring it down here, if not they'll clean the place out, as you know. Who'll tell them no. Listen, rugs, silver, furniture, anything you bring down you take for yourself.

So this is what Nayif wants. To put the apartment at the Gentleman's disposal so he can spread the sphere of his influence further and better, so he can be reckoned more highly in these bad times. And he grants me my piece of the cake, to empty out the apartment so they move into it empty and I benefit and he benefits and the young men benefit and the Gentleman's wife benefits and his mother benefits and joy and prosperity reign. And if not . . . who can tell them no . . . who can stand up to them?

Oh it's so clear . . . thought Khalil . . . but . . . what shall I do with Nayif my friend, with my friend Nayif, Nayif who is too much, who is my friend.

His name was Mustafa but Khalil always called him the Bridegroom, to himself, because his picture was always wed to the picture of the bride who lived on the fourth floor, with the high-heeled lace slippers.

Mustafa said to Khalil: I don't know what should be done . . . the smell's unbearable . . . it fills the whole place. Ahmad went to fetch her son and couldn't find him anywhere. Her son's wife said he'd gone away and that they couldn't go there and she asked us to sort things out . . . it's a strange time, my friend . . . you have to come up with me. I don't have to, brother, shall we call the Red Cross, it's hot, and this is really not on.

The *hajjah* was prostrate on her side, her eyes bulging and her mouth open wide. Her belly was blown up like a balloon and her arms and legs were spreadeagled. She was barefoot and her white flipflops were placed far apart next to her. Her white headscarf touched her slit throat where a spot of waxy blackness was covered in thick flies. Her bed was neat and the sheets were brilliant white. Her spectacles with the brown frames and an old copy of the Qur'an with thick pages were on her high pillow.

Only the cloying smell disturbed the calm there.

3

This is the most beautiful relationship that people can have. On his right was a woman of fifty with a large, warm, supple behind which quivered as she touched Khalil's hip and the top of his thigh whenever the taxi's worn out leather seat and springs shook. On his left was a middle-aged man, carrying a clear, plastic file in which there was a stack of papers and banking transactions. One of those people who works in private companies, who turn to them after they reach retirement age in their government jobs. His hands were soft, even though the backs were freckled with light brown spots. Every few minutes, he would take out a piece of paper from the file and look at it with his spectacles, then put it back carefully and neatly in its place and put the spectacles into the pocket of his white shirt.

We're great friends, me and the four passengers in the car. We make friends with each other's voices and each other's warmth with infinite lightness, not sullied or burdened by any consequences because we all of us know how transient our meeting is, how swift, how purely by chance. None of us will impose his memories on the other or his thoughts . . . we'll just chat for a while, like brother sparrows soon to fly the nest, we won't have time to fear evil from one another or to harm one another.

A passenger who was sitting by the driver got out. The man next to him settled in his place more comfortably, then started rambling on, saying that a man had to mind his tongue these days because the world was full of secret informers and that everything the passenger who had just got out had said was a kind of intrigue, making up rumors. Secret informers for whom? for which state? Khalil wondered, and he almost laughed out loud at the driver for being so absurd, as all the states are here and they don't need to send someone off to bring them back news, all the states, with their entire apparatuses, go along with one another and with us. There's a presumption in that "with us," thought Khalil. We're also: those states. All those states. Those that are on the maps and those that are thinking of coming into being. One of the things that would help their coming into being in the future would be for the groups to be ready-formed . . . like the Basque separatists, for example, or the people of Soviet Armenia, or the revolutionary Irish . . .

Why? asked the woman, I think what he said is right and these continual power cuts—and the gas, the driver interrupted her—it's not as straightforward as it seems. The fuel's there, why do we have to wait for the ships? We've got one foot on land and one foot in the sea. There's always a ship, carrying something, coming in to us so we follow the maritime reports. The man's right, there are reserves of fuel but the leaders quarrel with each other and put pressure on each other through the people. Khalil pictured the woman carrying a small transistor radio wherever she moved her large behind in the house, making use of words like "reserves" and "put pressure on." "They put pressure on" sounds to her as if the people are like strips of meat being boiled, squeezed up together in the heat and dark of the pressure cooker which she often has to use these days, gas is so scarce. And that one particular leader lifts the lid of another leader's pan and tips the people who are in it into his own pan and starts to put pressure on again and so . . . and so with this people who, tough as a boot, do not want to be cooked.

The passenger in the front said to her: Do you think so? This is what was meant: division. Dividing people, planting doubts and rumors until they come back and kill each other. The driver said: it's up to the people to stop being divided. It's up to the people to agree and change their leaders. Khalil thought, cheerfully, now the division's come to be between the people and their leaders.

The woman was silent as she nodded her head, unconvinced, as if to settle the matter and she looked at Khalil with a scornful smile which said: look at this ass, this revolting creature ... come on, let's agree to despise his stupidity and so Khalil gave her a conniving look of agreement and a smile to go with it, then turned towards the middle-aged man on his left and found him looking at his watch then craning his neck to see how congested the street was with cars, which were crawling along. Khalil remembered his appointment with the doctor and was afraid of missing it, since it might get rid of the acute pains in his stomach. The woman thought it might be quicker to walk, so she got out.

The driver got out of the lanes of traffic with some difficulty. He took a route through the backstreets so as to be spared the throttling traffic jam and everyone in the taxi felt relieved. But the driver discovered that there were plenty of clever people like him and he began turning around and around and cursing and turning around, until, as if by chance, he got to a roadblock made of barrels and he stopped in front of an armed man. The armed man rushed over and opened the door of the car and said: get out all of you. The driver got out and tried to explain but the armed man said: liar, as he aimed his machine gun at the driver's chest, if you were the driver of an ordinary car you'd have known that this road was blocked and you'd have known who lives in it, because the boot of the person who lives here is at the throat of your whole family and anything you try to do to harm this boot will fail, even if you stick flowers in it, it won't do any good. Get out all of you. The driver said that he was from this quarter and that his registration papers proved it, but he'd taken the wrong turning. The armed man pounced on Khalil but, because his face was so pale and because he gave him his identity card attached to the famous doctor's card where he had written down the appointment, he was soon convinced that he was going to the doctor. The middle-aged man said to him: my son, it's alright, let us go to our work. Your work? the armed man said . . . did I bring you here? Fuck your work. He struck the folder with his hand and the papers flew and fell, scattered, on the ground. When the man turned around to pick up the papers, the armed man kicked him on the backside, saying: now pick your work up. Then he turned back to the driver, pushing him by the shoulder: why were you speeding, you animal? Last week we escaped an assassination attempt, don't you reckon people might be on edge? Get out of here. Quick.

The driver reversed then went back and kept to the main road. The middle-aged man got out, still arranging the papers in the plastic folder. The driver said that he had taken the wrong turning, then he said that the armed man was afraid of another assassination attempt and that he was right.

Khalil got out and began walking along the road.

When his younger sister pinched him for sleeping in her bed, he opened his mouth as far as it would go and stuck out his tongue as far as it would go and began to bawl his eyes out. He enjoyed the wetness of the flood of tears that soaked his face so he bawled his eyes out again . . . his throat gives a graveling rattle then his voice rises in a long, high whistle which opens his lungs until it hollows them out and fills his head with a delicious heat. He takes a deep breath and screams again, a scream that keeps getting higher, as high as his pity for his weeping self can go until his mother comes to stuff sugar in his mouth and press his head to her bosom, so he gives a couple of little sobs as he looks at the place where his sister pinched him so as to remember it and to remind his mouth again of the delicious taste of the sugar.

All the ills of adults begin when they stop bursting into tears, that is, when they begin to stifle their voices, to keep them down as if they were forbidden substances, thought Khalil. So, the armed men have the healthiest and cleanest bodies. They don't scream and cry, it's true, but they use bombs and bullets to get the anger out of their bodies in the most beautiful way. He only has to feel the slightest annoyance and he goes up to the hill and loads his gun and, clear as clear can be: "bang." This is more beautiful than crying. Perhaps it is the way adults cry. They're authentic, the way they cry, to the point where they empty their bodies of life itself. They're exposed to death just by things not going the way they like.

Khalil noticed that there were no pictures of the martyrs who had been killed on the walls of the street. Only shreds remained. Shreds of lines and shreds of old pictures which the rain and children's hands had torn down. So then, the walls of the streets of our city will clean themselves, one day. The wheel had turned to where it should be now, its movement precisely regulated. The pictures of the martyrs, vainglorious, vying to outdo one another and rob a group of martyrs from another group . . . that is, like headhunters from big companies competing over the most valuable personnel. Now, there was no longer anything to make them go to all this trouble, especially given the material costs. They catch their followers and their armed men and their martyrs as they drop from between their mothers' legs. Just to be born into this sect means that you belong to it and that you have no choice, because the other sect will send you back where you belong if you try, if you're one of those who likes crossing to the other side and registering your opposition.

They'll clean themselves by themselves, the walls of our city, like a clever pedigree cat, thought Khalil, then he wondered when the middle-aged man would get home and who would be waiting for him there. He strolled through the iron gate into the huge building where the doctor had his clinic.

4

The nurse came hurrying in. She took some of the notices off the wall and pushed the bed next to his into the corridor and went away. A strapping male nurse came in and said to Khalil: sit on the chair now, we need all the beds, the wounded are laid out on the floor in the corridors, and he took away the bed. Khalil took this as a good omen as it meant they would put off the operation until the day after tomorrow.

Since Khalil had got to the hospital the pain from his ulcer, which the doctor diagnosed as serious and in a place that made it necessary to perform a quick surgical operation, had disappeared. When he noticed how confused Khalil was and that he was shaking he assured him that there was no danger to his life now, as long as he went into hospital the following morning or the morning after.

Is it the effect of the medicines and the injections or is it fear which makes the pain take wing?

In the evening they brought back his bed. They began talking again in low voices. The chaos that had spread on the ground floor was nothing but a passing emergency, so slight that one of the patients on the upper floors had not realized what was going on.

Khalil had not known that the city's real paradise was in its hospitals.

Everything inside was prepared with amazing precision. The hospital was one of the places most isolated from the outside, even the lighting did not acknowledge the light of day outside. The neon lights were on constantly. The hospital even manufactures its own, special air to break from the memory of the air everyone breathes. Air saturated with antiseptic and the special cold, neutral smells that the motors exhale just so. Inside the climate is independent and the temperature unchanging, pleasant enough not to have to weigh down the bodies of the sick with blankets.

It is an intensely white place without being dazzling. Intensely white to enhance the metaphor and the double meaning. A whiteness that washes the brain clean of any images of the blood and urine and vomit and bandages with dried skin and severed limbs which the sewers of the hospital, its excretory ducts, may send to the outside . . . a whiteness that turns on a new, fresh whiteness just now born in the eye and in the imagination.

They are so concerned to isolate us that they thought to provide Thai or Filipino nurses who speak no Arabic except for the short, functional phrases that they coo. What they say is so broken that they manage to make the patients forget their own language, so it does not provoke any sensitivity in them which a familiar dialect might provoke, to remind them or make them fear evil from those who supervise their rest.

The short, smiling nurses always roll along on rubber shoes which muffle the sound of their footsteps and they leave the room like the women of our families whom we have known since childhood. They look with the compassion of someone who has come from a distant country to do so. They dish out the trays of food with a look from their little slit eyes that says that a telling-off is certain, that whoever does not eat what is on his tray will be chastized.

Everything in the hospital makes the people staying in it revert to their childhood which they lost when all forms of care and protection went missing. They are in another time, completely different because it has its own, precise order. The day goes back to its original relationship with the light. Mealtimes, and the time for injections and drips and colored pills, bring the bodies back to the cycle of another day which does not recognize the foolery outside, brings them back to recognize the body's right to stretch out and knit the flesh together again.

The nurses pass in a steady stream as they spread through the rooms like the flow of blood pumped by a large and healthy heart. You need not even ask them for anything. Even speak. For the system of signals makes telepathic waves . . . it is as if the nurses knew how much the patients hated their voices. The nurse comes in with a sheet of paper and writes. She turns over the tired, humble body in its nakedness, like an ancient mother who knows the little secrets of how to treat it.

She brings the flipflops close to his pale feet. The man leans on her shoulder and she propels him over to the table or the chair. She quickly strips off the sheets, puts other, clean ones on and goes back to him. She jokes with him with vacant words which only touch on the extremities, which suck them up like a cold sponge. She washes his face and dries his hands. She does not waste any time. She stretches him out on his bed and covers him, she makes him feel that she remembers well the places where the pain is. She tells him when the doctor will pass by and when she is coming back. She brings the bell close to his hand, the bell that calls her and that he must not use for fun.

Here there is total recognition, without language, total compliance to an illness they could treat, which they could not ignore, or refuse to recognize or impose order on it to conceal it. Here, there is primitive time, time that is for your body, not against it.

On this white, floating island Khalil feels that he is above the city. That he looks over it from afar and so he only sees, if he stares, what a passenger in an airplane sees of a city over which he passes on a long journey. He only hears, in the bliss of his clean, warm bed swimming in disinfectants, a voice, fine and tender like the neon lighting that is lowered at night, echoing in the corridors with mechanical repetition calling doctors by their names and thanking them. A voice that vibrates with the muslin lighting and wanders over the quiet beds, quiet as a butterfly with measured heartbeat.

Khalil used to believe, in the past, that hospitals were vessels of pain. But now he knows that pain is not to be found here at all. The low moaning that he hears from time to time comes from bodies, like strands of small fungi that quickly separate out and lie in the little metal vessels. The pain leaves the house of the body like a runaway thief covering his face with his hand. No one sees him except the little pill or the injection that the nurse brings to push him out, to kick him out into the open. A tamed pain and small, outside the body and so known that it is extremely easy to find a good reason to wipe it out. A miserable, cornered illness, for which you almost feel sorry, the way you might feel sorry for a naughty boy who has been kept in detention.

Even the pain of those who die does not kick up a fuss. They die without pain. Only the following morning, their beds are empty and very neat, very clean. They leave them as if they had left with the breath of ether and with the drops from the dripbags whose walls shrink in on their emptiness. As if they breathe out spirits like the antiseptic sprays, the people who die leave nothing that leaves any mark on the bliss of this place, on its emptiness and its whiteness.

The Filipino nurse, who told him her name was Katie, came in: if you're still awake, I need you. Can you come with me a little while please. Don't worry, don't be afraid.

Khalil followed her along the passage. He saw a man walking, carrying a dripbag in his hand, to the waiting room, where there were some leather seats. She opened the door of a room with a single bed and went in, then turned to him inviting him to catch up with her. Khalil went in. It was a large room with one bed, lit up by the colors of the television which were reflected off the walls. A very thin man was sitting on a large sofa, with his hands on his ears, leaning over his knees and jiggling them nervously. Katie said to Khalil . . . please tell him that we won't find him a doctor at this time. And that the medicines that we gave him are all that it's in our power to do. Tell him that we aren't equipped to treat people in his condition. He's upset and doesn't want to understand me. He's making threats and I can't do anything to him. He mustn't go out of his room again. The young man said in English that he understood everything she was saying but she had to understand that his position was unbearable and that he was in pain and very sick and that the only solution was to find the doctor, even if he was on Mars.

Khalil was afraid of the young man. He turned to the nurse and she begged him to stay by the young man's side for a little while, if he was able to. The young man said he did not want Khalil to stay and the nurse went out.

Khalil began to watch the television. The young man got up and switched it off then wrapped himself around himself, moaning loudly. He went up to the basin and threw up. Khalil went up to him. He turned on the faucet and washed the young man's mouth and gave him paper tissues which he did not pick up. He pulled out the towel and the young man took it from him and sat on the bed again. Why don't you cry out loud? Khalil said to him as he closed the door properly and the young man looked at him for a long while, as if he didn't see him, then he said: I have to get out of here. I have to get out of here. Can he be a madman? thought Khalil, who was deeply surprised, does anyone ask to get out of here? Then he said: why don't you get out? The young man said: you don't understand anything. Khalil said: I do, I know that you're a junkie and that the doctor has recommended that you shouldn't even be allowed to leave your room because it was you who asked him to do just that. Aaargh, the young man began to shout. Aaargh, I'm in so much pain. It comes out of you, replied Khalil. The pain comes out of you. The young man said, as if he had not heard: they have to give me something so I can sleep. How did I get here, they don't know what's wrong with me.

Khalil thought that the young man was right and that the place for him was certainly not here. He opened the door and went out. He heard the young man saying behind him: where are you going? . . . he walked along the corridor. He opened the door to the neighboring room and found it was empty, he went along and opened the door to the adjoining room and found it was also empty. In the row of rooms opposite there was a middle-aged man snoring in a deep sleep with the pillow over his head, while the television in his room was making a hissing noise. He switched off the television and the light and closed the door. He walked to the end of the corridor on the second floor and closed the glass double doors, which were wide open. He went back to the young man's room and went in, closing the door firmly behind him. The young man was sitting on his bed with his head

161

curled in to his belly and his arms clasped over his head. Khalil sat on the sofa facing the young man, with his back straight, and said: I have a deep ulcer and my stomach hurts me. The young man looked into Khalil's eyes as if he were astonished by what he heard or by Khalil's sitting facing him with his head held high, like a cockerel. Khalil said: what's your name? The young man said: Issa. Khalil said: my stomach hurts me a lot, Issa, and he pointed to his stomach with his index finger then put his hand back on his knees. Khalil opened his mouth wide and began to weep out loud, began to howl. His tears began pouring down from his chin to the ground between his feet. A cry of pain came from his throat then his chest began to shake and convulse and he sobbed out loud. Issa opened his mouth wide and began to cry in a loud, broken, tremulous voice which soon stretched out long and regular like a cry of protest against a hard, bruising pinch. A sticky strand of mucus dangled from his upper lip.

When the morning nurse came in she found them sleeping next to each other on the bed. Their bodies had taken on the same curve, as if they were twins.

The trainee doctor came into Khalil's room and said hello. He said: my name is Waddah Ibrahim and he sat down, after he had drawn the chair up to the bed. He smiled and began to crack jokes with him: tomorrow morning we're going to open you up, then. You're really the most cowardly person I've ever come across. We've put it off until tomorrow because your blood is slow to clot, sir, and the reason for that is fear, just cowardice which, if it gets the better of the injection, will make everything more complicated . . . that's something else to be afraid of, isn't it? Your blood keeps flowing and running so it doesn't seal your wounds.

So I'm nervous according to the doctor who found the ulcer and a coward too, according to my blood which keeps on running . . . said Khalil, so the young doctor chuckled. What's to be done then? asked Khalil, the answer lies with you, the doctor replied, you have time ahead of you to think it over.

Don't go now, said Khalil.

Well . . . what do you suggest . . . shall we play cards?

Khalil agreed and followed the young doctor.

THE STONE OF LAUGHTER

The young doctor's face was not friendly but Khalil found something in it that made him feel like relaxing, like talking at length, something that told him that an evening spent with him could possibly, even pleasantly stretch perhaps for weeks. What could he possibly talk to him about? Khalil found no clear answer and he thought, as he followed him down the long corridor, like a hen following its mistress to where the grain is kept, he thought that perhaps it was because the doctor was young and capable of white laughter like this, when every day he saw unimaginable horrors. He rolls up his sleeves and plunges into the blood of mangled limbs and . . . then he can crack jokes with me and play cards with me. He has what I don't have, what I can't ever possess as I drown in my crumbling fragility and my perpetual wailing . . . his profession is the only one that has anything to prove its worth in this whole world, but where does he get the strength to do it, I wonder?

His name is Waddah and I've never met him before but we meet on the basis of an understanding that existed before we met. As if our meeting were of secondary importance, as if our names were nothing but trivial details, like our memories and our desires. We're here, with each other, for me to tell him that I'm in pain and for him to save me and there's no way that we could misunderstand one another. With no preambles, no ambiguity, no being smart, no guessing, and no surmise. He came directly to my stomach and my blood which no one knows anything about. There is no way they can. I say to him: look, I'm in pain and he puts out his hand and cures me, he takes out the pain and throws it far away.

Doctor Waddah felt very strongly for the patient, Khalil. Was it because he was still green, a trainee on a low income still motivated by the thing that had pushed him to go to medical school, or was it because there was something special about Khalil and his vulnerability, the emptiness of his big eyes, empty to take in the patter, the jokes, the smile, to do anything with absolute compliance. He follows him, he asks him questions and does as he tells him, like a little schoolboy or a disciple and reminds Doctor Waddah how close he is to the origins of his profession when a doctor was seen as a magician or a minor prophet. And who is not tempted by that?

More than that. Khalil makes him, despite himself, feel that he is needed, that he must protect him and that he is responsible for him, especially as the one visit that was allotted to this thin, young man made him see how alone and abandoned he was, for Khalil, after his friend the young man went out—Nayif, as he believed—threw the scrawny bunch of pink carnations into the wastepaper basket. When Doctor Waddah asked why, Khalil said: because he bought it from the flowerstall at the door of the hospital and he hadn't remembered to buy them before then . . . he passed by me on his way to somewhere else . . . and then, the sight of these simple, common flowers doesn't go with the thing I like in this hospital, which is its sterility.

This poor young man, said Doctor Waddah, like someone speaking about his son, he's always sad for no reason and his behavior doesn't get any better, he's too weak to play with his friends. But at the same time, he has an attractive strength and a distinctive resilience, I don't know what it is or where it comes from.

Doctor Waddah said to him: come on hero, I'm waiting for you downstairs. He rushed off. The nurse came in smiling carrying an injection and she said this is the "ouch" that will make you relax completely. Khalil thought, the whole hospital knows what a coward I am. He was assured of how deeply they understood each other. She gave him a gown that closed from behind and said come on, take off your clothes and leave them in the bathroom in the paper bag. He came out of the bathroom doing up the opening at the nape of his neck. The strapping male nurse came in pulling the stretcher. Khalil went up to the stretcher and left his gown open. He said, his lip trembling: is Doctor Waddah downstairs? The male nurse said: you'll see him very soon. The nurse lifted the gown from his bare bottom and gave him the injection, then patted the place where the needle had gone in. The male nurse took him out to the corridor then to the elevator, while a delicious torpor flooded his body. He reached the strongly-lit ground floor and began looking out for Doctor Waddah. He saw his eyes beaming from behind the open blue mask. His head was wrapped in a blue kerchief and he wore thick clothes like a space suit. Your surgeon is getting himself ready, said Waddah. Will you stay here? Khalil asked him. I won't be able to get away because my teacher's a hard taskmaster, Waddah replied from behind his mask, then he strolled over to a big glass door, raising his hands, and the stretcher caught up with him. Khalil found himself in a large room in the middle of which was something that looked like a table, or a large, stone sarcophagus. They put him onto it. Everything was pale blue, even the spotlights above his head. There were also pale blue voices, which did not say much, in the room. In this little paradise, the movement of things around him took on the same, watery rhythm that pumps out from his head, as if he had been here, among them, for an eternity until they had managed to attain such harmony and unity in their movements.

Best of luck, hero, the surgeon said from behind thick spectacles. They wrapped up his head and uncovered his body down to his groin. Khalil was not afraid at all. Waddah approached, whispering: now my friend, the doctor, will give you the anaesthetic . . . Khalil smiled to show how grateful he was for all of their love. An arm in a transparent glove reached out to his arm and held on to it. Start counting so we can see if you're clever at math, said a little boy's voice . . . they really love me when I'm a good boy and, although his tongue was dry and heavy, Khalil was easily able to say: one two three four. A needle sank into the fold of his arm, five, six, seven, eight . . . Khalil heard his blood rushing in his ears, nine ten, his heart gave one loud beat, elev . . .

—Breathe. Take a deep breath. Breathe. It's no. . .
—Breathe. Take a deep breath. Breathe.
Khalil heard the sound of a slap. He was completely awake but he knew that his body was outside him. In front of him. He did not see his body.
Khalil saw utter darkness, in which a few exquisite, radiant, phosphorescent blue haloes hovered around him. The haloes were them.
—Breathe.
Khalil's soul clings onto his mouth, lashes out and falls in its place. In it. Khalil's soul clings . . . to the lung. To the lung . . . it lashes out. It falls. You. You for me to breathe.
You do it.
I hear. I can't. Say that I can't hear. Hear. Hear. Here. I
I
—Breathe.

You Please.

Mouth . . . mouth. Hand. Hand. Eyelid eyelid. For a sign. To . . .

—Press press harder. He's not responding doctor. He's not . . .

Here. Don't go away.

I don't think it's my body. I don't know. I can get to me without it. And hear. Do it with him. You.

Now he slips backwards. Quickly. Fearfully. It isn't quick. It's not called quick. It doesn't have a name because anyone who isn't dying doesn't know it. The total darkness is a tunnel now. Not a tunnel.

The tunnel of a dying man.

It's gray. Horizontally backwards. The phosphorescent haloes are still close.

—He's not . . . no.

He knew.

They will not hear me.

I'm alone.

Very.

The "very alone" of a dying man.

Shame.

Khalil.

Alone.

Quick. Backwards he's leaning. Under.

The haloes suddenly shrink.

Quick.

His soul pulls away from his fingers.

All of them.

He finds not.

It's sucked up backwards and downwards.

They've gone away.

They've gone out.

Black.

A white dot ahead. Ahead.

Very small.

Backwards and downwards and towards it.

That's it.

I die.

Shame.

Shame.

This is his hand. He knows it.

His eyes see his hand.

His eyes see and this is his hand raised in front of his eyes.

So, his body moved before he knew it. His hand was raised in front of his eyes. Helped it up in front of his eyes.

On its surface there was the needle of a drip, stuck in place with white tape.

Khalil sees his whole body covered with a white sheet.

He hears a voice talking nearby.

But hearing is not . . .

His eyes are on the surface of his hand.

The blue lines under the skin are throbbing.

His blood is flowing in the veins of his hand and making them move. They move.

I'm alive.

Khalil looks at the surface of his hand and weeps.

Weeps. Weeps. Weeps noiselessly.

His temples are soaked with a cold liquid and his ears fill. And he weeps.

Waddah's face comes close over his face.

Enough, Waddah's face says . . . it's all over.

Khalil sees Waddah's hand lifting his hand with the pulsing veins. Khalil weeps.

He weeps

he smells the smell.

Warm milk drips from Waddah's face into his eye and turns the place white as snow falls behind the window.

Khalil, in his room, all afternoon, all evening, weeps. What's the matter, the effect of the anaesthetic wore off some time ago. Why are you crying? says Waddah. Khalil is on the point of speaking. He opens his mouth and the tears pour down. They flow and flow and flow. Khalil waits for them to be done, so that he can speak. As soon as he is on the point of speaking the tears come back. He wants to speak, as he has now recovered his mouth, but he cannot.

He looks at Waddah. He looks at his hand. He weeps.

Perhaps I've lost the power of speech, thinks Khalil, without feeling the least bit troubled or sad.

I'm weeping for joy.

I'm weeping and I'm so happy I can't speak. And I'm alive. I didn't die and I came back from . . . that agony . . .

But what can I say . . . what can I say . . . after what I tried to do in the darkness after that torture of pointing with my finger . . .

He moves his hand. His leg. With that fire blazing in his bandaged belly, he weeps.

Enough, says Waddah . . . talk to me . . . you must. Because for a few seconds you refused to come round from the anaesthetic. It's a chance in a thousand and we don't know why it happened.

We're afraid of brain damage. Something like a coma. Only a few seconds and it was alright.

But you're making me worried. Please say something. Say anything.

—My wound hurts me, said Khalil, laughing, drowning in his tears between sobs.

So that's how they die.

Oh my God.

Oh my God.

No matter how great the torture, it is not the torture of the language of the living. It's almost nothing like it. No matter how great the desolation, it is not the desolation of the living. It's almost nothing like it. What do the living know . . . what do all these herds of humanity that batter their horns against the rocks of the days know?

The mothers who love their sons. This—and this is all that is certain—is nonsense, this complaining and shouting and grumbling and beating of theirs. Nonsense.

Nothing is pure save love of the body. No one who has not lost it can love his body. Who loses it, cannot. He dies.

All these years that are called a life are nothing but nonsense, a folly, because they lack your dying for you to know.

All this wretchedness is not wretchedness if you do not know the wretchedness of dying.

All this torture, this desolation, this pain is nonsense because you have not died to name these things anew.

All this complaining, the despairing poets, the bereft, the grieving, the sick, rejected lovers, lepers, consumptives, the poor, the hungry tramps, slaves, the persecuted, the humiliated, all these who do not pay attention to their living bodies, to the light that rises with the dawn, to the breeze that pierces the blood, to the talk that springs from the desire to talk, all these arrogant fools who reject the blessing, who are ungrateful for the heat beating in their ears which you can hear when you listen to them from the inside . . .

All this because they do not know. And they will not have that . . . they will have nothing but a dark inkling . . .

If the king died and came back.

If the leader, the soldier, the despot, the revolutionary, the bureaucrat died, if the emperor, the communist, the mother died, if the sick, the lover, the tinker, and the philosopher died . . . and came back.

I came back from there . . . my chest rises, to breathe in the air and spread oxygen through every cell of my body, then falls, to expel what it does not need.

My living body is the blessing.

My living body is wisdom, all wisdom.

And nothing in this world is happier than I am. Nothing, as I hear the rush of blood roaring just by putting my head, my ear on my hand . . .

Katie changes the dripbag. She lifts the dressing from the wound then puts it back. Sweet dreams, she says.

She switches off the light and closes the door on the light in the corridor. The man in the other bed coughs. The white sheets are brilliant. Next to me is a living man, coughing and breathing because he, like me, is alive. What happiness, what happiness, what happiness.

Khalil sleeps . . . he begins to look at the drops that flow regularly from the drip and counts them, so that's the way the ones who die, die . . . those who commit suicide, how . . . then that regret added to the hell . . . oh my God. Oh my God.

So that's how the ones who die, die.

The severed head keeps listening, as it rolls from the guillotine, to the crowds of victorious revolutionaries cheer, keeps listening for a time that lasts much longer than the seconds before it fell. The armed man, thrown to the ground in the street, keeps hearing the bullets of the fighting, the advance of the enemy or the advance of friends while his companions do not drag him back with them, or drag him forwards, they say above his head leave him he's dead. Leave him he's dead. And he . . .

The dead man in his shroud hears the screaming of his children while he still keeps struggling to, torturing himself to, before he realizes that he . . . Khalil's hair stood on end. He pressed the button, trembling and cold. Katie comes.

I'm cold, says Khalil, and I can't sleep.

Katie switches on the little light. She comes up to him and puts her hand to his forehead. She goes out and comes back with a blanket. She puts the thermometer in his mouth. She takes it out and says, don't worry. Are you hungry?

Yes, says Khalil. She gives him an injection in his arm and says, you'll sleep now, and she puts out the little light. She puts the bell near his hand and closes the door on the light in the corridor.

5

J ust that you are alive. Just that you are alive. What wicked ingratitude . . . what denial . . . what misunderstanding. Understanding.
How happy I am. How happy I am, Khalil repeated, his eye
bathed with tears of gratitude for the blessing as he looked at
the street from the window of the taxi on his way to his room. He
loved his wound which hurt him and loved his body which was
stretched out comfortably on the back seat. He looked upon his body
as if it were a beautiful and beloved prodigal son. I love my beautiful
body.

The taxi driver stopped because the street was so busy. But that the
street was busy meant that there was no bombing. The people walking and the people who filled the shops, the people in cars and blocks
and buildings, the women in the kitchens and the children in school
and the workers and bureaucrats in their rooms, are all alive and will
not die now. The busy street is life and so are true, healthy bodies
which move with the will of the people whose bodies they are . . .

Then the driver began to huff and puff because of the smell of the piles of garbage. He closed his window then opened it again, because of the heat.

And the garbage? The garbage is a sign of life. There is no garbage in the graveyard, it is clean, absolutely clean, forever. It does not move, it does not murmur with life except when the living fill it, when children go to play by the graves and leave their garbage there, from sandwich and sweet wrappers to empty jam jars or tissues and empty bottles.

Garbage is what is left over from the lunch of the living and what it contained makes their bodies pulse and live.

What ingratitude.

What ingratitude and ignorance.

A woman throws a bag full of something onto the nearby vegetable stall. The stallholder curses at the top of his voice. She doesn't like his prices or his curses so she begins to shout and swear. Some passers-by gather and cars slow down and stop, the place gets more crowded and the sound of car horns rises. One of the armed men gets out and fires a bullet into the air. Then two bullets . . .

They don't let them chase thieves, the driver said. The thieves who robbed the bureau de change at the top of Hamra Street, I was there and I saw them get away. They block the traffic because of a fight over a pound of vegetables. What a dumb lot.

They're playing, thought Khalil as he smiled. They're making up games like children, and playing. All these are games to celebrate life.

All these games, operas, scenarios, jokes, swearing, they're a game, a game to celebrate life. When they see it, when they touch it, it walks among them and secretly hands out its sweet elixir to them all. They play in its lap.

Khalil closed the door of his room. He put his little bag on the bed. He was tired and sat down, happy that it was cold inside for the cold helped his heart and lungs bring his breathing back to normal and helped restore the rhythm of his heart.

He got up and went to the basin. He washed his face, he looked at his pale face in the mirror, he smiled and said, welcome.

Welcome Khalil.

I'm so sorry. I didn't know. I didn't know how much I loved you.

How much I loved life. He who hates himself doesn't love life. He who hates himself doesn't love life, Khalil my lovely.

The surgeon took out Khalil's stitches and said, smiling, great . . . the wound's fine. Thank God you're better. Look after yourself. And he shook his hand quickly.

Khalil went out of the little room saying thank you, after he had smiled at the nurse. He stopped in the hospital entrance hall and stood still, looking at the exit.

He went back to the information desk. He waited until the receptionist had his hands free and said, his heart beating violently: Doctor Waddah . . . Doctor Waddah went out a little while ago, the receptionist replied. Khalil stayed where he was, looking out at the street through the thick glass.

What shall I call this man? When he was holding my hand in the recovery room. His face over my face. What was that touch that went between our hands. Between the skin of our hands. The warmth of his hand gave me more than the umbilical cord that joined me to my mother. Much more, because I could see his eyes. Stronger than her smell. As if I were born from his two eyes and from the warmth of his hand. He stayed by my side a lot, for a long time. He sat on the chair in my room and began, while I was asleep, to look at me. More than my mother looked at me when I was asleep, as a child. As I was crying he was looking and smiling, he saw me and he knew what was wrong with me. He stayed looking at me a long time, saying nothing, doing nothing. He leaves and comes back and sits and looks at me. He was delighted when I came round from my coma. He believed that they wouldn't bring me round and I came round. Like my father, he was delighted with me, I came back and he stood by my side and held my hand and said: enough. It's all over. So he knew what it was all about. What was all over. They all left when I came out of the coma and he stayed. Near me. He was holding my hand before I woke up and opened my eyes and looked. He was looking into my face while my eyes were closed and before I opened them.

He was pressing my hand, calling my name many times before I opened them. Before I heard. And when I heard and opened my eyes his hand was the first to say: you're back Khalil. His eyes were the sign, the contact, the rope that raised me from the tunnel.

He used to ask the nurses, has no one visited Khalil? No. No one knew that there was no one to visit me.

So he comes and sits and smiles and it becomes more difficult to talk to me. He sometimes comes to see me in his spare time, he brings a tray to my side and eats, takes out his newspaper and reads, smiling.

The point where he touches my body opens up and shines. Opens up and light comes from it and lights up the inside of my whole body with the light of his touch. He changes my dressing and we both look at the wound as if it were our child speaking his first words.

He holds my wrist and the warm serum of his soul flows through my entire body, exuding sweet life like a gentle wave that spreads out and weighs me down until it comes out to settle in a fine layer on top of my entire skin. When I see him in my dream as a beautiful man I don't desire him because he is so far above my desire. When I see him embracing me, when my head is flung upon his full breasts, I don't desire him because he is more than a woman. I do not hunger and open my mouth because he is more than my mother and his eyes are so much more than her milk.

What point is there in my waiting for him. Does the strength, the density, of what there is between us have to say anything. I will be utterly wretched, when I do not find the words. And I will not find them. I will not find anything to say. What emptiness will language be after what was between us. It's violent and beautiful and intense to the point of no return. Does that mean there's no point in my meeting him now?

He whom I loved in that way, who loved me to that extent. Once, it happened. Only once. It's gone forever and nothing of it will be repeated save the torture of its passing, the failure of what follows it, its emptiness and its decline. What do I need him for now. He gave me everything. He gave me all that. I will not see him again, so my stockpile of memories of him remains intact, so he stays in my heart.

On his way to the exit Khalil saw the young doctor coming in through the other door. From the street he watched his back sinking among the people who gathered waiting for the lift. In my heart, repeated Khalil.

In the street he said to himself: his name is Doctor Waddah Ibrahim.

6

Khalil was filled with childlike delight with his new body, his strong body. He did not know how to express his happiness. He found no way to take his body out and use it, to show it things. He knows, but his knowledge needs to become deeper, richer.

He needs to be rehabilitated. To learn a new alphabet with which to love himself, the self he hated so long and abused. Needed many tools and various with which to change and see himself completely differently, as he desired, as much as he wanted to forget.

He sits in his room a long time, noticing and liking everything he sees and hears. The uproar of the children. The car horns, the sound of the electricity generators. He smiles at everything, even the cockroach that rushes down the plughole in the sink. He plays a lot with the cat that the *hajjah*, the Gentleman's mother, brought and which stayed after she left.

His stomach no longer hurts him, and he pays minute attention to what the doctor told him, taking diligent care of his food and medicines.

He began to take care of his room again, but without being neurotic or obsessive, he is tolerant when he should be tolerant and laughs at his old habits which have become, in any case, impossible now that the room is filled with the belongings he had brought down from the apartment upstairs.

He brought out his summer clothes and put them carefully in order. He waited for the electricity to come back on and he ironed his shirts and trousers, folded them and put them away. He took out the new clothes from their bags. He folded them again, proud and happy, and hung up the clothes which needed hanging. In one of the bags he stuffed the things he found had become dated or unfashionable, wondering why he had kept them all this time.

The Bridegroom, who had become an estate agent and a merchant and abandoned arms even though his friends had once again laid claim to the neighborhood, came to him one day and advised him to let the apartment upstairs. Ten thousand dollars just for the tenancy. Eight for you and two for me, or would you rather they occupied it. Five hundred dollars would take care of the young men. I'll be your guarantor and the rest is yours. Or would you rather they occupied it. Then two hundred thousand lire rent every year, and we can go higher. I'll speak to the group and come back in the evening. Think about it.

Khalil will not think for long. He had sold the two Persian rugs to get into hospital. He sold them both.

At that time he was spitting blood. To die or to sell the two rugs. The Bridegroom had brought the money the same day. He took the lion's share and ripped him off savagely. Khalil did not open his mouth because he was in pain and destitute and because he despised himself.

After he came back from the hospital he sold the television and the encyclopaedia and the refrigerator. He was not in pain and he did not despise himself at all. He needed money. He loved himself and his self needed money so he sold and bought food and clothes.

Morals cannot make a man hate himself.

High morals are to make you kind to yourself, to make you feel self-esteem and self-respect.

High morals are to make you generous and make you look around you a little so you see and so you bear witness until your self is no longer hanging in the limbo of torments to no avail, doing no good to anyone, only to punish yourself and abuse yourself for a crime you did not commit, to take revenge on the things around you by torturing yourself, more and more, endlessly, torturing yourself.

Madame Isabelle was not, herself, happy with that. She was not happy with that. What did she need the things in the house for. She had forgotten them and gone to her daughter or died after her son died. Why punish yourself, Khalil.

Does it hurt anyone if you sell things? Let the house? Is it better that it remains empty or that someone occupies it? That's silly. The principle is that there is a common definition upon which we all agree, towards which we strive and, true, we despise and scorn breaking the rules. But for me to be the only one who sticks to the principle, for me to be the single exception to the rule for the sake of the principle so that I come to scorn and despise and hate myself, must be nonsense.

Morals cannot be so against you.

It's disastrous, a disgraceful mistake. It disgraced me. It ripped apart my stomach and crushed my soul. My self, which I love, tells me that morals do not mean that a man hates himself but that he loves himself. That is because my self believes that someone who loves life is someone who loves himself and that someone who loves himself is someone who can love others.

And the only one who hates others, the world, life, is someone who hates himself.

Love me, love me, I am yourself Khalil my lovely. For the glory of life.

But Khalil, despite the deep sense of jubilation that his knowledge gave him, felt apprehensive that he may lose a little link in this chain, a link that he has never known, he had a faint, distant suspicion that his great knowledge of this was lacking in some way . . . a pale and frail and small and distant lack . . . but a lack all the same.

When he went up to the apartment with the Bridegroom and the woman he was slightly scornful of his excessive sensitivity, which had made him put off and put off going to check the place.

The apartment was empty except for a few large pieces of furniture swathed in dust.

It was so empty that Khalil was surprised. What had he been expecting to find in it? Who was he expecting to find in it? The spirits of those who had lived in it? Who had left it? Who had died in it? Even his sorrow as he walked around the rooms was a slender sorrow, paper thin and superficial. The place where the refrigerator had been and the place where the encyclopaedia used to be kept left two, neat marks on the floor, the marks of things that stayed, inert, in their places.

The Bridegroom was negotiating with the woman over the price of the remaining furniture and it was quite clear that she did not want it. Khalil left the two of them and headed for the bedroom.

Madame Isabelle's room had changed a lot, that kind lady who left with those who left, a long time ago. A very long time ago. Of her things, only the bones of her bed remained and . . . some nails she had knocked in, she or Naji's father, into the walls, to hang up the picture of a saint or a son or a brother . . . even the wardrobe with the door hanging off its hinges on which his little cousins had doubtless swung.

Life often becomes unhinged when you pass through places . . . only the hinges of coffins stay firmly in place, even if they turn to pure rust.

But although the room had been emptied of things, a presence remained there. It was full of many things. It was full of more things. And with more of those who had left it even after his uncle's household had left. Khalil wished that the Bridegroom would settle things on a friendly note with the woman.

He went into Naji's room . . . Naji who I love. Who died in the sniping from the eastern quarter, Naji who they said was an agent. Neither his bed nor his table was in his room because the *hajjah*, the Gentleman's mother, had moved them to the sitting room where the light was stronger for the sake of her eyes which were tired of reading and praying with her beads. Not even the little bedside table with its drawer and its little lamp was in Naji's room. Nor his clothes, carefully scattered until he comes back. Nor the smell of his clothes which used to speak of the sages of Tibet, of feminine and masculine foods, of the ordered turning of the stars which converse with our destinies. Did the stars tell of the destiny of your room and your bed, you little would-be Indian sage.

In Naji's room little metal stoppers were scattered on the ground, bottletops which his cousins used to collect and play with. There was also a little plastic flipflop on a rug which had been a wrap which his uncle's wife had folded and stitched up roughly, with a piece of string, to make a bed for one of the little ones. There was a cheap ball and broken pens and a scrap from a photo magazine. On the walls were drawings of men with huge heads, a sun, two houses, stunted trees, an airplane, the names of the boys and "Zahrah is an ass in school," in revenge, perhaps, for a hard pinch.

The *hajjah*, the Gentleman's mother, had left nothing more than he had seen when he found her on the floor of the house. The kitchen was so filthy that he guessed that she had never gone into it. She never ate in this house. She only performed her ablutions and prayed and read and slept and died. Her cat which now kept going back to Khalil's room remained, eating, playing, following him and looking at him a lot. And meowing and going out and meowing and yawning and meowing and sleeping.

Why had Youssef, Youssef alone, left no trace. No trace. Had he really stayed here? or somewhere else?

It's unbelievable, the woman said. It needs whitewashing and gloss, the plumbing needs redoing. Look. The water pipes are rotten and to fix them might mean taking up the tiles. Look at the water, how it's running from the kitchen floor all the way to the door. Look how shaky the kitchen cupboards are. I don't know how much all this would cost me. And without a proper lease. I'm not the way you think. I don't have enough money with me. The furniture's old and falling apart and broken, no one would buy it from me. You sell it and do the place up and I'll pay what we agreed.

Khalil had not seen her. He thought she seemed beautiful now because she seemed on the point of crying. Khalil went up to her and said, alright. We'll pay the cost of all the repairs, then we'll look into it. We'll think about money later. But I'm in a bit of a hurry . . . I have to go, she said with some embarrassment. She came back the next day.

Her hair, which came down to the top of her slender neck, was short and black and sleek. She was short with small, dark eyes and her large mouth was the color of a coffeebean, a little like Rita's mouth.

179

The Bridegroom said that her husband had died in South America. He fled the war to his family there. Their situation had gone downhill. He died and she came back with her son.

So it's self-defense then, these fixed smiles which size things up and value them precisely. She used to rush past holding her little boy's hand. She would kiss him before he got onto the school bus then stand, waving and laughing, until he disappeared. Her smile vanished as soon as she turned to the entrance of the building and hurried up the stairs taking firm, manly strides and holding her head high.

After a while she would come back and go out in the same haste. She would get into her little car and go and not come back unless it was with her son. It was she who brought him back from school. Whenever she met Khalil, in the entrance, she greeted him politely, a politeness excessive to the point of scorn. The simplicity of her clothes made him feel, likewise, that this woman despised him a little, for no reason.

No one used to visit her. Only rarely a woman of about her age came, and she only went out at the same regular, fixed times. No confusion in that infinite precision.

Once, Khalil lingered in front of the door of the apartment for a few minutes. He said if she takes me by surprise I'll ask her about the water. The dark, oily paint on the door was very shiny and was matched by the uneven green color of the new doormat. The bell was new too but there was no name above it. It was afternoon and Khalil knew that she was in, but it was totally silent. Khalil brought his ear a little closer to the darkness of the staircase and heard a faint sound of music.

What does this woman do? What does she work as outside and what does she do when she's at home?

In any case this widow is not grieving the death of her husband, she is not in mourning and she is not wearing black. Her clothes are dark but she does not wear black. Her son doesn't look like her. He has white skin and honey blond hair, he must look like his father.

Khalil rang the bell and took a step backwards. A long time passed and he decided to run downstairs, but the door opened. No trace of surprise showed on her face. Perhaps because she saw me through the little peephole, which is also new. She must be a very cautious woman for she opened the door in the clothes he had seen her going out in.

Did she stay dressed up like that at home or did she get dressed to open the door to me.

Khalil apologized briefly and politely and asked the woman if she had seen his brown cat with the white spots, which was used to coming up to this apartment, the woman who owned him was . . .

Yes, he's here, said the woman apologizing for not having let him know . . . he's inside playing with the boy, I'll make him bring him to you straight away. No no. There's really no need, I just noticed he'd gone and I wanted to . . .

What did this coincidence mean, Khalil began to think in his room, that the cat should be there and . . . all life's details are signs. Signs that mean something . . .

He was delighted with what had happened. He thought about her face again, which he had thought, the first time, would be on the the verge of tears . . . no . . . she was very tough, this little mother. Khalil was also delighted with what he had been able to see in the house, behind her face with its restrained smile. He had not seen much. Only a pale blue color on the floor and the air that the clean walls breathed out, a big, lush plant in a large brass pot, a dark, glassy light hanging from a black chain and a smell of perfume. He brings all this back now, he sees it in his mind's eye. Khalil was also delighted with the cat which comes and goes between them . . . and suddenly her bare feet lit up his head. Yes, she wasn't wearing shoes. Her toes were showing in flowered cloth flipflops . . . little bare feet with beautiful little toes.

One morning the woman knocked on his door very politely. He opened the door and was surprised to find her face and her big, brown mouth so close. She told him that she couldn't find Mr.— . . . the Bridegroom, said Khalil. The bath's full of dirty, scummy water. And the drain . . . perhaps from the apartment above . . . and the carpet might . . . please, what . . .

Khalil smiled to reassure her. The Bridegroom will bring a plumber this afternoon, when you come back. Thank you. She said. Thank you. She says thank you as if she was smiling at me . . . this woman despises me a bit, through Khalil, as he looked around what she might have thought of as his mean room.

Another time she stopped in the entrance of the building when she saw him, after she had said goodbye to the school bus and all the children had smiled at her and begun waving their hands until the bus disappeared. She stopped, or slowed down, she did not rush off with those manly strides of hers. She's giving me an opportunity, thought Khalil. He went up to her and asked her about the water and she said don't worry, I've sorted it out, we're a small family, then she did not rush to leave. Good, replied Khalil, then he watched her legs as she went up the stairs.

In his room he saw her hands. She has slender fingers and her nails are clipped short with a coat of clear varnish.

There's something like me in this woman. There's something masculine about her that I can't quite put my finger on. That's what makes me so curious about her. And I always see her after she's gone.

7

Nayif came twice to wish Khalil well. He was delighted and seemed relieved when Khalil told him that he had rented the apartment.

Khalil invited him to the restaurant to have lunch. The atmosphere between them was very intimate. After they had eaten they asked for two cups of coffee and two water-pipes and they smoked and talked. They remembered the years past like two old flames. Khalil talked about the woman in the apartment and Nayif gladly lent his ear, for friends have to talk about women. Khalil said nothing in particular but just his broaching the subject gave Nayif great pleasure as it held out the promise to him that their friendship would last, would go back to being almost as firm as it used to be.

In talking, Khalil found a way to welcome Nayif, something of a way to apologize, to soothe his troubled conscience for the bad feeling there had been between them. As if he were saying to Nayif that nothing had changed and that what had happened was just one of those things that happens between old friends, something he was eager to suggest was because of the nervous psychological state that the pain of the ulcer in his stomach had brought on. But Khalil felt some sense of loss. They had both grown up and, as much as they were two other people now, they were still extremely like the two they used to be. They turned a blind eye, quite on purpose, to the points of difference between them whereas, in the past, they used to discuss the points of difference and stay with them until they were attuned. Their collusion in turning a blind eye was now the strongest bond between them, memories aside. They felt a sense of duty, a cherished duty but a duty nonetheless, to keep their friendship going, like an old couple whom it no longer suited either to part their ways or to fight with each other. Just as an old couple so collude that they come to understand each other completely. Such an understanding is complete when love ends and their preoccupation with each other ends. They manage, to a surprising extent, to be totally empty while they are, for example, extremely compatible in bed, in their sexual relationship. Perhaps the most successful sexual relationship is that which begins after love has ended, for then anxiety ends. The pounding of the heart and head end and the body is empty, of all but the self. It is complete, completely for itself. So the beggar takes more pleasure in sex and savors it more, such that he cannot be compared with the philosopher and we, Nayif and I, have attained such harmony now, such success. We draw on the bubbling water-pipe and talk of trivial things and we steer clear of sensitive subjects.

Nayif said that the Brother, so he believed, was quite prepared to take on Khalil at the newspaper. Khalil said great, let me think it over for a little while.

See you soon.
See you soon, for sure.
I'll get in touch.
Be in touch.
See you.
See you.

Khalil dropped in on Nayif a few times at the newspaper and several times they sat in the Brother's office. Nayif visited Khalil several times in his room. They began to meet in the café, at the newspaper, with friends. Khalil did not work at the newspaper and Nayif did not press the point. Khalil was no longer as silent as he used to be in the past. Nayif was very eager that the Brother be pleased with Khalil and he began to be pleased with Khalil, he enjoyed himself, not feeling the weight of time upon him.

One evening the Brother invited the two of them to his party at the Summerland. Khalil got dressed up. Nayif dropped by with a new silk shirt. In the car with Nayif, Khalil said how pleased he was with the shirt. Nayif opened the glove compartment and pointed to a bottle of perfume. Put some on and give it to me, said Nayif. He turned on the little radio and sweet music poured out.

When they arrived, the balcony of the Brother's wing was crowded with party people; it was not quite packed, but Khalil had not been expecting so many guests. The men stood up and greeted them. The women stayed sitting and put out their hands.

Khalil knew most of the people there, who gave Nayif an uproarious welcome. Nayif slipped in among them. One of the women fetched him a drink and he kissed her hand as laughter rose from Nayif's whispering circle.

The Brother went up to Khalil and said to him: I know all Nayif's jokes. Now's he's telling the story of the man who went to the lavatory. When Khalil seemed not to know the story, the Brother seemed surprised and began to ask Khalil how well he knew Nayif. He just doesn't tell me many jokes, said Khalil, and he asked the Brother to tell the story of the man who went to the lavatory. The Brother said that a man was sitting on the lavatory in the bathroom like everyone does. There was a sudden, violent round of bombing then things quietened down again. People went out into the street and looked at the building that was worst hit when they saw the man, on the fourth floor, still sitting on the lavatory. The balconies and the walls of the house had been destroyed, right up to a yard from where he was sitting. Of course, because he was shocked by the surprise bombing and because he was afraid that, if he moved, the ground under his feet would give way, he stayed sitting, perplexed, holding onto the belt of his trousers, which were around his ankles, while people burst out laughing and shouting at him. He didn't hear until the people came to stare in their dozens and the whole street was blocked up . . .

What a scene, said Khalil, laughing while the others began to shriek with laughter. The Brother said, smiling, it's the way Nayif tells them, he spins them out for half an hour or more, haven't you noticed that he's enjoying himself more now that his wife's gone away. Do you know her? Yes, I know her, said Khalil, she wasn't happy here. Women have become very demanding, said the Brother, and times are hard. And you, why didn't you bring your wife with you.

You know I'm not married, said Khalil. I know, the Brother replied, I mean your girlfriend. Khalil was a little confused as he tried to think of something sensible to say. The Brother interrupted him, saying: don't worry. And he filled his glass.

The balcony looked out over the pool. On the surface of the water, lit up by the spotlights on the side, was a little boat made of artificial roses and carrying lighted candles, swaying in the warm, heavy autumn breeze. The hotel waiters were clearing up after a riotous wedding party, sweeping up briskly, then the lights faded. The wide, clean expanse fell still and the glow of the crescent moon shone down.

The waiter knocked politely and came in. He picked up the remains of the food, then carried a large tray full of clean glasses to the balcony and put it on the table. He leaned towards the Brother to make sure he had understood the sign he gave him then came back, with a big tray of beautiful, shining fruit and a big bucket of ice. The Brother looked at him and the waiter made a sign with his index finger, meaning now, and he came back from the door pulling a little trolley laden with all kinds of sweets, then he rushed out, smiling, placing his hand on his head as a sign of his gratitude and closed the door behind him.

Nayif put a cassette of oriental music in the big cassette recorder and Salaam, Said's girlfriend, Said who was the senior man in Nayif's party, got up to dance. She was barefoot. Nayif tied a long scarf, which her friend had pulled lightly from her shoulders and tossed to him, around her hips. She danced beautifully because her body was well-proportioned, because the opening of her dress rose up whenever she lifted her hands, because the way she swayed, with her breasts and her long thighs, made the fine, pink scarf swing.

Khalil looked around for Said to see how he was enjoying his girlfriend's beautiful dance and he did not find him. He leaned over to the Brother and asked him about Said. The Brother said, he's not very far away. Then he began to watch Salaam's dance.

Salaam was becoming more and more absorbed in her dance and in the music and it began to be clear from her face that she had forgotten everyone completely, that she was swaying as if she were alone in her room except that, from time to time, she looked at Nayif who sat, cross-legged, on a little cushion on the ground and, laughing, she began going up to him to push him away by the shoulder with her bare foot while he pretended that the flood force of her femininity had knocked him to the ground.

Said came back to the balcony, clapping to Salaam's dance, to the rhythm of the music. He sat down and lit a cigarette and, after a while, after she had rearranged her hair, Fatimah the actress came up to him. When she became aware of Khalil's eyes fixed on her she said, in a loud voice: has anyone seen my handbag . . . I can't find it, then she sat next to Khalil and, when she found that he was still looking at her, she said: yes? Khalil leaned his head towards her and said: you're very beautiful, and she said in an emphatic way: thank you. Thank you, Prince Charming.

She's got beautiful thighs, hasn't she, the Brother said to Khalil as he pointed with his eyes to the thighs of a woman of whom Khalil knew nothing except that she was a prolific poet whose name he had often read in the newspaper. She was stretched out as if she were posing for a sensitive artist. She's a bit boring, added the Brother. Khalil said that she drank a lot and the Brother laughed and said: that's to prove that no matter how much she drinks it doesn't affect her. She wants to show that she's one of the boys, that she has a strong head and can handle it. Her husband's a *hajj*, a pious man, and he never goes out with her. He travels a lot because of his business which she despises and she squanders her money to punish him. How is she boring, asked Khalil . . . because she's desperate to be like the men. You know she's now the editor-in-chief's mistress. I don't know how that man can put up with her in circumstances like these, when death is so close to people, they don't know what they're doing any more, they don't even know what they like . . . said the Brother.

As if the war came down on them like a blessing from heaven, thought Khalil, all their flight now from the moral restraints, morals which used to impinge upon their memories. With malicious innocence, they put it all down to death being so close . . . they find that the more they continue to flee the more they are inclined to see themselves as victims of this brute destiny, that they are more sensitive than other, ordinary people to the gravity of things. That somehow, they constitute an elite of sensitive people who love life so much that they refuse all forms of death. They've just found a good excuse for things that, in their memory, in the depths of their upbringing, are not allowed at all . . . it's a devastating war, you can only live until tomorrow . . .

But they're little desires, scattered. They're a lot less than the love of life, thought Khalil . . . desires cut to their size and why should I worry about it. He raised his glass and drank to the health of them all . . .

Sumayah's hand stretched out a fat, smoking cigarette to Khalil. Khalil took it and said: I don't smoke, thank you. Pass it on then my friend, said Sumayah, laughing at Khalil's poised politeness which was out of step with the increasing instability of the things around him. Khalil passed it to the Brother. The Brother smiled at Khalil and said: I'm like you. I don't smoke either. And he gave it back to Sumayah who thanked them both for their good taste.

Sumayah finds you upsetting, Khalil, said the Brother. You've been hard on her since you've been coming to the newspaper offices during the bombing . . . I don't mean to be, said Khalil . . . I didn't realize. The Brother laughed loudly and Khalil began to look at Sumayah who was smoking with her eyes closed. She opened her eyes and said, so Khalil, don't look at me . . . look somewhere else. Then she said: I think there's something unnatural about you my friend. Perhaps you've often been told that you're handsome, enticing, so you act however the fancy takes you. Never mind. You are handsome, you're very attractive but, well, I'm a realistic woman. Never mind. Your glass. But let's see you from time to time. And rest assured, I don't want to get married again. Thank you.

Nayif stood up, nibbling on an apple and the poetess said, put down what you have in your hand and answer me . . . I'm not . . . Nayif went back to her side, frowning. The woman's a donkey, said Sumayah, a donkey with innumerable ears. Whenever she opens her mouth she brays "I'm not" . . . she'll spend her whole life explaining what she isn't . . . it doesn't occur to her that it's no use speaking in the negative . . . if she woke up one day and began to say I am . . . they'd notice that she didn't have much time any more . . . perhaps that's why she's turning in an empty circle. She's begun to show her age . . . do you like her Khalil? . . . well, say who do you like, Khalil. So far you haven't found a woman you like, I mean to sleep with more than once or twice . . . do you listen to Umm Kalsoum . . . you're making the hashish fly right out of my head. Put your finger on the vein in my throat and you'll see how my pulse is racing. I don't like this at all. Good. Tell me with whom . . . name me one that you've slept with so I can get an idea of who you like.

I'm not, the poetess began to say again. Nayif stood up and began to thank the Brother for the party. The Brother put his hand on Khalil's shoulder and said: stay here I want to speak to you. Nayif avoided Khalil's eye when he asked who wanted a ride in his car . . .

The Brother left the empty balcony and said to Khalil let's go in, it's better inside, it's got very damp and the breeze has turned cold. They went in. The Brother switched on the light in the corner and made himself comfortable on the large, leather chair. Khalil sat on the little sofa as if he were waiting for something.

The Brother got up. He carried the tray of fruit and two clean glasses inside and closed the balcony door. He opened a little cupboard and brought out a dark bottle from which he poured a few drops into two glasses. He sat down. He looked into Khalil's face and said, I hear from Nayif that you want to work at the newspaper . . . and he fell silent, waiting. Not exactly, replied Khalil, it's Nayif's idea, he wanted to help me out financially. I'm not very pressed any more.

The Brother went to the drawer of the cupboard. He opened it, took a wad of dollars from a wallet inside, put them next to Khalil's glass and said: take what you want. His eyes bored lecherously into Khalil. Khalil felt very confused and a hot rush of blood raced to his head. I don't want you to be shy, the Brother said, take what you want. But I don't need money, said Khalil. And . . . and I don't see why I should take money from you.

The Brother took a deep breath as if in pain because he had not been understood. You can take anything from me, the Brother said, and you know. It's no use you making me suffer more.

Yes, Khalil knew, but he said, struggling for breath: no. I don't know. Well, said the Brother as he took the wad of notes and threw them on the bed. I don't want you to get me wrong. To hell with money. Forget about it completely . . . he took a sip from his glass. I was supposed to go abroad a month ago but you paralyzed me and I couldn't move. I'm still putting it off hoping that I might see you. Am I that stupid? do you like women? I don't know, said Khalil.

No . . . you don't like women . . . I know. Listen . . . you're a lot younger than me, perhaps that's what's tormenting me and making things complicated. I used to sleep with women as well, in the past. But now that's all over. That's to say I didn't know for sure, and to give up women altogether worried me a little. Well. Of course I won't lay a finger on you unless you want me to . . . well . . . what will you do with me . . . I know that your head's full and that you're con-fused . . . I can help you. I mean, you can ask me for whatever you want. Whatever you want.

The telephone rang. The Brother lifted up the receiver and said: don't worry, you can both come up, no, I'm not asleep.

Two women came in obviously amused, asking if their coming at this time was bothering anyone. Not at all, said the Brother, smiling, and he began to ask them where they had been all evening. The staunch one, who clung up to her political principles which, as far as Khalil knew, did not go hand in hand with the principles of the Brother, said: we had dinner and we talked about her latest book, then we thought of dropping in on you . . . she took off her shoes and said: I want to go for a swim . . . I left my costume here . . . it's still where you left it, the Brother replied, warmly. She went into the bathroom and came out with the costume and said to her writer friend are you coming? She replied no . . . I want to stretch out a little and she stretched out on the bed then started saying over and over again . . . are we bothering anyone . . . without waiting for a reply . . . by the way, she added, will you get rid of that vile creature for me or not . . . he doesn't let me work, I can only work my own way. Where did they get him from. The Brother promised her the best and turned to Khalil and said: I'm going abroad in a couple of days. I'll see you when I get back of course . . . I'll call a taxi for you.

8

Khalil woke to the sound of bombing. It was two in the afternoon. What was new? The last period had been a period of calm and optimism, as they say.

He heard the woman's voice in the entrance of the building. He washed his face and went out. Abou Ahmad was by her side. She was very pale and glanced around her distractedly. No, stay here. You can't do anything now, Abou Ahmad was saying, then he said to Khalil: the boy's at school and she wants . . . no way, said Khalil, wait until the bombing calms down a little. The children must be in the shelter if it's like this. There's no shelter at the school, replied the woman. He'll be very scared . . . maybe he's the only child left there . . . perhaps the bombing will get worse. I must get to him.

That's fine, we'll call the school, said Khalil and the woman rushed to catch up with him. Her hands were shaking as Khalil took the receiver from her and began to dial the number that she dictated to him. The line was constantly busy. The two of them remained silent. Khalil thought of going with her in her car to fetch the boy but quickly thought better of the idea. The school answered and he gave her the receiver. She spoke anxiously then put down the phone. She calmed down and sat on the chair nearby: they're alright, she said, and in a safe place, well, said Khalil, let's wait a little while then. Would you like some coffee? The woman stood up apologizing, thanked Khalil and went up to her house.

The bombing started again in the evening, violently. Khalil went up to the landing and found her there with her son and some of the neighbors. They were silent. She was mending her cloth flipflop and her son was clinging to her, silently. Once in a while he asked her about the cat and she replied that he was hidden away. Her soaking hair hung, dripping, over her shoulders.

The electricity had been cut off. The flame of the only candle guttered and almost died the draught was so strong, so Khalil put it in the corner. She asked her son if he was cold and he said nothing. She walked over to the door of her apartment, fetched one of her thick jackets and put it around his shoulders. The bride, who had abandoned her former elegant ways, was yawning loudly. She no longer wore the slippers with the high heels and the fluttering lace. She was wearing the velvet robe, but the opening at the chest gaped more because she had grown a lot fatter. The opening did not reveal her chest because the cotton shirt went up to her neck.

The boy nodded off on the woman's shoulder when the intensity of the bombing grew less. Sleep well, said the bride and went up to her house. What's the matter with you and with her, said Abou Ahmad, don't leave here until they've all calmed down.

The woman began trying to support her son's neck, which was twisted over her shoulder. Khalil got up to help her by holding the boy. His hand touched the top of her breast and their faces came close in the smell of fresh soap which filled Khalil's head instantly. He went back to his place on the step. His heart was beating violently as he looked towards Abou Ahmad. For a long time he did not look at her and, when Abou Ahmad said: alright we can sleep now, Khalil turned around to go downstairs and he saw her looking at him. She quickly turned away, trying to lift up her son in her arms.

How strong she is, this woman, how strong she is, Khalil kept saying, alone and sleepless in his room. They're so repulsive, women. So repulsive.

Wicked witches and good fairies. Because they know the power of attraction that they possess, whether clean or dirty, clever or stupid.

How disgusting their bodies are, which are always secreting something. Always secreting blood, filth, rancid milk, urine, sweat, pungent white juices, tears . . .

A cavity that's always sucking. Always sucking. Like the hidden pit of their sex. Beautiful women know and flirt and walk and send out the smell of their knowledge . . . and the ugly ones. The ugly ones are more seductive. A lot more seductive. You know them in the darkness of their stifled, unconfessed lust. They send your imagination a lot further and urge on your members. Repulsiveness comes to be the way they move their bodies, not the way they look. Something more intense. Something pure. Don't waste your time wooing her. In the darkness of her stifled lust sits pure lust that says just touch me. The ugly ones are the most scary.

And this woman upstairs, when she walks in the street everyone agrees: she's an ugly woman.

Where is he waiting for me, asked Khalil. In the Ramlah Baydah area, replied the Brother's henchman as he drove at a speed that Khalil found alarming. He made a comment and brought the driver back to his senses.

When did he come back? asked Khalil. He came back about a week ago, he replied, I came yesterday but you weren't at home.

He calls it home, he despises me in the depths of his heart. He must have picked up lots of young men from streets like these, and he can guess the reason why the Brother asked about me on two consecutive days, I who live in a room like this. Never mind.

Khalil followed the Brother's henchman down the long stairs underground, then they reached a heavy iron door, inlaid with large pieces of leather. The Brother's henchman knocked on the door then went back up the stairs. A woman opened the door and Khalil followed her along a corridor that looked like a hall, then they came to be in a large hall divided into what seemed to be rooms by thick, wooden partitions. He saw the Brother sitting at a very long bar which was, in its turn, divided into little bars with cupboards while from the corners came soft, low music.

The Brother welcomed him, shaking him by the hand for a long time. He invited him to sit down on the bar stool nearby. Where am I? asked Khalil, a note of protest in his voice. What is this place?

The place had, in the past, been a nightclub. They had fitted it out as an emergency shelter and the walls had been rebuilt. Here they relaxed. Withdrew from the word like saints and hermits and had meetings or parties. All his keys, his cupboards, looked like his secret way of communication, the drugs in which he deals were, by and large, lines of cocaine which banish sleep and clear heads sapped of energy by fatigue and late nights.

In that place, Khalil realized that what drew him to the Brother, what drew him like a magnet, was that he knew how intensely the Brother desired him. Desire so strong that it began to be reproduced in its object, that is, Khalil, for to ignore it was no longer possible. People desire and lust for those who realize the extent of their desire for them.

The Brother was very kind and tender in a reserved, shy way. But Khalil sensed that the place had a purely sexual soul . . . and sordid, which made him shy away from imagining even the touch of the Brother's skin. Desire mingled with acute nausea. With hatred verging on the pleasure of torture. More torture from this man who is often tormented in his attempts to reach me, stamp his imprint on my soul and possess it, so I become like him. Khalil thought: we certainly become like the people we have sex with and I do not want to be like this man.

The Brother was looking at Khalil, the beautiful and agonizing object of his desire, and he despaired more. He knew that Khalil's youth would quickly scatter his confusion and make his despair total. He knew that Khalil saw in him that public figure, who had deplorable and dubious powers and, so, that he despised him. He was still at the age at which, if we despise someone, we do not desire him or crave him. This made the Brother's torment, his feelings of powerlessness, worse. The Brother felt so feeble that he preferred that Khalil should go. He said, go home today, Khalil, and come back tomorrow. I'll take you on a special errand.

The following day Khalil went to him, desiring. He went in spite of himself.

They set out in a yacht from a place near the Club Militaire. The foreigner who had been kidnapped was there. Said was there as well, and others. Opposite Jounieh Beach a man called Habib caught up with them. No one took any notice of Khalil except, perhaps, to give him a few looks bordering on disapproval for his being there. The Brother also seemed preoccupied. It was night when the yacht fell still.

The Brother said to Khalil: now we're unloading our cargo of hashish and opium and taking weapons on board. Today the deal's being done on account of the Sikhs in India. Habib bought heavy weapons from the army and we struck a deal that he would guarantee a cover. The source today is a Canadian Mafia. They're the guarantors. We go back to our areas with trucks loaded with light weapons that pass the crossing points as potatoes. Habib guarantees the cover. He's negotiating with the Israelis now. The Israelis here. In the water. They're the most difficult because they play on the quota. They may be greedy, they may make things awkward for us and they may sell retail. They may not make any profit, just to be perverse. Today Abou Ali is with us, he's an explosives expert. The Israelis have known him since the '48 war and they don't play around with him . . . Said, of course, will take his share and his party's share, and he'll justify it as being a tactical move to beat the enemy at his own game. Khalil, what do you think?

Khalil said to himself this man is really infatuated with me. Like in a storybook. He felt sorry for the Brother when he realized the risk that the Brother was running by bringing him along. He said nothing, thinking. He said to himself: the Brother finds me a little foolish in my innocence. He wants me to grow up, he wants me to see. I'm like someone taking an airplane for the first time. I'm surprised and on edge when it takes off, when it rises up from the ground although it passes over my head every day without my thinking about it. He said to the Brother: your secret is public knowledge, you know. The Brother smiled and said but today you're seeing it with your own eyes. Your problem is in your head, Khalil. All my cards are in your hands now, so will you grow up?

Before the Brother got into his car he gave Khalil a card with all his telephone numbers on it and said: don't throw it away . . . I'll wait for you to get in touch with me.

Dawn was just about to break . . . Khalil started walking up the hill to the Club Militaire, keeping his eyes open for a taxi . . . he kept walking until he reached Hamra Street. As he was walking up it . . . he saw three boys running then splitting off into the alleys. He heard a rain of bullets so he stopped in his tracks . . . then the huge explosion rang out.

I'd better go back the way I came, said Khalil, walking faster until he almost broke into a run. He heard running behind him, and bullets. He stopped. A hand on his neck then a strong blow to his jaw. He fell to the ground. Another blow from a rifle butt on his shoulder then the armed man picked him up by the shirt and dragged him to the wall. He propped him up against the wall and began to kick him in the legs and the small of his back. Two armed men watch him as he is thrown to the floor spitting blood. A car stops and they drag him over to it.

You've made a mistake, says Khalil, I'm not . . . then he remembers. There's a card in my back pocket. The armed man pulls it out and reads what is written on it. Khalil does not know what is written on it.

Stop, says the armed man to the driver. Stop the car. Why didn't you say? says the armed man. Never mind, says Khalil.

How can we apologize to you now? Our nerves are all a-jangle, sir.

He's a lawyer, from a group of our friends . . . oh God . . . we'll take you to the hospital.

No, says Khalil . . . let me out at the end of the street.

No, we'll take you home, the armed man insists.

9

What choice, what choice, what choice?

What are you thinking of, Khalil, you noble creature, as you walk around your room like a mad cat with a scorched tail?

Oh, Khalil who came back to praise life, to love yourself . . .

This is the missing link that you were afraid of, the thing you did not know, this is the thing that was lacking. It's time for your confusion to end, for your delight with the arteries of your hand which pulse with life to flower and open and lean over the lush branches.

It's not enough . . . it's not enough . . . it's not enough for you to love yourself Khalil.

It's not enough for you to love yourself because your self is exposed and swift to perish . . .

Your self which you love so much needs a nuclear shelter.

Learn how to love it now . . . preserve it . . .

Preserve me so that you can love me, Khalil's self was saying to him.

Love me love me little Khalil . . . more and more, for you to love me.

Because I really deserve it. I deserve to multiply, to grow, for you to love me.

Look around you what choice what choice.

Khalil was talking to himself, the self that began, from afar, facing him, to talk to him like an understanding teacher: those disabled sons of yours, those who do not die in the bombing kill each other in front of the bakeries, they kill each other.

And my brothers in the civil defense?

Your brothers in the civil defense die in the explosion, or they rush to the dead to plunder the corpses, they pull the gold rings from severed hands.

And my mothers? Khalil said to himself.

Your mothers, who bear so many children, sit cross-legged like Sultanas while their children work, take arms, kill. They are quick to forget, they collect the salaries of the dead as they earn the takings of the ones who are still alive.

Get it straight, Khalil, everything is organized in advance, or after the event, as the Brother told you. You're the only one who's floundering around in chaos. A silly little chaos like novice writers get themselves into. The Canadian guarantee is solid. The Sikh group pay up on time and Israel is torturing us with the quota.

Who do I have apart from you, don't I deserve it, aren't I worth it?

What about me, who protects me, while you reap the harvest of being so serious? As you are utterly convinced that you are on the side of life, and that the most beautiful thing we can do is praise life.

Praise life Khalil.

Praise life.

There is no life there, Khalil. There is life. Tell me, confess do you love someone other than me, more than me? Is there another woman?

Then Khalil's self tried to control herself.

Well, what are you doing? Work as a prophet, work as a messenger, start a war, set up a party? Have you found a comrade for yourself, a brother, a soldier?

You haven't found one because they don't exist. They are the way they are, you ass. Sorry. Khalil's self apologized . . . she drew a deep breath, crossed her legs, and straightened her skirt.

Is the Brother vulgar? Tell me that the human race is vulgar! Did he have to be hanged by a kangaroo court over a failed attempt at revolution? Did he have to stay in his far off countryside, disguising his malnutrition as he disguises his swollen eye?

What do you think if we start from here? From the malnutrition? We must find a solution for ourselves. You know the end of the line. Start from there if you can. I don't want us to become divided. Let's confess, we're still infatuated with each other.

Sit down, Khalil . . . Khalil's self put her hand on his hand. She said in a last, desperate attempt: let's spell out every word in the sentence and lay it on the table:

We know now that there is no choice: for you to love yourself means to hate others.

Khalil's self slammed the door behind her and stood, panting heavily, in the entrance to the building.

In the distant heights the wolves roam inseparably in a long, transverse line, leaving sinuous, parallel tracks on the broad stretches of snow and on the mounds and dips which the light of the moon puffs out to make them domed and hollow.

The wolves do not roam in packs. They meet, they separate. When they meet, they walk side by side. There is no leader in a pack of wolves. None walks in front of the other because he knows that whoever follows in his footsteps will devour him.

The wolves meet when they are hungry. A male and a female. The male does not trust his female for she is stronger and more fearless than him. He mounts her, briefly. She does not fear him nor he fear her because desire paralyzes strength for a few seconds, replaces it with another strength before the first returns.

If the wolves are lucky enough to find prey they attack it together and tear it apart instantly. He who is not appointed a share weakens: they recognize his weakness and devour him instantly.

The wolf does not sleep.

If it does sleep it is alone and far enough from the smell of the other wolves. The wolf stands on the crest of a hill. It looks around.

The wolf stands on the crest of a hill and begins to howl out the depths of its despair.

Hatred, hatred.

Hatred is my mother who loves me.

Hatred does not breathe easily, it does not breathe.

Hatred makes life flow in my veins. I stick with it as my self should stick with me.

Khalil walks in the city now and hears his regular footfall on the soaking tarmac.

He walks in it as if he were walking over it, above it.

This hideous city,

this uniquely hideous city.

How can the poets sing of its beauty. This depravity.

They just don't want to get caught up in seeing it in its hideousness. To see it in its hideousness would take them back to their own hideousness, its vileness would take them back to their own vileness and so they prefer to fabricate stories about it and to keep the stories going . . .

Khalil was innocent of the city. Khalil and his self, who had been so radiantly beautiful in her youth, were both completely innocent.

He was completely innocent. And completely free. So he knew how to hate the city.

He hates it not as the son of a beautiful woman hates his mother, his mother who used to be beautiful and who belonged to the General. The son simmers his hatred long, over a low flame, until it is cooked. Then it is ready. He loves his mother and hates her for being beautiful, for a long time. The beautiful mother is not our mother. She is a mother and she is beautiful and there is something of the General in her beauty.

She kisses us in our beds before we sleep, with lips hot and full so that the General, who is waiting in the sitting room, will see them. Any man waiting in the sitting room acts the General to us, we are boys who play games about soldiers and thieves who were afflicted by having such a beautiful mother.

But when we grow up we become leaders, we hate her and we crush her beauty. We also crush the beauty of her lips. And whenever we remember her beauty and sing praise to it we crush and mutilate her more.

That's what the leader does.

But what does that have to do with Khalil.

This city was not his to grieve over and hate as the leader or the poet hates it. It gave him nothing and had promised him nothing, it had not betrayed him nor was he its lover.

Love and betrayal. You must be sick to be using words like these to speak of the city.

That is how the city was when he came to it.

That is how they fooled him, without meaning to at all.

He believed, for example, that Fayrouz's voice was angelic and that he was listening to the angels singing. But soon he realized that this woman's songs had nothing to do with him. That it was nothing more than a slight mistake. This woman who was singing for a loss that he did not know and could not imagine, in an old harbor which turns around as she turns us around with words empty to the core. Because it was a symbol to the core. A symbol that symbolizes nothing to him.

Fayrouz's songs belong to our families, perhaps, to those who are full of longing for Kfar Hala and the mountains of flint. But the singer does not reach me, nor does she lift me up to skies like those who weep whenever they hear her voice, who weep for that generation that was over before it began, before it inherited, as the successive generations do, the rites of assuming power and surrendering it, they departed in agony and the memories are many. Me, no one gave me anything to thank anyone for, I was born as if I hatched from an eggs as my paternal uncle sings to his brother in the Hejaz then tearfully tells me to listen to Fayrouz and to pay heed to her songs...

Fayrouz who continues to gather together the skies of the nation, crossing the frontier, the pelican that flies to and fro in its skies, always blind in one eye or the other: what heresy, how much of the hot air of hatred and empty promise do I need to lift the zeppelin of my soul above your skies with its angelic singers and vile smells. How high. How high? for me to be free of you all?... free because I'm free. Because my hatred is pure.

Perish, all of you ... perish.

Even the slave. The slave is only a slave if he wants to be. If he loves his master, and the slave may love his master as he loves himself. The slave may love his master more than he loves himself. This slave is a slave forever.

The slave who hates his master, even were he bound hand and foot to that master, is a free slave. A free slave because he hates, because he fences in his hatred day after day. Stronger. Stronger. Dug in as deep as it can go. Season after season . . . the slave who hates his master loves himself and is free. More free than the master. Higher than his master and the master cannot reach him. The master's freedom is like a foul old maid.

In the siesta, in the heat of the siesta, everything calms down.

The master comes in to lie with the woman he chooses, damp, her legs cold. In the siesta, on his way out, the slave sits down outside in the afternoon shadow, in the buzzing of the flies which he likes and then continues, even if he is exhausted, his unrelenting labor. He fixes his eyes on the master's door until his eyes pierce it. He sees the master, he sees the master looking at him. He begins with the more difficult stage so that he does not let himself down in the middle of his exercise. He starts with a smile from the master's eyes or with a kind word from him. He begins to sway backwards and forwards until the movement becomes smooth and his breathing becomes even. Backwards and forwards with a regular tempo, to make the talisman move in a straight line. The talisman which protects him from the smile, from the kind voice, which blocks up the cracks through which his master might seep in. So that the hatred remains clean and pure. So that he stays bolted shut on himself, so that what is his remains his.

Only after that does the slave take his eyes off his master's door and come out of the master's siesta cloaked in hatred. And, free, the slave begins to rhyme and sing as he prepares the bathwater and a glass of wine for his master who will awake shortly. The city will not reach me because I will rise, I will ascend. I will be the hymn that rises from it.

My real, burning fear is that I might come to look like the flocks of people down there. That I will wrap myself in a thick casing and I will not hear them nor get wind of their smells.

Khalil feels disgusted because a shoulder bumped into his shoulder in the street. He feels disgusted, his stomach shrinks, nauseated, don't touch me don't touch my purity . . . don't touch me.

Khalil prefers to walk back to his room so that he does not smell their breath in the taxi.

V

Epilogue

A light rain was falling but, at this hour of the night, the cold was biting.

The Bridegroom stopped in the middle of the street to help a truck driver park straight to the curb.

The men came up and began to unload the heavy crates.

—Bridegroom, said Khalil, do you think there's enough room?

—Of course, sir, replied the Bridegroom, it's swallowed up two big tanks and there's only one oil heater with rusty joints left, it's being stubborn but there's a cure for it . . .

Fine, said Khalil and he walked over to the entrance of the building to get out of the rain.

He saw the woman coming down the stairs in her nightclothes, wrapped in a thick dressing gown . . .

—What's this, Mr. Khalil . . . I didn't imagine that you could be happy about it . . . these crates have arms and ammunition in them, you know . . . there have been some accidental explosions in residential buildings recently . . . this isn't . . .

—Go upstairs, go inside, things aren't the way you think. I'll come up in a minute, if you'll allow me, and I'll explain what's going on. Trust me.

—But Khalil . . .

—Don't worry, I told you . . . go upstairs and get out of this cold. Don't worry, go upstairs . . .

She opened the door and waited in the entrance. Khalil closed the door behind him and went up to her. He saw a still hidden fear shining in her eyes. Fear or was it desire.

He took her head in his hands and kissed her. She tried to slip away . . . she put her hand on his arms and began to pull at his arms to free her head. Khalil bit her lips. She lifted her head: you bastard, she said, as if she were crying. Khalil held onto her hair and slapped her hard.

She won't scream, her son is asleep inside.

He threw her to the floor and ripped her nightshirt from the bottom. She began to kick and writhe and crawl until they reached the middle of the sitting room. He pinned down her thighs with his knees, on top of her, and she started to hit him. He hit her hard across the face over and over again and her hands fell . . . then she fell still . . . she went limp, like a corpse.

That won't do you any good, he said, and slapped her again. Kiss my hand. Kiss my hand. Then he moved down on to her chest. Kiss me . . . kiss me . . . kiss my neck . . . my neck . . . lift your head up . . . take off . . . this dressing gown. Take your nightshirt off.

Spread out here.

Khalil looked in every corner of the house as he did up his flies, blue and lush green and paintings on the walls and lights in the corners . . . she was playing house . . .

She was playing at being a family and security.

She was playing house.

Now things are even. Now I begin the real story of humility, of submission, submission to my belonging to my brothers, submission to the glorification of life, to the general misery of life.

Khalil said to the Bridegroom: listen to me. Either she pays what's over and above the repairs or she finds her things in the street.

I've had an excellent offer. You'll take your share, of course. Thirty thousand dollars and this time with a contract, of course.

Take these crates to the car and the rest can stay here. I'll give you the key.

The Bridegroom caught up with Khalil in the entrance to the building after he had closed the door.

In the entrance, the *hajjah*'s cat was meowing and rubbing itself against Khalil's leg. Khalil kicked it viciously and the sound of its meowing shot up like a scream.

Khalil's henchman opened the back door of the car.

God be with you, sir, said the Bridegroom.

The henchman got in and turned over the engine.

I went up to the rear window . . . Khalil had a mustache and a pair of sunglasses. Where are you going, I asked, and he did not hear me.

It's me, I told him, and he did not turn around.

The car moved off and, from the back window, Khalil seemed broad-shouldered in his brown leather jacket . . .

The car moved off and began to draw away. Khalil was leaving the street as if he were rising upwards.

You've changed so much since I described you in the first pages. You've come to know more than I do. Alchemy. The stone of laughter.

Khalil is gone, he has become a man who laughs. And I remain a woman who writes.

Khalil: my darling hero.

My darling hero . . .

Hoda Barakat

In 1974, Hoda Barakat was awarded the Licence in French Literature from the Lebanese University. She taught for a year in Al-Khaim village in South Lebanon. After the beginning of the civil war in Lebanon in 1975, she moved to the village of Bashara in the north. In 1975–76 she went to Paris to start a Ph.D., but because of the civil war she decided to return to her country where she worked as a teacher, journalist, and translator. In 1985 her first collection of short stories, entitled *Za'irat*, was published. In 1985–86 she worked at the Center for Lebanese Research. In 1988, she helped establish *Shahrazad*, a women's magazine. *The Stone of Laughter*, which was written in Lebanon during the civil war and which won the Al-Naqid Literary Prize for First Novels, has also been translated into French and Italian. Her second novel, *Ahl El-Hawa*, came out in 1993. In 1989, Hoda Barakat moved to Paris, where she now works as a journalist.

Fadia Faqir

Fadia Faqir was born in Jordan in 1956. Her first novel, *Nisanit*, was published by Penguin in 1988 and her second novel, *Pillars of Salt*, is forthcoming. Fadia Faqir is a lecturer in Arabic language and literature at the Centre for Middle Eastern and Islamic Studies, Durham University, England. She is at present working on her third novel, *The Black Iris Crossing*.

Sophie Bennett

Sophie Bennett studied Arabic and Persian at the School of Oriental and African Studies, University of London, and won the Goodwin Adams Persian Prize. She has a Ph.D. in Modern Arabic Literature and works as a freelance translator.

Other titles in the series

From Chile:
The Secret Holy War of Santiago de Chile
by Marco Antonio de la Parra
trans. by Charles P. Thomas
ISBN 1–56656–123–X   paperback $12.95

From Grenada:
Under the Silk Cotton Tree
by Jean Buffong
ISBN 1–56656–122–1   paperback $9.95

From India:
The End Play
by Indira Mahindra
ISBN 1–56656–166–3   paperback $11.95

From Israel:
The Silencer
by Simon Louvish
ISBN 1–56656–108–6   paperback $10.95

From Jordan:
Prairies of Fever
by Ibrahim Nasrallah
trans. by May Jayyusi and Jeremy Reed
ISBN 1–56656–106–X   paperback $9.95

From Lebanon:
SamarKand
by Amin Maalouf
trans. by Russell Harris
ISBN 1–56656–194–9   paperback $14.95

From Palestine:
A Balcony Over the Fakihani
by Liyana Badr
trans. by Peter Clark with Christopher Tingley
ISBN 1–56656–107–8   paperback $9.95

Wild Thorns
by Sahar Khalifeh
trans. by Trevor LeGassick and Elizabeth Fernea
ISBN 0–940793–25–3   paperback $9.95

A Woman of Nazareth
by Hala Deeb Jabbour
ISBN 0–940793–07–5   paperback $9.95

From Serbia:
The Dawning
by Milka Bajić-Poderegin
trans. by Nadja Poderegin
ISBN 1–56656–188–4   paperback $14.95

From South Africa:
Living, Loving and Lying Awake at Night
by Sindiwe Magona
ISBN 1–56656–141–8   paperback $11.95

From Turkey:
Cages on Opposite Shores
by Janset Berkok Shami
ISBN 1–56656–157–4   paperback $11.95

From Yemen:
The Hostage
by Zayd Mutee' Dammaj
trans. by May Jayyusi and Christopher Tingley
ISBN 1–56656–140–X   paperback $10.95

From Zimbabwe:
The Children Who Sleep by the River
by Debbie Taylor
ISBN 0–940793–96–2   paperback $9.95

Titles in the "Emerging Voices: New International Fiction" series are available at bookstores everywhere.

To order by phone call toll-free 1–800–238–LINK. Please have your Mastercard, Visa or American Express ready when you call.

To order by mail, please send your check or money order to the address listed below. For shipping and handling, add $3.00 for the first book and $1.00 for each additional book. Massachusetts residents add 5% sales tax.

Interlink Publishing Group, Inc.
46 Crosby Street
Northampton, MA 01060

Tel (413) 582–7054
Fax (413) 582–7057
e-mail: interpg@aol.com